# The Aydin Trammell Chronicles

## Volume One

# Shiny Lies

---

By
Ruairí Cinéad Ducantlin

# Copyright

© 2021 by Ruairí Cinéad Ducantlin



# Disclaimer

This story is a work of fiction and is provided exclusively for entertainment purposes. This means everything written came from the author's imagination with the hope of entertaining you, the reader. Names, characters, businesses, places, events, and incidents are products of the author's imagination or used in a fictitious manner. Any resemblance to actual persons, living or dead, or actual events is entirely coincidental.

# Table of Contents

# Preface

The Aydin Trammell Chronicles were originally conceived as a five-part mini-series. Reviewers liked the story enough to insist I re-write the scripts as novellas. The collection of novellas became Volume One.

This story may be disturbing if you are a consumer of social media. The tale of Aydin Trammell is essential if you are a user of TikTok, Facebook, Instagram, or anything else hosted *In The Cloud*.

Maybe not. Immerse yourself in the threat of global tracking. Ponder the implications of computer algorithms being able to track anyone, anywhere, for any reason, and scoring you for review. Consider this concept: *There is no longer an expectation of personal privacy.*

Also, contemplate those who are conceived, trained, and nurtured to be above their peers. Ponder the consequences of a chosen few failing to meet expectations. What is the depth of worry if the selected elite turn against the governments and corporations who monitor *every aspect* of our lives?

Please, read on, immerse yourself in the threat of fascism being taught under the guise of improved intelligence through social media. Contemplate the possibility of governments and corporations nurturing generational oppression.

Or not.

It is, as always, your choice.

The story of Aydin Trammell begins now.

# Ptarmigan Lane
## Dark and Stormy...

*"And he'd hated himself, and hated her, too, for the ruin they'd made of each other."*

Dennis Lehane

**Denver, Late Night, Sidewalk, Hard Rain**

*Damn, it stinks. Trash and dog shit. Mental note: Never run and hide on a trash day.*

*Phil never shuts up. The rain and the stench are making him worse. What the fuck is wrong with people who let their dog shit on the sidewalk? At least the rain will wash it into the gutter.*

*Stopping here was a bad idea, but we needed to get out of that place.*

*Hanging around with dead people is never a good idea.*

"Phil, don't put this on me."

"It is on you, Aydin. You and Allison. Do you think it will stop raining soon?"

"I hope it never stops raining."

"Are you planning to stand under this awning forever?"

"I might."

Like a moth drawn to a flame, Phil is staring at a neon beer sign. High up, out of reach, the sign is three letters ringed in a red oval: OLY. The Y is intermittently flickering, and the red oval has dimmed considerably.

"That neon light buzzing is annoying me. My dad used to drink that beer because it was cheapest by a penny. Do they even make that beer anymore? The Gray Dog café, up on Colfax, is open and only about three blocks from here."

"Okay, I'll walk in the rain, but you have to promise not to talk about it."

"Not talking about shooting people is good. Quiet is good unless the police ask about the dead people. You know what you did. You know what Allison did. Aydin, I think we need to talk about it."

"Fuck it, let's go. Just try to shut up."

Aydin and Phil pull up their hoods, hunch over, and step into the downpour. Not small, Aydin's six-three, two-fifteen dwarfed Phil's five-ten, one-eighty-five frame. Being shorter, Phil maneuvered to put Aydin's large frame between him and the driving rain. Outwardly, Aydin is composed, intelligent, and an all-around good guy. His thoughts, however, are never far from the truth, and his anger is perpetually simmering just under boiling over.

*Fuck her.*

*I know what I did, and I know what she did. Phil was there, standing around. He'd get three-to-five. I'd get ten-to-twenty. Ten-to-twenty without. The Service will fix it. I hope the Service will fix it.*

*She will skate. Snakes always slither out of trouble.*

*This mess is just like the deal on the island when she fucked over the seller. Pops warned me about her. Pops knows trouble follows her because she invites the demons.*

*She missed shooting that prick and will slide right on by. She missed the meathead because she knew I wouldn't.*

*I had to clean up her mess.*

*Fuck her.*

"What's that Phil?"

"Are you listening to me? Aydin, you never listen to me. You should listen to me, and maybe next time, this won't happen."

"I don't listen because you never shut the fuck up. There won't be a *next time*."

*Phil knows me better than anyone. He knows that is not true. There is always a next time.*

"Where do you think Allison is now?"

"Who fucking cares where she is? She's not here."

"You care, Aydin. That is why you are swearing. You care where she is."

*I am swearing because I like swearing.*

*I know where the bitch is.*

# No More Family BBQs

**Denver, Gray Dog Café, Window Booth, Whipping Rain**

Phil is mildly surprised at Aydin's grumbling and griping, but he is letting his friend ramble.

"Bitches be crazy."

"Did you quote The Big Bang Theory? Yes, Aydin, they are crazy, but you married her. Pass the pink packet."

Stirring the sweet powder into his coffee, Phil is eyeing Aydin across the booth.

"What are you doing on your phone?"

Realizing his questions are being ignored, Phil swatted at the flies while eyeing Aydin's unfinished breakfast. There is no sense in letting the flies have at the buttermilk and walnut goodness.

"Are you going to eat that?"

Without looking up from his phone, Aydin pushed the remains of his three-am breakfast toward Phil.

*Damn, that rain is sideways.*
*At least it is warm in here.*
*What a dive, these vinyl seats are sticky.*
*Phil loves dives.*
*He never stops eating.*

"Did she text you?"

"No."

"Did you text her?"

"No."

"Then, what are you doing on your phone?"

"She is at her mother's house."

His fork stopped, hovering just short of the next bite enter his mouth. The fake maple syrup dripped off the pancake and onto his thigh. Phil knows Aydin was not telling him something.

"What did you do?"

"I can track her phone. She always goes home to her parent's place in Lone Tree. She feels safe there. She thinks I won't go there and drag her ass out into the street."

"You won't, and you know it. Allison's dad won't let you do something stupid, like dragging her into the street. That didn't go so well last time. Her dad loves you more than he loves her. He won't let you do something stupid."

"Yeah, Pops is good people, but her mother is a bitch just like her. Two peas in a pod."

"Why did you marry her? You have known her family since you were five. What's the deal with her mother and your father? How come they kept getting stationed on the same bases?

"Pops I get. He was spying before we were born. Why did Pops marry Allison's mother?

"Never mind, I'll ask Pops. You had to know what Allison is like before you married her. You knew why you were saying the forever *I Do*. What's the deal?"

*Phil's timing is terrible.*

"Phil, those questions are for the beach and too many cervezas. You know why I married her. What are you getting at?"

"Nothing. Everything. Something is not right. Allison knew the buyer's goons were going to be there. How did she know? Did she cut a side deal? That's it! She cut a side deal."

Aydin looks up and gives his only friend a wry smile.

"Took you a long while. Yes, Allison cut a side deal, which is why we have no money and no way to track the bastards."

Aydin is checking for a response to the text he sent thirty seconds ago.

**Me**: She did it again. Condition uncertain, suggest be ready.

**Pops**: Understood. Be safe.

Phil dives back into his second breakfast and resumes chattering between bites.

"How much do you think she took?"

"She got our share."

Phil grunted in disgust.

"All of it?"

"Yes, all of it."

"Why would she do that? We are her only friends. Why would she burn us?"

Aydin's tone is bitter.

"Because she could."

"'Because she could.' What do you mean?"

"Phil, to Allison, this is all a game. It is not about the code or the money. It is about a sport she loves playing and winning. Right now, she thinks she is winning."

"She *is* winning."

"No, Phil, she is not winning. The code doesn't work."

Phil's mind is reeling. He is pushing the dregs of syrup around on the plate with the knife. His next question soft and confused.

"What?"

"The code doesn't work."

"Yes, it does. I saw it in the simulation. It improves the results of the base code anywhere between 26 and 46 percent."

"No, you saw the simulation I rigged."

"What did you do? Wait. You knew! You knew she was going to double-cross us."

"Yes, I knew, which is why I manipulated the simulation. The base code I gave them is missing the core."

Phil had stopped eating, put his coffee down,

and focused across the booth.

"Aydin, we are in trouble. Allison is in trouble. What are we going to do?"

"We are going to get our money. When we get our money, I will give them the core. The new deal is 70-30."

"70-30?"

"Yep, 70 for me, 30 for you."

"What about Allison?"

"She's not getting a dime. She can have the fucking house."

*She will get half of everything in the divorce.*

*The money will be waiting for me when I get out of prison.*

"Where are we going to live?"

"We?"

"I got no place to go. I like the apartment."

"I don't know Phil. We'll figure it out. But that's the deal. We get the money, she gets the house, and everyone walks away. The buyer will force her to hand over the money to us. If she doesn't hand it over, no core."

"Okay. What now?"

"Now, we go to the office. We can sleep there, on the floor in the conference room. I suspect we will be getting a call in the morning."

*She will call, or the buyer will call, or both.*

*Everyone will blame everyone else.*

*Dead people do that: They put everyone left alive in a panic.*

## Denver Technical Center (DTC), Mid-Morning, Constant Rain

Entering the small offices of Fírinne, Ltd., the sign above the reception desk explains the company name but does not describe the business.

***Fírinne*** *(fi-rin-ne)*: Old Irish for **Truth**

*Cad í an fhírinne? / What is the truth?*

The small lobby is stark with a simple reception desk but no receptionist. The two tiny offices are as plain as the lobby. On the left, Aydin's office. Next to Aydin's office, is Phil's even smaller office behind the reception desk. The software development company is authentic. Aydin and Phil are the owners and the coders.

The intelligence agent spy work for the Service is an excellent side job.

A small closet and the head are to the right of the lobby. The conference room is to the extreme right as you enter the lobby. Aydin's office and the conference room have windows facing the parking lot.

The office used to smell like a nail-salon until they cut-loose the receptionist. It has the persistent odor of the cleaning crew's antiseptic solution used on the head and terrazzo lobby floor.

Aydin and Phil are asleep on the conference room carpet when the office phone chimes. Neither complained. The industrial carpet was softer than the rocks they slept on their desert missions.

"I told you they'd call. I forwarded my cell to the office line. I'll put it on the speaker."

Wiping the carpet impressions from his face, stretching the pain from his thigh and the old wound from the terrorist's bullet, Aydin pulls himself up to the conference table and the ringing phone. Phil grunts and does not move from lying on the carpet.

"Good morning, Thank you for calling Fírinne. How may I help you?"

*"Cut the crap. What I want to know is: How are you going to fix the mess you created?"*

"Mess? What mess? If you have a problem, maybe you should talk to Allison."

*"We talked to Allison. She says you double-crossed everyone."*

"Double-crossed? Me? HA! Fuck you and that bitch who took my money."

The long silence told Aydin the buyers just learned Allison played everyone against the middle and walked away with the money.

*"The code doesn't work."*

"Correct."

*"What are you going to do about it?*

"Me? I am not going to do anything. You are going to get Allison to give me the money. All of it. Then, I might decide to give you the working version. Until then, I am going back to sleep."

Aydin pressed the red icon, disconnecting the call. He laid back down, knowing Phil would be unable to remain quiet.

*Thirty years old, and he looks at the world as a teenager.*

*How does he do it?*

*I need to be more like Phil. Phil's life is simple.*

*I need simple.*

"Aydin?"

"Yes, Phil?"

"They might kill her."

"I considered that, but it is not likely."

"Why not?"

"Because the buyer is a middle-man and didn't offer a deal to get the working code. He is out of money and can't ask his buyer for more. They have to get Allison to play nice. If they don't, we are all fucked."

"It's still raining."

*Son of a bitch.*
*Phil must be worried about the mission.*
*When he is anxious about the mission, he acts like a kid with ADD.*

"What's the rain got to do with anything?"

"Nothing, just saying. What if they go looking for her?"

"Why do you think she went home? Pops will shoot first, then ask why."

"Yeah, that's true. Maybe you should give Pops a call."

"I already did. I sent Pops a text while you were eating."

"You send Pops a text at three-thirty in the morning. Has he responded?"

*Pops loves this shit.*

"He responded when I sent the text. He knows Allison only goes home when she needs him to protect her. He kind of likes it when she screws up badly. It reminds him of Iraq."

"That is one crazy-ass family, and she is one crazy-ass woman... Umm... Ugh... Sorry."

"It's okay, I know. I *married* the crazy-ass woman."

"What do you think she will do?"

"I don't know, but her buyer will call again soon."

"What makes you sure they will call?"

"We are their only out. I have the working core code, and they need it. The buyer needs me, and Allison is their path to me."

### DTC, Early Afternoon, Raining

The rain continues to pelt the windows, but it is not why the conference room smells like wet dogs and body odor. Phil had run out for burritos and iced tea.

Aydin was working on something using the laptop PC he pulled from his office into the conference room. On his PC, Phil is looking for episodes of Diners, Drive-Ins, and Dives that he has not seen. Frustrated because he has seen them all, he begins reading the news.

Looking down, Aydin ignores his phone, which is receiving text messages about every minute.

*Let her stew.*
*She deserves it.*

"Are you going to eat that?"

"Phil, do you ever stop eating?"

"Why would I stop?

Phil peels the foil from another breakfast burrito.

"I heard, on the radio, the rain isn't going to stop until tomorrow or the next day, maybe longer."

Aydin is head down, not responding.

Phil is eyeing Aydin between mouthfuls, feeling happy. The running and adrenaline rush from twelve hours ago made him too tired to dream. The carpet felt like a cushion in the few hours he was asleep.

"When are they going to call?"

"How should I know that? But if the text messages from Allison are a clue, it will be soon."

"Messages from Allison?"

"Yes."

"Well? What do you think she is doing? Freaking out?"

"She sure is. Let her."

The conference room phone chimed but had not routed through Aydin's cell phone. The direct call caused Phil to raise an eyebrow toward Aydin. Without emotion, Aydin pressed the green button.

"It is about time you called."

*"Fuck you, Aydin. What did you do?"*

*Allison is trying to be hard, but I know her, and she is not hard.*

*For someone so smart, she tries to be tough.*

*She's sharp but not harsh.*

*Well, not harsh, like shoot a guy in the face harsh.*

"Allison, I'm sure a marriage counselor would

love to pull apart your language directed at me."

"*Nice one, smart guy. There's no counseling in our future. How are you going to fix this?*"

"Fix what?"

"*Don't play games. You gave them bad code.*"

"You stole my money after you missed shooting that goon. He is *your* buyer. How are *you* going to fix this?"

Phil stopped eating, watching Aydin, trying to figure out why his friend was calm. Allison's tone changed from aggression to gentle pleading.

"*Aydin, come on, we need to fix this, right now.*"

"Oh, so now *we* need to fix this. I didn't give them anything. You stole the code because you thought I didn't know you had access. How will *we* fix this? Two minutes ago, it was *my* problem. Allison, *you* created this, and *you* are going to fix it."

"*Aydin...*"

When Allison paused, Aydin pushed the mute button.

*That bitch.*

"Phil, stay away from the windows, but take a look around the parking lot."

"What am I looking for?"

"You will know it when you see it."
*"AYDIN!"*

Phil stepped cautiously out of the conference room. Aydin presses the unmute button.

"You need to keep your voice down."
*"Don't patronize me. Tell me how we are going to fix this."*
"I told you *we* are not fixing anything."
*"Aydin, please. These are not nice people."*
"Not nice? I am shocked you would be friends with *not nice* people."
*"You know what I mean. The buyer is dangerous but not as bad as the guys at the end of the chain."*

Aydin muted the phone, letting Allison continue to whine. Phil slid back into the conference room, crouched over, away from the windows. Silently, he pointed to the parking lot directly outside the conference room windows.

He held up two fingers and then mimed driving a car, followed by holding up four digits and mimed shooting a pistol. Aydin nodded and unmuted the conversation.

"Allison, shut up."
*"What? Are you listening? We are in trouble!"*
"No, Allison, *you* are in trouble. Your friends are

here. Excellent plan, by the way. Keep me talking while they attack. What is the objective, kidnap, and torture me to turn over the core code?

"Fuck you, Allison."

*"What are you talking about? Aydin..."*

Aydin pressed the red phone icon, terminating the call. Using hand signals, he and Phil morphed their thinking from technology weenies sucked into a bad deal. They reverted to the special forces commandos that brought them together a dozen years ago.

Sliding from the conference room, they duck-walked to the vault behind the secure wall panel. Pulling on advanced Kevlar vests, holstering a pistol, loading, and racking two M4 tactical rifles, inserting TCAPS ear defenders, they did not speak.

Bumping fists, Aydin crawled to the far end of the lobby and took a position behind and to the right of the reinforced reception desk. Phil's position, behind the reinforced wall panel, was purpose-built for his left-handed shooting.

Using a shaped charge, the attackers blew the lock off the exterior lobby door. Four armed threats infiltrated the lobby and stood in an overlapping field of fire. Aydin's first thought is calm and straightforward.

*Fucking idiots.*
*The fucking door was unlocked.*

Four headshots left four dead wanna-be commandos.

Aydin's dark thoughts returned.

*The cleaners shouldn't complain.*
*They can replace the ceiling tiles.*
*The blood won't stain the terrazzo.*
*Dead people follow that bitch around.*

"Phil, make the call."

"Roger that."

Grabbing their PCs and more tactical gear, Aydin and Phil did not look back.

# Family Time

***Aydin's Mercedes, South Bound on I-25, Raining***

"Phil, check my phone."

"Use the car. You know, for a super-smart techno weenie, nerd, dude, you can be kind of dumb."

Aydin ignored the insult and slid his hand over the touch control. Linked to his phone, the Mercedes displayed his text messages. Fortunately, the newest text appeared first.

**Me**: Threat confirmed. Ready One.

**Pops**: Confirmed, ready one. Be safe

"Do you think she is safe?"

"Define safe."

"Don't be a prick. You don't want her dead. Besides, she has our money. You're going to take C-470 to Lincoln and come in from the backside?"

*I know where the money is.*
*She is predictable.*

"That's the plan."

"Maybe, you drop me on the north side, and I'll recon down to the rear of the house."

"I'm not sure the neighborhood would appreciate an armed commando sneaking around their back yards in the rain."

"What is the plan?"

"I am going to park in the driveway..."

*Pops will help.*
*He loves this shit.*

Aydin pressed the touch control, and the voice activation appeared.

"Send a text to *Pops*."

**Me**: Pops, open garage door, arrival in 11 minutes

Aydin's mind reeled, waiting for a response from Pops.

*Pops will know to keep quiet.*
*...*
*What is taking so long?*
*...*
*He's moving the cars.*
*Moms? What about Moms?*
*Relax.*
*Breathe.*

> **Pops**: Garage cleared ETA four
> minutes. Sent collateral to buy
> groceries.

*Pops loves this shit.*
*Allison is going to freak out.*
*Good, she deserves it.*

"Do you think Pops sent Allison shopping with her mother? We can surprise her when she returns. Probably not. How do you want to handle it?"

"We need to be quiet. Do you have a taser?"

Phil reached into the calf pocket on his right pant leg and pulled out a taser.

"Good, keep it ready. We'll probably need it. Allison is either on the pool deck or in her old room. It doesn't matter. We'll zap her, zip-ties, then look for the money."

"Why would she be on the pool deck in the rain?"

"Under the gazebo, under the tanning lights. You know how vain Allison is. My bet is she is tanning on the pool deck."

"Don't be a prick. You think the money is at the house?"

"No, but we'll look anyway."

"Then what?"

"Then, we take her to the safe house and figure out how to get our money."

Aydin pulled into the open garage and turned off the engine. Neither he nor Phil closed their car doors. Pops is waiting, holding open the entry from the garage to the house.

Not a word is spoken.

Pops motioned toward the rear of the house and the pool.

Moving to stand either side of Allison, both men admired the bikini.

*Damn, thirty-one, and she still rocks it.*

Changing his mind, holding up his hand, Aydin indicated Phil was to fire the taser when he dropped his hand. Aydin woke Allison with something she could not mistake.

"Hi, Red."

Allison hates being called Red by everyone but Aydin. Before she could react, he reached down and toppled Allison from the deck chair onto the hard, Cool-Deck concrete surface. The sleeping woman banged her right elbow and right knee but remembered to reach for her pistol under the towel.

Phil zapped her.

### Aydin's Mercedes, North Bound, I-25, Raining

Allison's hands and feet are zip-tied together, with her hands behind her back. Her skin is sticking to the cool leather of the rear seat. Pops packed some of Allison's clothes into her small duffle while Phil and Aydin moved Allison from the pool deck to the Mercedes' back seat. What annoyed Allison most was not being hogtied and dumped in the car in her bikini. What upset Allison was her father duct-taped the gag.

"It wasn't in her room, and Pops said she showed up with nothing but the duffel. Aydin, where do you think she hid the money?"

"I know where the money is."

*She gets the house, and I'll take the property.*

"Okay, smart guy, if you know where the money is, why did we have to drive over here and pick her up?"

"She is the contact with the buyer."

"You lost me. Why do we care about that?"

"Allison leads us to her lover. He will lead us to the real buyer, the guy at the end of the chain. From the real buyer, we will learn who is behind the plan."

"Did you say, *lover*?"

"I did. Isn't that right, Red?"

Phil glanced over the seat at the bound woman. Allison rolled her eyes with a 'What did you expect?' shrug. Her eyes returned to the small duffle and her clothes on the floorboard.

"Aydin, when this is all over. I am going to find a nice quiet bar, on a beach, someplace where no one knows my name. I am going to sit on a barstool until my ass is bonded with the Nogahide. Then, I am going to drink some more.

"I liked it better when the missions were simple. Hike in. Blow something up. Hike out. Simple. Life was better when it was simple. Now, we got all kinds of trouble."

Phil's tone is never dark for long, which is one of the things Aydin likes most about his friend. Phil's pause told Aydin his friend was about to say something cheesy to break the tension.

"So much trouble they should call us the Trouble Magnets."

*Phil is right.*

*It might be time to get away and not think about spies, advance facial recognition code, and who is screwing over who for fun.*

"I'll go with you to the beach. Remember why we are here."

"I remember. How much longer?"

"Forty minutes."

### *Safe House, Longmont, Blustery Rain*

*I hate this place.*

*Everything here feels fake.*

*I am going to find another safe house.*

*Maybe someplace up in the mountains.*

*A place that doesn't have lousy art and doesn't smell like a musty hotel room.*

Pulling a taser from the gun safe, Aydin returned to the den. Phil is sitting to Allison's left, and she is still bound, in her bikini, lying on her side on the cold faux leather sofa. Aydin tossed the duffle on the floor in front of Allison.

"We are going to let her get dressed. Phil cut the ties. If she burps or farts funny, I'll zap her again. When she is dressed, tie her hands and feet again."

In silence, Phil cut the ties. Allison pulled off the bikini without an ounce of humiliation, opened the duffle, and put on red lace panties and bra. Phil looked anywhere but at the red-headed spy. She took her time dressing, her eyes never leaving Aydin.

*She is putting on a show for me, like the first time.*

*She wants me to remember the good times, and there were a lot of good times.*

*This is not one of the good times.*

When dressed, jeans, a cream-colored silk shirt, and Ariat boots, she placed her wrists and feet together for the zip-ties.

Phil pulled her hands behind her back before binding her again.

"Remove the gag."

Phil gently pulled the duct-tape and wadding from Allison's face. He gently rubbed the red marks left by the duct tape. Allison watched Aydin's eyes for a hint of affection. Knowing the rage in his mind, she tried to break Aydin's focus.

"I used to think it was fun when you tied me up."

Stretching her jaw, wiggling it side to side, opening and closing her mouth, Allison is overacting for Aydin's benefit.

*She thinks she is getting to me.*

"I won't be able to contact Marco without my phone."

Her eyes focused on Aydin, rubbing her tongue on her dry lips. Allison was playing every card available.

"Can I get some water?"

*Aw, fuck.*
*It is working.*
*What is wrong with me?*

Phil stepped away and returned with the water, holding the glass for Allison to sip. Aydin remained silent, watching. Allison nods a thank you to Phil but has a question for Aydin.

"Did you send your Dad a note? It is your mother's birthday."

*Son of a bitch.*

"No. I'll call him later."

Phil eyed Allison's smirk and wink before turning back and waiting.

"Like I said, without my phone, I can't contact Marco. You brought me here for nothing."

Phil's raised eyebrows let Aydin know Phil was paying attention. Aydin rolled along.

"I have Marco's number."

Allison's shoulders slumped. Phil sat, watching.

"Marco's real name is Terrence Albert Macron. He goes by Terry. He uses Terry unless he is criming, then he is Marco. You didn't know that, did you? Allison, why do you think Terry, or as you know him, Marco, was so friendly and *generous*?"

Phil's years of training were thorough. While on a mission, and this was a mission, his training allowed him to control his ADD and remain silent, observing. Aydin continued when Allison ignored the question.

"Allison, your friends at The Service played you and Terry. Terry is a double agent. Working with you was the plan to blow his cover. Well, a plan to blow it on our side. The Russians, Chinese, and Iranians might not know Terry is playing everyone. I don't think they know that we know so much about their assets."

Phil's head was bobbing with new understanding. Aydin had been playing a long game. A very long game. Phil is wondering if Aydin marrying Allison was for the mission. Aydin continued with his summary.

"You missed the shot at the goon on purpose. You wanted me to take the shot. If it all goes dog-fucked, your cover is still good.

"Allison, your cover is still good. Except at home. I think it will take a long while for your father to forgive you."

*Pops would not shed a tear if we whacked her right now.*

*He's paid too high a price because of her.*

"Dad, won't forgive me? Forgive me for what?"

"For trying to get me killed."

"Fuck you."

"Thanks for the offer, but no, our days of fucking are over. Allison, we need to get Terry out in the open, and you are going to help. Why are you going to help?

"Because if you don't help, you will lose your cover. What happens when you lose your cover?"

Phil shifts in his seat, causing the faux leather to squeak, pulled at his chin, before blurting nonsense.

"Damn, I need some popcorn."

Allison and Aydin, without taking eyes off each other, simultaneously respond to Phil's snarky comment.

"Shut the fuck up."

Allison shrugged, sat back, then continued.

"What do I get out of helping you?"

"You get an uncontested divorce. You get the house. I keep all of the cars except your Rover. I keep the money, all of it, except Phil's cut. And, this is important. You get to fuck off and never talk to me again.

"That last part is for me."

*That should get her attention.*

"You don't know where the money is, you lied. Fuck you. You're not as smart as you think you are."

"7125 Ptarmigan Lane, Elbert County. No thanks on the fuck."

"Son of a bitch... What is your plan?"

*So smart, so beautiful, and ignorant to simple facts.*

*That is why she needs me.*

*Since we were little kids, I have pulled her out of too many troubles.*

*She doesn't think things through like I do.*

*Phil, also, I know he doesn't like to read, but he needs to understand the mission briefs.*

*She needs us.*

"I thought it would be obvious."

"You can't be serious. Marco won't do it."

"Yes, he will."

"Uh, guys, the movie is really, really, good, but

something happened to the storyline. The audience doesn't know what you are talking about."

Allison and Aydin yelled together.

"Shut the fuck up."

"Terry will cooperate, he will give up his buyer, and you know why."

"Aydin, we don't do that."

"Yes, we do, and you are going to help."

"I won't do it."

"Then, I will blow your cover. FirstBio and their cartel would love to know it was you who brokered their billion-dollar global deal that went south."

"Fuck you."

"The answer is still no. Allison… Red, we need to get Terry to give up his buyer."

Allison's pouty expression is ignored, feigning disappointment at being rebuffed, so she answered.

"I didn't seduce him, but he thinks there is candy at the end of the game. Marco won't give up the buyer."

"Why not."

"Because Marco is an idiot. There is no *buyer*."

# Riding the Stupid Bus

"That is the part I missed. I knew there was a hole, but I couldn't figure it out. How did you do it?"

"I used a digital answering machine. The Cloud is amazing. You can hide anything if you work a little bit."

*She is smart and on-point when she wants something.*

*Too much of her is the show designed to bend men.*

"Terry never spoke to the real buyer?"

"No, he left messages. I'd create a response using a digital voice. He'd get a text to retrieve the response."

"Nice work, but you will have to do better. Who is *your* buyer? What did you say, who is at the *end of the chain*?"

"If I told you that, they'd kill us all."

Phil's unable to control his ever-present snarky comment.

"Not getting dead is good."

Allison and Aydin together with a softer tone.

"Shut the fuck up."

"Allison, what did you do?"

Allison shrugged and looked away.

"Grifter. You played Terry in a long-con grift. He didn't seduce you. You seduced him. Where did you get the seed money?"

Allison refused to look at Aydin or answer his question.

"The house! You mortgaged the house."

"No, not the house."

"Where then? Allison, where did you get the money?"

Turning away again, Allison refused to be intimidated.

Aydin turned the taser sideways and fired. The probes each struck one of Allison's breasts, searing little black marks into the cream-colored silk. Aydin kept his finger on the trigger until the discharge was complete. Allison is out cold, laying on the floor, on her side, gently foaming from the mouth.

"Why did you do that?"

"Because she deserved it."

"Aydin, what did she do?"

"She took a kickback from FaceTurn, the firm building the prototype."

"Who the hell is FaceTurn? What are you talking about?"

"FaceTurn is owned by FirstBio. She is in the middle of a long con. Remember when we received our orders? The orders emphasized 'compartmental need to know.' That is a message telling us someone close is the target."

"Allison?"

"Yes, Allison."

"Holy shit. That means... What does it mean?"

"Phil, it means Allison was setting up everyone, including us, to take a hit when she skipped with all the money."

"You lost me. How is Allison going to get all the money?"

"Allison talked Terry into fronting the seed money. She then talked FaceTurn into believing the code I developed was under threat. She offered to protect the code for a fee.

"She planned to burn Terry, claim victory with FaceTurn, then walk with everything. But Terry got smart and demanded she convinces us to deliver the code to him. Allison figured out Terry planned to kill us all, take the code and the money."

"You are making some suppositions, but, wow, you can't trust anyone anymore."

Aydin ignored the comment and stepped over to check on Allison. Lifting her to the sofa, he noticed the open duffle was oddly shaped. Aydin's soft tone was shockingly firm.

*Ah, fuck, not again.*

"Perimeter check. Now!"

Phil did not speak, jumped up, and began the ordered surveillance. Pulling open the duffle, Aydin's K-Bar sliced the inner lining. The transponder's LED is blinking green.

Holding up the transponder, Aydin turned to see Phil standing with his back to the wall, to the left of the front door. Phil held up three fingers forward, then turned his hand a one-eighty and held up three more digits.

*Six bogeys.*

Phil pointed toward the rear of the house with two fingers, followed by two pointing to the front and two toward the garage door.

*Here comes the flash-bang.*

Aydin draped the couch blanket over Allison's head and torso before he moved to a location diagonally opposite Phil. His new position created an overlapping field of fire. From their spots, Phil covered the rear of the house. Aydin, the front, and bay windows. Both fire zones included the entry from the garage.

In a whisper, Phil is unable to remain quiet.

"Who are these guys?"

"Terry's people."

"He doesn't give up."

"Would you give up if one-hundred million dollars was on the line?"

"A hundred million? I thought the deal was for a million upfront and nine more on delivery?"

"That's Allison's fee for stealing the code from me. FaceTurn will make billions from the code."

*Here they come.*

Aydin put a finger to his lips, causing Phil to release the safety on his M4. The experienced commandos opened their mouths and let the TCAPs in both ears absorb the shockwave.

The infiltrators did not blow the locks. They silently open the front door and the large glass slider and rolled in two flash grenades.

Aydin and Phil quickly absorbed the concussions and waited. The four attackers rushed into the large open area and received four quick headshots.

Holding up a stop sign, Aydin then pointed to the garage entry. Seconds feel like hours when your adrenaline meter is pegged at eleven. Both commandos waited for the door to burst open but did not fire until the last of the attackers was visible in the door.

One round from the first attacker entered the wall next to Aydin's head. Both attackers received shots to the head.

Allison sat up, letting the couch blanket slip away, and looked around.

"They will keep coming."

"That is why you are going to call Terry and arrange a meeting."

"Can I pee first?"

Holding her feet up, Allison expected Phil to cut the zip-ties so she could walk to the bathroom. Aydin refused to cut the plastic cuffs. He picked up Allison, took her to the bathroom, stood her in front of the toilet, then pulled down her jeans and lace panties.

"You'll have to wipe for me."

Aydin returned Allison to the sofa. Phil had moved the bodies to the dining room.

"Did you two have fun?"

Together, Allison's and Aydin's tone is almost inaudible.

"Shut the fuck up."

Aydin grabbed his backpack, pulling out a burner phone. Powering it on, he placed it on the arm of the sofa, nearest to where Allison was sitting.

"Tell Terry we took out his team. Tell him we are coming for him unless he stands down. He is going to write it off, and everyone stays alive. You got that?"

"Of course, *I got that,* you moron."

*She is beginning to understand.*
*If I can, I will keep us all alive.*

"Marco, the deal is off."

*"No, it is not off."*

"Your guys failed."

*"Bitch, what did you do?"*

"I didn't do anything. Aydin figured it out. He is offering a deal."

*"No deals. I want my money, and I want the code. Working code. That is the deal."*

"Marco…"

Aydin cut off Allison's pleading.

"Terry, you are blown. Allison screwed us all. The deal is dead. Cut your losses, and everyone lives. By everyone, I mean you."

*"Master Sergeant Aydin Matthew Trammell, it is nice to meet you. I have heard so much about you. The story is, you took out an active cell in Kunduz province by yourself? That was some kind of badass mission."*

"I had help…"

*Two can play this game.*

"Terrence Albert Macron, Central Directorate of Internal Intelligence, retired. What happened, Terry? I supposed even the Frogs have some scruples. They sent you into the cold when you burned their Moscow mole. Terry, you don't have a lot of friends. Call it even, and I will be your friend."

Ignoring the insults, Terry continued in an even tone.

*"Give me Allison and the money, and we are done."*

"Allison? I am not going to let you kill her."

*"Kill her? You do not understand."*

Phil's shock at the realization erupted.

"Oh shit!"

This time, Allison's and Aydin's tone is whispered but firm.

"Shut the fuck up."

Allison shrugged, shook her head in the negative, and nodded toward the phone.

"Terry, I don't think Allison wants to see you again. You are not getting the money, and you are not getting Allison. I assure you. She does not love you despite what you may think. Geez, Terry, I thought you'd be smarter than to fall in love with a two-timing, back-stabbing, red-haired spy."

The silence told Aydin that Terry was undergoing a small epiphany.

*This jamoke fell for her bullshit and smiles.*
*She can be magnificent when she wants to be.*
*Magnificent and deadly like Cleopatra's asp.*

"Terry, no money, no Allison, and we all walk away alive. My word is I will not hurt you. If you don't take the deal, I will hunt you, find you, and hurt you."

*"No deal."*

"That is too bad. Now I have to worry you are going to do something stupid. Do you know what happens when I worry, Terry? Don't answer, I will tell you. I get cranky when I have to worry. I don't want to worry. Last chance, walk away, and everyone lives."

*Take the deal.*
*Take the deal.*

*"No deal."*

Aydin reached down and killed the line. Looking at Allison, he waited for her to speak.

"I am not going to tell you where he is."

"No need, I know where he is. What I am trying to figure out is what to do with you."

"Yo, Aydin, you seem to be in the knowing of a lot of details that, somehow, I never learned. Mission briefs usually contain details about targets, target locations, defensive capabilities, and how to take out the target. I'm a little blind here. Help me out. Don't be a prick because you are two steps ahead."

*I've been tracking her phone for months.*

*Do I tell Phil and give up the information to Allison?*

*No, let that be a secret.*

*Phil will figure it out eventually.*

Glaring at Allison, unblinking, Aydin answered Phil's question.

"Allison has been playing the long con for at least two years. Early on, she made a mistake. She didn't know or didn't care that Terry and FaceTurn were under every type of surveillance possible.

"When The Service determined she was playing games, they contacted me. They knew she and I grew up together on military bases. They knew we had been a couple, on-and-off. They asked me to help."

Allison's eyes squinted, not believing.

41

"Yes, Allison, I played the long game too. Part of me wanted it to be real, but I knew better. Pops came to me about you, he knew. I had his clearance reactivated."

Allison's shoulders slumped slightly at the realization of disappointing her father.

"That's right, Allison, everyone knew what you were doing except Terry. What I want to know is simple. What were you going to do if you got away with the money?"

Allison looked at Aydin, gave a dry, sideways smile, then stared out the bay windows at the Rocky mountains. She is missing the sun and sunnier days. Phil understood it was time to make some choices and some calls.

"The cleaners are on their way. We need to be gone in five. What are we going to do with her?"

"She comes with us."

"What are we going to do?"

"We are going back to the office. First, we are going out to Elbert County and pick up her cache."

"Good idea, pick up the money."

"We'll get the money, but that is not why we are going to her cache."

# All In or All Dead

*There are two types of stupid.*

*It sucks to have both.*

### Elbert County, Steady Rain

"That one. You said: 7125 Ptarmigan Lane. That must be the place. We are so far out the GPS couldn't find it."

"No, Phil, the GPS works. This address is too new for the maps."

Allison is sitting in the middle of Aydin's Mercedes' back seat, staring out the driver's side rear window. Aydin noticed her focus in the mirror and adjusted his plan. Pulling up short of the electronic surveillance, he parked two hundred yards east of the gate and turned to his friend.

"You or me?"

"I'd go, but my guess is, we are going to need your tech skills to open the gate."

"Okay, I'll go. She goes in the trunk first."

The two commandos pulled Allison from the rear seat, expecting her to kick and scream. Allison took it all calmly and allowed herself to be locked in the trunk after the bugout bags and weapons were moved to the back seat. The lashing rain soaked everything in the three minutes it took to relocate the spy to the trunk.

Phil sat in the driver's seat and watched his

friend climb through the barbed-wire cattle fence.

Twelve minutes later, two flashes of light coming from the road near the gate was the signal. Phil started the car. He pulled up, slowed enough for Aydin to open the front passenger door, and jump into the moving vehicle.

The long gravel driveway abruptly ended with no structures visible.

"Aydin, what is this place?"

"It is a 65-acre cattle ranch."

"Where are the cattle? Where is the ranch house?"

"There are no cattle, and there is no house."

"Where is the cache?"

"Use your light, you search left, and I'll scan right. Look for anything."

Allison hollering and banging raised the commando's eyebrows. Opening the trunk, Phil put the beam of his light in Allison's face. Squinting, she sighed calmly.

"Find the pink ribbon on the cactus. About a foot off the ground. Probably fifteen yards, at two o'clock. The cache is buried about a foot down. The code is zero-six-one-one-two-zero-one-five."

*Does she think she is funny?*
*She is trying to let me know something.*

Aydin's response oozed bitterness.

"Our wedding day."

He slammed the trunk and shone his light in the two o'clock direction. Phil spotted the ribbon through the rain haze.

"There."

"Careful, it is muddy, and there is a lot of cactus."

Arriving at the ribbon, Aydin scanned the area with his light.

*She bought this land for our retirement.*
*She did this on purpose, the pink ribbon.*
*She wants to know if I remember.*
*I remember everything.*

Again, Phil spied the goal first.

"Here, the ground is soft."

"Yes, but that is not the cache. It is a diversion."

"What? How do you know that?"

"When we were about twelve, her father and my mother were stationed at Cheyenne Mountain. Allison and I build a fort in the forest behind the base housing. It was our base camp. She would set up missions to see if I could solve a puzzle. The same as when we were kids, this is one of the puzzles. A misdirection."

Aydin continued to shine his light back and forth. The rain and mud were beginning to soak through his boots before he found the spot. Stopping, he focused his light on a small depression under a dead cactus.

"There."

Stepping over, Aydin pulled a cactus, which was attached to a cover. After tossing the plant and attached sheet metal to the side, the rain quickly washed the dirt from the cache's control panel.

Phil continued to scan the area, peering through the rain and mist. Spying a small structure, Phil started to walk over to the odd shadow.

"Aydin, what is that?"

"It is a cattle trough."

"A cattle trough for no cattle?"

"Stay here, Phil. Leave it alone."

Phil stopped, turned back to his friend, and shrugged.

Squatting, Aydin entered the code, which resulted in a green light. Pulling the handle, opening the safe, handing two money bags to Phil, he reached deeper. He pulled the false bottom and grabbed the small safe. Closing the outer safe, he replaced the cactus cover, not bothering to check the surrounding ground cover's look.

*The rain will blend everything.*

Opening the trunk, letting the rain pelt Allison, he held the small safe under the trunk's light. Allison's expression faded and turned from confidence to fear. Aydin closed the trunk lid without a word and tried to clean the mud from his boots before driving away.

Aydin pressed the touch control, and the voice activation appeared.

"Send a text to *KTF*."

**Me**: Need Extraction: Target Two, immediate threat.

### *DTC, Conference Room, Rain Unrelenting*

Standing in the lobby, pulling off his rain slicker, observations briefly replace Aydin's dark thoughts.

*Whatever they use to clean with is some powerful stuff.*

*At least there are no bloodstains.*

*The odor is burning my nose hairs.*

*Too bad we can't prop open the door and air this place out.*

*Dead people do that.*

*They find ways to annoy you for days.*

Allison's feet are zip-tied again, but now her hands are strapped to the arms of the conference room chair. The entry door is repaired, the lobby has no signs that four people were lying dead on the terrazzo hours earlier.

Phil returned with burritos and iced tea to find Aydin head down in his PC. The small safe Aydin pulled from the cache is sitting on the conference room table.

*They've been quiet for too long.*

*Allison is mentally grinding.*

*She is trying to find a way out of the cluster-fuck she created.*

*Phil is trying to figure out our next move.*

*I got ten bucks on Phil speaking first.*

"What are we going to do today, Brain?"

*I win.*

Without looking up, Aydin completed a *Pinky and the Brain* quote.

"'Same as every day, Pinky. World domination.' She's probably thirsty and hungry. Give her some tea and a bite."

"You want me to feed her?"

*No, Phil, we want her to starve to death.*

"Untying her is a bad idea. Feed her something. ... I got it!"

Allison's glare is on Aydin but is being ignored. Phil continues to try and catch up to Aydin's plan.

"You got what? The combination to the little safe?"

"No, we don't need that."

"How do you plan to open the safe without the combination?"

Aydin stood, picked up the small safe, and threw it on the carpet from over his head. The top corner's angle, hitting the thin industrial carpet and the concrete below, popped open the small safe.

Aydin didn't bother to pick up the spilled contents. Phil eyeing the contents while holding the bottle of iced tea to Allison's lips was a mistake. The iced tea dripped and stained Allison's silk blouse.

"Oh, sorry, but the taser holes made it trash anyway."

"Just give me a bite of that burrito."

Pulling the foil back on the burrito, Phil continued his inquiry.

"Passports and flash drives? What's in the envelope?"

"Phil, put that burrito down and put the money bags and flash drives in the vault. Give me the envelope. Close the vault and change the code. Leave the passports."

Phil shrugged toward the hungry Allison but turned to complete the ordered task.

Returning to the conference room and the colder burrito, Phil resumed his questions with Allison's burrito in one hand, his in the other.

"Aydin, I'm going to need a little more info."

"FirstBio and Faceturn. Allison has been playing them also. Faceturn is owned by FirstBio, the founder of Faceturn sold out when FirstBio paid him in cash and told him to go away. He went away. The Chairman of FirstBio has a hardon for the Chinese."

"Isn't he Chinese?"

"Vietnamese. Tran is his name, and he escaped with his parents just before the fall."

"This seems like a lot of dead people for a guy who just hates the Chinese government. What am I missing?"

Aydin looked up and focused on Allison. Staring, he did not avert his gaze until she spoke.

"Tran hates the Chinese because of what they did to his family. He has built his empire with one goal: Hurt the communists."

Phil turned and responded to Allison's chin thrust, requesting another bite.

"What does that have to do with the code?"

"He's not after the code, not exactly. He wants what I did to the core."

"Wait. What about Marco? Terry. Whatever the fuck his name is. I thought we were going to take care of him first. What happened to that piece of this mission? Ad hoc missions end up with the wrong people dead. Will it ever stop fucking raining?"

"Your ADD is kicking in."

"Eat shit. Now tell me why I should not be worried about you making up the plan on the fly."

Allison sat in silence, internally beaming and remembering. She may have double-crossed everyone, but she did love Aydin and Phil. Aydin brought her focus back to the room.

"One, Terry is out of the picture. Check my texts."

Aydin slid his phone along the table quick enough that Phil had to drop his burrito to keep the phone from sliding off the table. Shaking his head, he opened the phone and read the message.

**Me**: Extraction requested. Target two. Immediate threat.

**KTF**: Extraction, target two, confirmed.

"KTF?"

"Kermit the Frog. … Done."

"Done with what? You are doing it again, charging ahead, making plans, and being the only one who can magically solve problems. It is not our fault you grew up going to schools in military towns with teachers who couldn't spell *teacher*. We know you are too smart by half. Stop being a prick."

*Ah, fuck snacks.*

"I arranged to meet Tran."

Raised eyebrows from Phil and Allison did not phase the smiling Aydin.

"We are going to the house to clean up for dinner. Shanahan's at 19:30. Allison, Tran, and me.

Phil will be at the bar. That is unless Allison doesn't want to play nice. But my guess is, she has already figured out how I am going to salvage this cluster-fuck."

Smiling, Allison responded.

"I agree."

"You don't know what I am offering."

"You are going to broker the deal with Tran directly. You are going to tell Tran you brought me along to prove you have control. Cut a deal with Tran, hand over the code, and everyone walks away. Nice and clean."

"Almost."

"What did I miss?"

"I am not handing over the code."

# Clarity Takes Planning

***Trammell House, Rain Lessoning***

"Are you going to watch me shower?"

"You used to like me watching you shower. You are not leaving my sight until this is over."

Without a hint of awkwardness, Allison quickly stripped and stepped into the open concept shower stall. Hollering over the water, Allison was curious.

"You picked Shanahan's because you don't think Tran will start shooting in a nice place."

"Nope."

"Then why did you pick it?"

"I like their steaks."

"What if he starts shooting?"

"He won't. He'll have his people follow us, create a roadblock, or an accident, then ambush us."

"How do you know that?"

"Do you *ever* read your mission briefs? You are so fucking lazy."

Aydin began texting while waiting on the long shower he knows Allison prefers.

**Me**: Pops, need support. Corner of South Syracuse St and Syracuse Cir

"What are you saying? It is hard to hear over the water."

Shutting off the water, stepping forward, pulling the oversized towel off the hook, Allison continued.

"I was saying, what are you going to do when this is over?"

"Phil said something about a beach."

"Yeah, right! You'll be bored on day two and asking for a new assignment."

"Maybe."

Aydin glanced at his phone when it vibrated with a new text.

**Pops**: Support confirmed, 20:15. Be safe.

Phil entered, dressed in slacks and a clean shirt.

"Phil, watch her while I shower. *Do not* let her near the back wall of the closet. Her dress and shoes are on the bed. All she needs is underwear from the drawer in the closet.

"I don't need underwear."

"Good, put on the dress, then sit down."

"Phil, I am not kidding. If she does anything funny, shoot her."

"Got it. Dead Allison if she picks her nose."

*Phil won't shoot her, but she doesn't know that.*
*He might shoot her, but he won't kill her.*
*I hope he won't kill her.*

Phil enjoyed the view of Allison dropping her towel and wiggling into the red silk dress.

Aydin was in and out of the shower in four minutes. He shaved in another three and dressed in two minutes. His dark thoughts returned to when he and Phil did not think about the consequences of their actions.

*Nine minutes.*
*It used to be six minutes max and four in the field with a dry shave.*
*I like the cream softening my beard.*
*Sue me.*

"Two cars. Phil, you follow us. Our table and the seat at the bar are reserved. Remember, Tran won't try anything while we are inside. He'll wait until we are on the road."

## Shanahan's, Rain Lessoning

The folded bill did not go unnoticed when Aydin handed his keys to the valet. When the valet looked up with a bright smile, Aydin nodded to the reserved spot.

*The life of an international intelligence agent is never dull.*
*A thread-bare diner for breakfast.*
*Cheap take-out burritos for lunch.*

*An expensive restaurant dinner.*

*All in forty-eight hours.*

*Damn, I like this place, good steaks and the chairs are comfortable.*

*Phil loves this stuff, and it beats going home to the desperation of the holler.*

*How did someone as smart as Phil come from a dead coal town?*

*The internet is the new educator.*

*We'll go to the beach and find Phil a girl.*


Tran didn't wait for introductions or permission to sit. He walked directly to the table, pulled out a chair, and relaxed while the waiter set his usual drink on the table.

"You know a lot about me, Mister Trammel. Shanahan's is a good choice. Some rain, huh?"

*Wow, these guys are dumb.*

*He thinks I don't do my homework.*

*The scar is the clue.*

*I'll play along like I don't understand the game.*

"Yes, a lot of rain. Call me Aydin."

"Call me Tinh."

If Allison was annoyed at being ignored, she didn't show it.

"Aydin, you have what I want. I know you cut out Terry, and now, it seems, you are cutting out your wife. Very well done. Exceptional."

"What is it you want, Tinh?"

"The core codes. I already have what you gave Terry. I know where you got it. Although I am impressed, I have the same code but a couple of versions older. Getting the current working version through the firewall is no minor effort. Again, well done."

Both nodded to the compliment and sipped their drinks, allowing Tinh to pause before getting to the point.

"You also know the base code is useless to me without the core you created, which is why we are here. Aydin, what do you want?"

"One-hundred million Euros in my account by noon tomorrow."

Tran did not flinch at the enormous demand.

"That might not be possible by noon. Fifty by noon. Fifty when I confirm the core code."

"One-hundred million Euros in my account by tomorrow noon. Also, a free pass for Allison, Phil, and me."

"Seventy-five by noon, free passes for Phil and you. Allison comes with me."

"One-hundred million Euros in my account by tomorrow noon. A free pass for Allison, Phil, and me. Your jet to take us anywhere we want to go, and back, for one year."

"Aydin, we seem to be going in the wrong direction with the terms."

"No, Tinh, you should have agreed to the

hundred-million. Every time you try to play me, I am upping the terms."

Tran smiled, nodded, sipped his drink, and paused.

"One-hundred million Euros in your account by tomorrow noon. Allison comes with me."

"No can do."

"You are loyal after she tried to burn you? She thought Terry's idiots would kill you. There is no way she thought we'd be here talking. She comes with me."

*His boss wants her.*

*Why does everyone want the crazy bitch?*

*Bitches do be crazy, but the men who want them are fucking nuts.*

*Does that include me?*

"Yeah. No."

"I am sure your bosses at The Service will like it if you end up dead, and I end up with the core code."

*Stupid.*

*That was a mistake.*

"See, you just had to be stupid. Why does everyone always have to be stupid?"

Out of the corner of his eye, over Tinh's shoulder, Aydin noticed Phil tap the rim of his drink glass six times.

Allison put her napkin on the table, announcing she had to use the bathroom. Both Tran and Aydin put a hand on Allison's forearms. She sat back down.

Aydin noticed Phil put his knife and fork down at odd angles. Tinh had two people behind Aydin. Two people behind Allison. That left the remaining two at the bar. Aydin's tone was almost jovial.

"We are done here."

Standing, Aydin firmly grasped Allison's upper arm, lifting her from the seat. Not letting go, he led her to the exit. The valet had done what the fifty bucks up-front ensured. He parked Aydin's Mercedes across from the main entrance.

Looking in the rearview mirror, Aydin saw Phil's signal as he pulled out of the parking lot.

Turning right on to South Syracuse, Aydin spied Pop's Silverado across the street. Pops didn't make it the block to Belleview Avenue before Tran's people surrounded the trio of vehicles. One good guy Mercedes in the front, with two bad guts trailing. Then Phil's pickup and a bad guy with Pops bringing up the six.

Waiting at the traffic light, Aydin pressed a unique icon before sending a text.

"Send a text to Pops."

**Me**: Three bogeys, 2 and 1, friendly trailing. Red with me. Option B.

Seeing the text pop up on the screen, Allison wondered aloud.

"Option 'B'?"

"A location."

"Where are we going?

"First, we are going around in a circle."

Allison sat quietly. Aydin made a few unusual turns but did not try to lose Tran's people. He successfully maneuvered, so all three bogies were trailing his Mercedes. Turning back on the SB I-25, Aydin sped up, moving to the extreme left lane, forcing the trailing cars to match his speed.

The trailing vehicles didn't know Aydin was racing to catch Phil and Pops already on SB I-25.

Crossing Arapahoe Road, Phil and Pops merged into position, in the second from the left lane. At County Line Road, the bad guys knew something was up. Next to the concrete center divider, traveling 95 in a 65 mile-per-hour zone was a clue.

At the last minute, Aydin veered right, crossed three lanes, and entered the C-470 onramp. The convoy scrambled to follow. Phil and Pops were each able to insert their vehicle behind one of the bad guys.

From the right lane on the onramp, at the last second, Aydin veered left and entered East Bound C-

470. The Mercedes handled the rain soak maneuvers with ease. The first of the bad guys was able, barely, to adjust direction. The second car would have made the turn except for Pops. Aided by the torrent of rainwater running down the ramp, Pops bumpered him into the concrete Jersey Barrier. Phil hesitated just enough not to hit the panicked driver he was following. When the driver figured out the plan, he tried to speed away. Too late.

The industrial strength brush guard on the front of Phil's Silverado pushed the bad guy into the barrier next to his boss' crumpled SUV.

After losing contact with his cohorts, the remaining bogey vehicle immediately veered off C-470 onto the South Peoria Street offramp.

*I do love this car.*

**Me**: Go for target three.

**Pops**: Target three, confirmed. Be safe.

# Winning Feels Like Losing

### *Trammell House, Rain Howling Again*

Aydin is texting, pacing, and listening to the big-screen television tuned to the local news.

## BREAKING NEWS

TINH TRAN, FOUNDER, AND CEO, OF FIRSTBIO, WAS KILLED IN AN AUTOMOBILE ACCIDENT THIS EVENING. DETAILS ARE STILL COMING IN, BUT IT APPEARS AS IF MISTER TRAN'S VEHICLE MISTOOK THE OFFRAMP SIGNS AND WAS HIT BY ANOTHER CAR BEFORE COLLIDING WITH THE ABUTMENT.

STAY TUNED TO KRDN FOR ADDITIONAL DETAILS.

Allison's hands and feet are zip-tied, but her hands are in the front so she can eat and drink. Allison is sitting on the sofa, Phil in the overstuffed chair. Aydin continues pacing. Allison is quiet, listening to Aydin and Phil. Phil is mumbling between swigs of beer.

"Well, that sucks."

"Except, Tran's not dead."

"What are you talking about? There it is again.

You and Pops are keeping us in the dark. Keeping *me,* the guy who was there, in the desert with you, keeping me in the dark. I know you don't trust people. Hell, I don't trust people and people *like* me. You trust Pops. I know you trust me. You just don't know how to break the cycle of growing up alone. Aydin, I believe in you. You need to trust me. Stop being a prick.

"What are you talking about?"

"He's not dead."

Phil stared at the standing Aydin, demanding an answer.

"The guy we met with was not Tinh Tran."

"Tran sent a go-fer? How did you know?"

"I look at faces all day for a living. Tran has a scar on his left eyebrow. The guy we met didn't have the scar. You two should read the mission briefs."

Aydin's cell phone chimed.

Placing the phone on the sofa's arm, between Allison and Phil, Aydin pressed the green icon, followed by the speaker icon.

*"Well done, Mister Trammel, well done."*

"Hello, Tran. Did your doppelganger give you the terms of our arrangement before he gnawed on the road barrier?"

*"He did. I am surprised you did not ask for more."*

"I don't need more. I needed you to know I am serious."

*"I believe you are serious, Mister Trammel.*

*Very serious."*

The large double-paned glass of the slider shattered, sending shards into the house. Before the glass shards stopped rolling, Phil and Aydin had Allison pulled behind the couch and the zip-ties cut.

Phil is commando crawling toward the pantry and the hidden door leading to the crawl space under the house.

*"Are you still there, Mister Trammel?"*

Pulling the phone down, Aydin responded.

"The price is now two-hundred million Euros by tomorrow noon. I will text you the account number."

*"Mister Trammel, you don't think you are in a position to bargain, do you?"*

"Two-hundred and twenty-five million."

*"I like your style, Mister Trammel."*

"Fuck you, Tran. We are not friends. Two-hundred and fifty million."

*"Let's be reasonable and discuss this like businessmen. I am not going to allow you to extort me. I am going to let you live if you give me what I want."*

"A sniper with a lock on my house isn't extortion? If you kill me, you'll never get the core code. Why are you trying to kill Allison? Never mind, I will ask her. Two-hundred and seventy-five million."

Another shot hit the sofa but was blocked by the barrier hidden in the custom-made furniture.

"Tran, you should hire better shooters. This one is terrible."

*Phil must have gotten a lock on the sniper's position.*

Aydin heard the distinct muffled sound of a silenced rifle.

"Tran, are you still with me?"

*"I am here Mister Trammel."*

"Call me, Aydin. Since you just lost your sniper, I feel generous, two-hundred million Euros by noon tomorrow. I get the money, and you get the core code. Is it a deal, Mister Tran? Wait, listen to this."

Aydin stood and pointed his cell phone at the wall-mounted television and the local news.

### Breaking News

Our report earlier indicated Tinh Tran, Founder, and CEO, of FirstBio, was killed in an automobile accident this evening. The identification of the deceased has been corrected. Tinh Tran owned the vehicles in the multi-car accident. The person mistaken for Tinh Tran is his nephew, Duy Tran.

Stay tuned to KRDN for additional details.

*"Mister Trammel, do you think it is a good idea*

to extort millions from me?"

*He is trying to threaten me.*
*Everyone takes stupid pills then calls me.*

"Is that a threat?"

"*No, Mister Trammel, it is a statement of fact. I suggest you ask Misses Trammel.*"

Allison shook her head in the negative.

*She is beautiful.*
*Beautiful and deadly, like a copperhead snake.*

"We are done here, Tran. Enough talking. I get the money, and you get the core code. I know it is worth at least one-point-seven billion to you. A couple hundred million is chump change.

"You wire the money. I will confirm the money and tell you where to meet. You, Tran, not one of your boys, you come, or the deal is off. Any questions?"

"*Mister Trammel, I am unable to get to Colorado easily.*"

"Then, no deal. Look out your window. What do you see?"

Fearful, barely moving the edge of the vertical blinds, Tinh Tran glanced out of the corner of the hotel window. Seeing the flashes of light from the neighboring rooftop, Tran let the shutter slats close softly.

"*Two-hundred million.*"

"I am glad you understand the situation. Two-fifty. What's fifty mil between friends?"

*"Two-hundred and fifty million."*

"I will text the account number. When the money is confirmed, I will text the meeting details. I am not stupid enough to think you won't have protection.

"Tran?"

*"Yes, Mister Trammel?"*

"Your protection stays back. Me and you. Do you understand?"

*"I understand, Mister Trammel."*

Aydin pressed the red icon, ending the call.

**Me**: SQ-913-076-2771-523-98-7-AB.

**Tran**: SQ-913-076-2771-523-98-7-AB

**Me**: Situation secure. Stand down. Beer on me.

**Pops**: Stand down, confirmed. Be safe.

*Pops loves this shit.*
*I hope I love this shit when I am his age.*

# Not Dead is Good

*Hell is for those too stupid to stop when they are winning.*

### Trammell House, Early Morning, Lite Rain

The cleaning crew worked all night to remove glass shards from the carpet, apply plywood covers to the shatter slider, and dispose of the sniper's body. Allison and Aydin are sitting at the breakfast bar. Phil is cooking breakfast but eating as much as he is putting in front of his friends. He is enjoying listening to Allison pester Aydin.

"Will you help with Dad?"

"No, Allison, you have to fix it with Pops."

"He listens to you. He won't listen to me."

"That is because he is tired of pulling your ass out of a jam. Remember when we were sixteen? He knew I took the heat for you. Luckily, he and my mom called in the markers and got me released.

"Allison, you can fix it. Tell Pops you got caught in a long game. You were in too deep and forgot which way was out. That is true. Tell him the truth, but not the details."

"That is not why he is mad at me."

"No, that is not why he is mad at you."

"Yeah, Pops loves our Aydin."

Both refused to look up but responded to Phil's interruption.

"Shut the fuck up."

Phil just grinned and shoveled the scrambled eggs onto their plates. After finishing breakfast, Phil picked up the dishes, loaded the dishwasher, then headed to his apartment in the pool house.

## *DTC, Conference Room, Late Morning, Lite Rain*

"Tell me again, why we came back here?"

"Phil, I told you, the high-speed, secure internet."

"Oh yeah, why do we need the secure connection? What are you doing that probably involves me getting shot at some point shortly?"

*Ah, fuck snacks.*

"Something is out of place in this deal. I know why Tran wants the core code, and I know why he wants Allison. Someone is playing a different game. What I don't know is who is pulling strings."

Allison is watching Aydin closely from the conference room chair, her left wrist zip-tied to the chair. She decided to break her silence. Her goal is to distract Aydin before he figured out the truth.

"It is about time, mullet."

"Mullet, that's good."

Only Allison responded to Phil's snarky comment.

"Shut up."

Aydin did not look up from his PC.

"Allison, are you nervous about what I will

find?"

"You won't find anything."

Immediately she knew the comment was a mistake. It confirmed there was something for Aydin to find. She knew he knew it from his sideways glance.

Interrupted by the timer on his phone, Aydin realized it was noon. Switching to a secure browser, he confirmed the deposit of two-hundred and fifty million Euros. After confirming the money, he pressed the icon he created to initiate the transfer. It required 37 seconds to confirm the funds and transfer them to an alternate numbered account.

Aydin expected what happened next. The text message arrived.

**Tran**: ???

*How did I know he would be monitoring the account?*

*Criminals are predictable.*

*Not all.*

*The smart ones are not predictable.*

*It is a good thing most of them are stupid.*

**Me**: 17 Rio Grande Blvd, 14:00.

"Two o'clock. The warehouse."

Phil nodded and went to the vault behind the

false panel. He returned wearing his vest, putting Aydin's Kevlar vest on the table. While Phil was laying out the weapons, Aydin sent another text.

**Me**: Mission go. Target one confirmed. 14:00

"Come on, Aydin, help a bro. How are we going to play this?"

"Classic exchange. We'll open the big doors and park inside, facing out. Tran pulls in, his guys jump out, and fan left and right. You stand with Allison while I walk forward to meet Tran.

"Tran's guys will start shooting when I hand him the flash drive."

"I hope you have more than that because that is a plan that sounds like we get dead."

Aydin did not respond. He stood, began checking his weapons, smiled, and glanced at his phone.

**Pops**: 14:00. On your signal. Be safe.

*The rain and wind will affect ranging.*

**Vacant Warehouse, Overcast**

"It stopped raining."

"Yeah, for the moment. Phil, get her out of the

car.

*Sweet, we finally catch a break, no rain.*

The three are standing in front of Aydin's car, facing the cavernous warehouse's large open doors. The opaque windows behind the trio are bright, with the sun over the mountains.

Pigeons have begun using the one broken window to nest in the rafters and on the personal lockers on either side of the main floor.

*Chuck Yeager had it right.*
*Keep the sun to your back and the enemy to your front.*

"Do you want me to shoot those birds, so they don't crap on your car?"

"Forget about the birds, Phil."

"Here, he comes. Didn't you say just Tran?"

A black sedan pulls in, flanked by two black SUVs. Before Tran exits the vehicle, armed guards pour out of the SUVs and form a line on either side of the sedan.

Tran's driver exits the vehicle, then turns to open the rear door, allowing Tran to exit the car. Tran pulls off his sunglasses but changes his mind when he experiences the glare from the windows' western wall.

Aydin stepped forward two steps, and without

looking, he waved Phil and Allison back. They retreat to behind the open front passenger door.

*This is not good.*
*One, two… eight.*
*Tran brought eight fucking guards.*
*Oh well, we came all this way, might as well dance.*

Slowly reaching into his breast pocket, Aydin pulls out a flash drive. Holding the flash drive close to his chest, he does not move.

"Tran, there is something I don't yet understand. You have everything you need but the core code I wrote. I get that part. What I don't get is why you didn't steal the current version of the base code? Why did you wait for me to steal it?"

"An excellent question, Mister Trammel. Aydin, I wanted to know if you had both the intelligence and the connections to pierce the Bamboo Firewall."

"You were testing me? Fuck you, Tinh. I don't believe you. I think your back doors are all closed. Your guy on the inside was executed for treason. You lost your pathway into the intelligence service and figured I'd be your new supplier."

"They told me you were smart, Aydin. I didn't know how smart."

*Holy shit snacks.*
*I wonder if Allison understands what is going*

*on.*

*No, of course not.*

*She didn't read the mission summaries and updates.*

*Pops knows.*

"Yeah, they have been telling me I am smart since I was five. Here I am, standing in front of a firing squad. How smart is that?"

"I see you understand the situation."

"I understand it entirely. One, your first plan was to get the core code and recruit me to work for you. You realized you could never trust me.

"Your second plan is to get the core code and kill me. But that doesn't work either. Too many people, on both sides, would not like a dead Aydin.

"Third, you figured, I would be useful as a contractor when you need my backdoor into the intelligence service. Finally, you realize there is too much trouble in brokering with The Service. You decided to write-off the money. Kill us. Then sell the core code."

Tran waves his hand in a forward circle, requesting Aydin continue his explanation.

"You missed something important."

"What is it you think I missed?"

"The core code doesn't work without the decryption cipher. Go ahead, Tinh, guess where the decryption cipher is stored."

"Aydin, your premise is well reasoned and

thoroughly detailed, but *you* missed an essential element."

"Humor me."

"I don't need the decryption cipher."

"Tinh, you have been given bad advice. You were told your guys could decompile and reverse engineer the compiled code, bypassing the cipher. The core code is not compiled into an executable. It is still raw and encrypted.

"You need a cipher for the raw code and a cipher for the executable.

"Checkmate, Tinh. I give you the core code. Everyone walks out of here alive. Tomorrow noon, I will text you the ciphers."

Tran turns and waves at his vehicle. A man exits the sedan, steps up, and bows toward Tran.

"Is he telling the truth?"

"Yes."

Tran waves the small man away, who hurriedly climbs back into the sedan.

"Very smart indeed. My intelligence sources will need an upgrade. They failed to inform me just how dangerous you are, Mister Trammel.

"One question, if I may?"

*He's going to make a threat.*
*Be cool.*
*Breathe.*

"What makes you think I will not agree to your

terms. Get what I need, then send my team after you?"

"You can't threaten me, Tinh. I know where you live."

Threatening Tran was the tipping point.

"Give me the damned code. I get the ciphers tomorrow at noon. Then, you will start looking over your shoulder."

Aydin could not remove the grin from his face. Turning to Phil and Allison, Aydin winked before turning back to Tran. Phil grabbed Allison's hand tightly and gave a gentle tug.

After years of living in the USofA, Tran thought he understood the nuances of American communications. He did not understand why Aydin was smiling. Stepping forward, Aydin held the flash drive at arm's length. Holding out the flash drive was the signal.

Pops pulled the trigger releasing the round through the one broken window. Pressing the trigger also activated a servo release mechanism.

Tran's head exploded at the same time machine guns opened up in the direction of Tran's people. Phil yanked Allison down and pushed her to the rear door. They both climbed into the car.

One weapon on either side of the warehouse, concealed in old personal lockers, the automated guns swept back and forth across the front half of the warehouse.

The arc of the weapon's sweep was long

enough that several of the gunmen began to turn and run. None made it two steps.

After scanning the target zone, perched across the railroad tracks, eyeing the downed gunmen, Pop's pressed the control. The automated weapons stopped seeking targets. Aydin walked to the sedan, opened the rear door, and peered inside.

The small man was alive, having taken one round in the leg, one in the arm, and one in the upper right chest. Aydin's stern face frightened the small man.

"You know why?"

"Yes. Will I die?"

"You will live."

Aydin nodded and walked away. The trio is driving away as the cleaner's van came screaming into the warehouse behind them.

In under a minute, the cleaners had the automated weapons removed and were out of the building.

Phil was unable to remain quiet.

"That was cool. Two sweet .30-cals with netting for the spent shells. Computer control and battery mounted under the tripod. Nice and tidy, the rig makes for easy cleanup. Fully automated laser range finding mounted above the receiver. Flawless target acquisition. That kind of automated targeting requires three reference points for target acquisition. The two .30-cals are pinging each other for ranging. Where's the third point for triangulation?"

Aydin held up the flash drive. He pointed it at Tran.

"Hot damn. Where did you get the idea?"

"Breaking Bad."

Allison grunted.

# Never a Good Idea

*Hanging around with dead people is never a good idea.*

***Trammell House, Early Evening, Overcast***

## Breaking News

We are updating our report on the underworld shootout in the warehouse in Baker. Tinh Tran, Founder, and CEO, of FirstBio, and eight of his entourage were killed in an abandoned warehouse. One man survived with life-threatening gunshot wounds.

Officials indicate the deaths are the results of a drug deal gone bad. At this time, there are no suspects.

Anonymous sources tell KRDN that Tran's history of trouble with the Chinese government finally caught up to Vietnamese immigrant.

Stay tuned to KRDN for additional details.

Aydin reached across the counter, grabbed the remote, and pressed the mute button.

"No, Aydin."

"Yes, Allison. It's either that or I turn you over to The Service."

"You wouldn't do that. The Service would send me to Leavenworth."

"Yes, they would. Treason is a serious charge. Talk to your father or go to Leavenworth. Allison, this is all on you. All of it. I can spin it if you make up with Pops."

"Aydin?"

"No buts. Yes or no?"

"Okay, I'll do it."

"How did you know? The little guy in Tran's car, what's that all about."

"You need to read the mission briefs. That guy is Liu Wei. He's a data scientist."

*She will figure it out.*

*She's smart enough to know I just gave her a clue that connects everything.*

Phil intercepted Allison's anger, calming her down.

"Don't be a prick."

After a deep breath, Allison made the connection.

"Isn't that a Chinese name? Oh... It was Tran?"

"Yes, it was Tran."

"He is a Chinese sleeper agent. No wonder he became so successful. The Chinese backed him. How long? What was he going to do with the core code?"

"Analysis says: He was recruited before his family joined the boat people. He wanted my core code for a specific reason. The Chinese facial recognition software is the best in the world. Their recognition AI can identify anyone in their database in under twelve seconds. But the accuracy is somewhere in the mid-seventies to low eighties as a percentage.

"My core code bumps up the accuracy to the high nineties."

Aydin paused, waiting.

*She's figuring it out.*
*Finally, she may understand what she did.*
*Damn, Pops will know what to do.*
*He'll tell me if I should cut her loose or not.*
*Bitches be crazy, but more so when you love them.*
*Trust and love.*
*Is there one without the other?*

"What are they going to do with all the data?"

"That is the real question. My core code makes the base code almost as accurate as a tracking chip. It can track you anywhere there is a camera connected to the WEB."

"TikTok?"

"TikTok is just one source. Facebook,

Instagram, Google, all of them. Every selfie taken and loaded to the Cloud is used as a comparison source. Tagging photos with names make the recognition that much easier. Every time you look at your phone, the augmented AI could ID you."

"Well… fuck. I almost screwed up. Bad."

"Yes, but almost doesn't count."

"I will talk to dad. Whatever you want. We can fix this. Did you say something about the beach? Two hundred and fifty very large can buy a lot of beach time."

Phil's sing-song tone was bright.

"Aydin and Allison are sitting in a tree…"

Smiling at each other, Aydin and Allison loved Phil also. Their response came with a smile.

"Shut the fuck up."

# Mandarin Pith
## Winter Snows...

*"Let those who know know,
and let me keep what little privacy I can."*
*Lisa Bonet*

### DTC Conference Room, Mid-Morning, Snowing

Aydin and Phil are in the Fírinne conference room. Together, they are working to resolve the catastrophe that was the mission to keep the Chinese from turning their facial recognition AI into a global tracking service. Using Aydin's core code to augment their AI, the Chinese could identify anyone. With the advanced algorithms, anywhere there is sufficient technological infrastructure, a person can be identified.

Using the existing GPS and a cell phone, anyone can be tracked. Anywhere. It is a good thing the Chinese did not get Aydin's core code.

Allison, Phil, and Aydin's debrief with their sponsor, The Service, did not go well. A week ago, during the AAR, the After-Action Review, Aydin's mind kept wandering to the same thought.

*These fucking eggheads have no idea what fieldwork requires to be successful.*
*They think staying alive is a game.*

Kermit and his team of cleaners pulled another

miracle. He and his team from The Service confirmed everything was tidied up. Critically, Kermit's team *managed* to ensure local and state law enforcement did not look beyond a local drug deal gone bad. The trio of longtime friends resumed their daily routine. Their mundane daily routine. Coding and testing. Rinse and repeat.

Phil convinced Aydin to cut Allison a break. Phil knows Aydin and Allison love each other and have been in love since they were kids. He was not going to let a screw-up by the beautiful red-haired spy destroy a life's worth of memories.

Aydin says he married Allison for the mission. Phil knows the truth: Aydin genuinely loves Allison.

They have been in love since first grade. Warm winter days are rare in the middle of nowhere, Montana. One memorable day, Allison kissed Aydin on the playground. He has known Allison is the only one for him since he was seven years old.

Outwardly, Aydin took Phil's gentle pestering and suggestions in stride. Internally, he is seething.

*She never reads her mission briefs.*
*Phil never reads the entire summary.*
*I am the only one who reads.*
*I almost got shot.*
*What was she thinking?*
*She almost burned Pops too.*
*Pops.*
*He says he can get her set straight.*
*We killed the connection.*
*Which means we burned the buyer.*

*Now the Russians are sniffing around.*
*Where in the hell do we go from here?*

"Yeah, Phil, I get it. Pops will make it right. Allison will stay with Pops and Moms for a couple of weeks. Then she will come home as if nothing happened.

"Didn't you say the rain was supposed to stop? It is snowing! Did you check the messages?"

"Aydin, you know this is spring in Colorado. Snowing in the morning, seventy degrees, and sunny at two in the afternoon. No, I didn't check the messages. That's a receptionist's job. Are you going to hire another receptionist? What's bugging you?"

*He always knows.*
*What is with him?*
*His Hillbilly blood must be psychic or some damned thing.*
*He was like this in the desert.*
*He'd say 'no, this way' or 'hold' and every time he was right.*
*Phil kept us alive with whatever it is he learned hunting squirrels.*
*Whatever he brought out of that holler is a good thing.*
*Fuck it.*

Aydin reached for one of the breakfast burritos, his second large black coffee, and scanned the list of voice messages before responding.

"Seventeen messages. Does it feel like we are

playing poker, and we keep waiting for cards that are missing from the deck?"

# Crossfire Array



Phil is bored with reviewing the failed mission and looked forward to getting back to the predictable coding. He willingly headed out in the storm to bring back burritos and iced tea. To Phil's annoyance, Aydin has been quiet for too many hours.

Their offices go unused because of the isolation felt in the small rooms. Phil hates that his office has no window. Aydin supports Phil's need for community and a window by almost always sitting in the conference room. Aydin sits in the middle of the long table, facing the windows. Phil is at the end of the table, on Aydin's left. His back is to the wall and the windows to his left.

Phil understands, Aydin's access to secured materials far exceeds his own. He wishes Aydin would open up, discuss options a little more often, and ask for advice. Eyeing his longtime friend, Phil understands. When Aydin is tapping his upper lip with his right index finger, he is analyzing whatever he just read.

*Ah, fuck snacks.*
*This sucks.*
*Allison is read-in on the new mission summary and going to have to help.*
*Pops too.*
*Son of a bitch.*
*Phil is going to love this.*

*He hasn't even read the damned thing.*

*We have too many voicemail messages, too much on our plate.*

*I'll get us some help.*

**Me**: Need replacement receptionist. Prior military preferred.

**KTF**: Source receptionist, prior military. Confirmed.

Aydin glances sideways. Phil tilts his head in a gesture of 'it is your turn.'

*He wants to know what we are doing next.*

*He needs to stop watching Diners, Drive-Ins, and Dives and start reading the mission summaries.*

Before Phil can speak, Aydin cut off the questions.

"Shut up and read your mission summary. I've requested a receptionist."

Phil raised an eyebrow, put down the burrito, wiped his hands, and opened his PC. Aydin let him read, knowing Phil would figure it out.

Phil figured it out and erupted.

"Fucking losers. They are about as useful as tits on a bull."

Aydin tried to calm his friend.

"They know we are close to finding something.

The only option is to keep going. It looks like the Russians want to reach out to Allison. The Service wants the same play with the Russian as we ran with the Chinese."

"What do the Russians want with your core code? The Russian AI sucks. Will your code even work with their AI?"

Aydin's tone always lightens when he talks about coding.

"Theoretically, the API tweaks we made will allow the core code to integrate into any sufficiently sophisticated AI."

Phil sighed in disgust but pressed forward.

"Theoretically? You mean if the creek don't rise, on a Tuesday with the full moon, it'll work?"

"I tested with the hacked version of the Chinese AI, and it should work with the Russian AI."

"Do you have a version of the Russian AI?"

"No."

Aydin realizes a truth.

*Phil is avoiding talking about Allison.*

Phil's tone is confused.

"We do not have a working version to test. Theoretically? Should? That is a whole lot of thin. We made a lot of dead people. What is different about this mission? Is this a different mission? Is this the same mission part two?"

*Phil has figured out this might be a setup, but he is trying to get me to tell him the details.*

*I don't have fucking details.*

*There is a primary and a secondary motive.*

*One: Use Allison to get a working version of the Russian AI.*

*Two: Figure out if she has been turned. If she is a double agent, I'd know.*

*She may be crazy, but she is not a traitor.*

*I hope Pops is wrong.*


"First, I think Allison made a mistake. I don't think she understood Terry was going to try and kill us. Allison was in over her head, and now she knows it. The question is, why was she playing the grift, and what pushed her to deal with the Chinese?

"There is something else going on, and The Service wants to know if she has turned. They are testing her, and it is our job to find out. One way or the other.

"Second, if she can get a working copy of the Russian AI, I can test the API. If it works, the Russians will pay."

*Another two-fiddy would not hurt.*

Phil snorted at the information.

"When ifs and buts are candy and nuts, every day will be Christmas. Why do I think this is something else?"

"Did you read the second page?"

Exhaling, Phil returns to reading his PC. Waiting for Phil to catch up, Aydin's dark thoughts continue.

*At least the snow is pretty.*

*It will be melted by noon tomorrow.*

*The roads are going to suck.*

*There is no way the Russians will walk into a warehouse.*

*The automated ranging and target acquisition worked perfectly.*

*The key is the flash drive.*

*You can reposition it within the target zone, and the algorithms take over.*

*The Service says the DoD is interested.*

*That will be another nice paycheck.*

*It will be nice to have Allison back.*

Phil breaks Aydin's thoughts.

"What the actual fuck? We can't do this. Why do they think we can do this? Bunch of slackers whose cornbread ain't done in the middle. Next time I see that son of a bitch, I am going to jerk a knot in his tail. Aydin, what is wrong with those fuckin' morons?"

*I see Phil has figured it out.*

"Reading is good for you, Phil.

"Fuck you. What is he thinking?"

"How do you know it is a he? Have you met our handler? Our handler could be a woman. Or, worse, a fucking committee."

"My recruiter was male. But I see your point. We never see faces."

The cloud cover was thick enough to create a

misty, dark afternoon. The dull afternoon light let headlights shriek into the conference room. A tall car pulled into a parking spot directly in front of the large windows. Huge, late spring snowflakes are blowing at an angle in the bright high-beam lights. Not expecting a visitor, both former commandos dive under the table and its reinforced center partition. Aydin issues orders before their knees hit the carpet.

"You get to the closet. I'll tip up the table while you get us some machinery. We move on go.
"Three.
"Two.

The headlights go off, and the ambient light from the ceiling returns. Quizzically, the longtime friends look at each other. Phil is unable to remain quiet.
"What the fuck?"
"The same plan, on go."
"Two.
"One.
"Go!"

Aydin tips up the table while Phil duck walks through the conference room door and begins his dash to the hidden panel. Hearing the electronic lock on the main door release, Phil dives behind the reinforced reception desk before he can reach the secret wall panel and the safety of being armed.

The small, stark lobby is stark is a terrible place

to hide.

Phil can see Aydin through the glass of the conference room door. Aydin mimes a simple plan. Phil is going to draw the attacker's attention so Aydin can rush them from behind. Aydin's mind is complaining.

*This is not good.*
*We need to be armed all the time.*
*What was I thinking?*
*Stupid fucking civilian life is going to get me killed.*
*Probably today.*

The lobby door pushed open, and in walked a woman in a Canada Goose, Blakely Down Parka, and matching gloves. Hearing the laugh, Phil stood up and slow-walked back to the conference room. He helped the silent Aydin stand up the large table and align the chairs. In the desert, Phil learned to read Aydin's clues. His eyes are looking at you but not focused on you, and his lips are a thin line holding back the rage. Phil could see on Aydin's face the simmering pain.

*What the hell is she doing here?*
*What does she want to know?*
*The mission is for her to make contact.*
*Are we estranged?*
*Is that the right word?*
*Yes, I think so.*

*She isn't living at home.*
*That is strange.*

Allison pulled off her parka, shook the snow onto the terrazzo, and laid the parka and gloves on the reception desk. Walking into the conference room, she is striking in her fire-engine red turtleneck sweater and matching spandex leggings. She acted as if the incident with the Chinese was forgotten.

Kissing Phil on the forehead, she walked around the table and sat in the chair opposite Aydin.

"You should have seen your faces when I pulled up."

*She knows I like that sweater.*
*She is making a point.*
*She wants to make up.*
*HA!*
*Let's see.*
*It is time for someone else to squirm.*

"You should have called. This isn't over, and you know it. We could have shot you."

"But, you didn't."

"No, and that is on us. It won't happen again. Phil?"

Without a word, Phil exits the conference room, headed to the hidden vault. He returns with sidearms and shoulder holsters for himself and Aydin. After strapping on the protection, Phil sits silently watching, and Aydin looks up.

*Let's see what she thinks.*

"Did you read it?"

"Yes."

"All of it?"

"Yes."

"Well?

"We can do it. But it won't be easy."

Phil burst out laughing, His undiagnosed ADD kicking in, Phil is trying to talk, laugh, and sip coffee that is too hot. Aydin and Allison waited until Phil was calm enough to speak clearly.

"Tran was an idiot. There's a tree stump back home with a higher IQ than his security team. No one, and I mean no one the Russians send at us, will be that stupid. Allison, do you realize what you have to do?"

"Of course, but I never give up the candy. It is all about the promise of something more."

Her face taking on a stern look, Allison turned from Phil to Aydin and continued.

"Only Aydin has ever tasted this candy."

*She is supposed to be squirming, not me.*

# Build the Labyrinth

**_Late-Evening, Trammell House, Heavy Spring Snow_**

Phil and Allison are sitting on the leather couch with Aydin in the overstuffed leather chair to their left. Allison is sipping red wine while Phil pounds back Fat Ale. Aydin is drinking Navy Strength Gin with a lemon squeeze and downing it too fast because his mind is reeling.

*She is trying hard to tell us something without words.*

*I need to slow down.*

*Those fuck-nut military shrinks didn't have a clue.*

*One hundred percent fit for service.*

*HA!*

*Stupid fuckers.*

*They thought they knew what six straight months in the desert and too many missions did to you.*

*Doctor missing dick and doctor ass licker didn't know shit.*

*I need to slow down.*

*I want to know what Allison is driving toward and why.*

*Is this another game?*

*Am I being played again?*

*Bitches be crazy, and damn, she is their queen.*

"Allison, you said, 'Tran was never the target.'

Tran was always target number two. Or three. … Three. It doesn't fucking matter."

*I need to slow down with the gin.*

Looking through eyes beginning to blur, Aydin continued.

"Back up and explain to me what you are talking about."

"The mission. My primary mission was always about Terrence Macron. They wanted to sweep him up and turn him over to the Central Directorate of Internal Intelligence. The French wanted him bad for getting their people in Moscow killed."

"So, there were two missions?"

"Yes, and you should slow down. You're not nearly as sexy drunk and slurring as you are sober."

"Fuck you."

"Maybe."

Phil heard the clue, leaned forward, collected three of his empty bottles, and stood to leave. Aydin stopped him.

"Phil, sleep in the guest bedroom. There is too much ice and snow out there. You'll drown falling into the pool on the way to the guest house. I am not diving in to save you."

Phil just nodded, kissed Allison on the forehead, and headed to the kitchen and the guest bedroom.

*Here we go.*
*She is squirming now.*

"Aydin, there is something else you need to know."

Phil stopped, waiting. Aydin bit.

"What's that?"

"The guy you killed at the first meeting with the buyer?"

"Yes?"

"He was one of ours."

Phil grunted and disappeared into the kitchen. Outwardly, Aydin appears unphased. Internally, not so much.

*Ah, fuck snacks.*

*Games within games.*

*I should have seen it coming.*

*Allison is getting a different mission brief.*

*She plays dumb on the summaries and objectives to hide that she is getting alternate targets.*

*Be cool.*

*Breathe.*

"I figured you must have had *an out* in place. When were you going to tell me?"

"Now."

The tiny eyebrow twitch told Allison she had reached Aydin's heart. Allison might be the only person capable of seeing Aydin's mental darkness vanish.

*Allison, Phil, and Pops are the only people I trust.*

*I trust me,*

*Hellfire, sometimes*
*I don't trust Allison or me.*
*Hellfire?*
*Where did that come from?*
*Phil used to say that word.*
*What the hell do they teach kids in the holler?*

Allison slid along the couch, closer to Aydin and the overstuffed chair before he asked.

"Does Pops know about the friendly?"

"He knew from the beginning."

"Of course, he did. He is one smooth fucking spy. You know he loves me more than he loves you?"

"Fuck you."

Aydin's mind flew back to the fort in the woods when he and Allison were young. In the fort, away from the families, she said she liked how he smiled and kissed him. He never forgot her smile or the kiss.

"Okay."

Allison saw the smile her love keeps reserved for her.

### Mid-Morning, Trammell House, Light Snow

The trio fell easily back into their routine. Morning workouts completed, showered, dressed, they had finished the breakfast Phil presented. Aydin's attitude is all business.

*Last night was fun.*
*Today will be ...*
*What did the Brits in the desert say all the time*

*...*

*I miss those guys.*
*Dog's dinner!*
*Today will be the dog's dinner.*

"Allison, you follow us to the office in your Rover. Phil, on our six in the Silverado. Everyone is armed from now on. Questions?"

*Of course, there are no questions.*
*They are in mission mode.*
*Mentally and physically ready.*
*Are we ever not in mission mode?*
*There are no missions on the beach.*

In silence, the longtime friends clean up, close the armory vault, hiding it in the rear of the pantry, and bundle up against the cold.

### NB I-25, Clearing Snow Flurries

Allison is in her Rover following Aydin's Mercedes with Phil in his Silverado several car lengths to the rear. Crossing under Lincoln Avenue, Aydin was sure three dark vehicles on the northbound onramp, using the shoulder, had run the traffic meter red light,

*No way they are on us this soon.*
*Did Allison do something?*
*How would they know where we are?*
*The dog's dinner.*
*Be cool.*
*Breathe.*

Realizing the three vehicles were increasing their speed on the dryer, well-travel lane next to Allison, Aydin moved to the extreme inner lane. Allison followed the maneuver, trying to stay on Aydin's bumper.

She was a few seconds late in moving over one lane. One of the new pursuers was able to force his car between Aydin and Allison. The other two behind Allison. Aydin notices the dispersion.

*These Bozos made a mistake.*

Aydin pushed three icons on the small touchscreen. One of the images connected him to Allison and Phil. Hearing the communication connection chirp, Allison just started speaking using her 'I'm on a mission' voice.

"It seems we picked up some friends."

Aydin grinned to himself and issued orders.

"We will let them think we are either not aware of who they are or don't care. When Phil takes out number three, we cut-over and exit at Orchard Road."

*It was simple in the desert.*
*There weren't any of these pretty civilian vehicles and entitled mall-hair soccer moms.*
*Fewer people to worry about making dead.*
*Everyone got out of our way.*
*Civilian life is going to get me killed.*

"Allison, stay with me. I am going to try to find a larger gap in the traffic."

"Will do."

"Phil?"

"I'm good."

Aydin altered his speed until fewer civilian vehicles were to their right. Passing under Dry Creek Road, the travel lanes are wet but free of snow and ice. Phil provided an update.

"Confirm, four bogeys. I am being trailed also. At Arapahoe Road, I will engage."

"Confirmed, four bogeys. Allison, be ready. If you have to, drive on the shoulder or wherever you need to keep moving."

Allison's response oozed cynicism.

"Yes, dear. You know this is not my first rodeo?"

Aydin and Phil heard the sound of a pistol being racked.

*She does know how to take care of herself.*
*Damn, she is hot.*
*Like when we were twelve, she loved to shoot.*
*We wore out my grandfather's .22 single shot.*
*She made me clean the squirrels, but she knew how to cook them.*
*I need focus, or I will be the dog's dinner.*

Aydin altered his speed, flipped on his turn signal, but did not change lanes. Anything to put the slightest doubt in the pursuer's minds. Eventually, Phil chimed.

"Passing under Arapahoe Road.

"On go.
"Three.
"Two.
"One.
"Go."

Aydin and Allison did not look back. They veered right and darted between cars onto the Orchard Road off-ramp. Phil followed after nudging the third bogey just enough. The bogey driver overcorrected, lurching left, before bouncing off the concrete divider.

At the end of the off-ramp, the green traffic lights allowed the trio to turn left, pass under I-25, and begin their circuitous route back to the office.

"Hey, Aydin?"

"Yes, Phil?"

"They didn't follow."

"No, but I am sure we will see them soon."

"I guess your little hack for the traffic management system worked. All the lights are green."

Ignoring Phil's comment, Aydin remained intent on the mission.

"Allison, park on my right, Phil on Allison's right."

"Confirmed."

"Confirmed."

"Going silent, stay behind me."

Reaching up, Aydin pressed the icon, closing the connection to his friends. He repositioned the second icon down and pressed it three times. The traffic signals in a one-mile radius of the office resumed normal operations.

Aydin made a half dozen turns, remaining on the perimeter of the DTC.

*That should be enough time.*

Reaching over, he repositioned the third icon down and pressed it two times. When the text message appeared, he drove directly to the office.

**KTF**: Ready one, completed.

*Kermit and his cleaners are excellent.*
*They never miss a standing order.*
*With the two-fiddy, their Christmas bonuses are going to be fat.*
*Assuming dead doesn't come along first.*
*I'll set up the Christmas bonuses now in case dead is an option.*
*Dead is always an option.*
*I wonder what Allison wants for Christmas.*
*Her birthday is in ten weeks.*
*I wonder what she wants.*
*Beach.*
*She wants a vacation.*

Pulling into the parking lot, the plowing followed Aydin's standing order. The snow from the parking lot was a nice, neat pile on the sidewalk. They piled the snow to the left of the main office door, in front of Aydin's office. The snowbank is half the height of the windows. The sidewalk is shoveled from the main entrance, down the short path, and right across three parking spots.

Parking on the left of the office door requires walking around the vehicle's rear to enter the office.

Aydin stopped in the first spot on the right of the office door. Allison and Phil followed orders and parked to Aydin's right.

While holding open the office door, waiting for Allison and Phil, he noticed three cars pulling into the complex.

Allison had entered the office when three cars parked, facing the snow pile. Three black Mercedes S-Class sedans, with blacked-out windows and temporary plates. Phil began to pull his weapon and turn toward the threat, but Aydin's hand to his chest stopped him.

"Relax, they are here to talk. Ready two."

Without a word, Phil entered the office, allowing Aydin to close the door.

While Phil pulled an M4 from the hidden vault, Allison understood the situation and repositioned the conference room chairs. Phil spoke to the conference room.

"Azima?"

With the tiniest hint of being artificial, a silky-smooth female voice emanates from the overhead speakers.

*"Yes, Phil?"*

"Send priority one text, code alpha-zero-one."

*"Please confirm priority one text, alpha-zero-*

*one."*

"Confirming priority one text, code alpha-zero-one, black."

*"Confirmed, sending priority one text."*

"Thank you, Azima."

*"My pleasure."*

Allison's quizzical look while holding her Walther PPK amused Phil. He spoke softly to explain.

"Azima was the daughter of one of our guides in the desert. She was a sweet girl with some serious health problems. Her father said the illnesses were from the chemical bombs. She was a beautiful girl. Ah, fuck it."

Emotional, Phil turned back to the task of positioning his M4. Allison helped her friend change his thinking.

"Alexa or Google wasn't good enough?"

"You know how Aydin is. He hacked their AI, merged the best parts, cranked down the security, and created Azima."

Aydin waited on the sidewalk for the *guests*.

*These guys are good, and they know it.*

*They are trained well.*

*I hope Allison knows just how dangerous this mission is.*

*The Chinese middlemen were amateurs compared to these guys.*

*Well fuck, look who it is.*

*I was right.*

*This day sucks worse than the dog's dinner.*

Aydin watched the steam rise from the three cars park to the left of the office door. Two men got out of each vehicle and formed a perimeter. One of the men walked to the rear of the center car, opened the door, and out stepped their boss. Walking around the closest car, avoiding the puddles of melting snow and road slime, the leader approached Aydin while his security fanned out.

"Hello Mister Trammell."
"Hello Mister Goncharov."
"Very good, you pronounced it correctly."
Extending his hand, Aydin shook it but did not move.
"Were your family potters before the revolution?"

No hint of a Russian accent, five-foot-eight, short-cropped hair, Goncharov's biceps pressed against the thin winter coat. Borya Vikentiy Goncharov is built like a whiskey barrel. Round, hard, with a nasty bite. His Cro-Magnon appearance hides a sharp mind and is an aide to his vicious reputation. Aydin knew the game's intensity had been turned up to eleven.

*This is one serious mofo.*
*Be calm.*
*Play nice.*
*I hope Allison and Phil are ready.*
*Wait!*
*I know that face.*

*Son of a ...*
*No ...*
*It can't be him.*
*This guy's face is all fucked up.*
*Stop worrying and being a pussy.*
*Allison and Phil are ready.*
*What does this motherfucker want?*

"I see you are an educated man. Please, call me BV."

"Borya Vikentiy Goncharov, the Fighting Potter, is not someone I expected to meet today. Call me Aydin. What can I do for you, BV?"

"You can invite me in, offer me a coffee, and allow me to discuss with you the new mission you were assigned."

*Fuck me.*
*Oh well, if BV wanted us dead, we'd be dead.*
*What the hell, let's dance.*

"Sure, send one of your boys to Starbucks, three blocks that way. A large black for Phil and me. A mocha latte for Allison."

BV smiled, turned, and waved to his designated go-fer. He turned back to find Aydin holding open the office door.

# Blinding Daylight

**Early-Afternoon, DTC, Bright Sun, and Windy**

Phil has his back to the inner corner, left of Aydin, and opposite the windows. Allison is to Phil's left, on the other corner of the table, with her back to the windows. She has closed the section of the vertical blinds behind her chair.

Seated at the other end of the table, BV is flanked by two bodyguards. Aydin turned his chair to face the Russian. Two of BV's security are in the lobby. The final pair outside.

The large coffee half-finished, Aydin is wondering how long it will take the Fighting Potter to get to the point.

*He is making a show of it.*

*He wants me to think he is in charge, and I am to fall in-line.*

*When was the last time these guys showered?*

*They smell like a three-day-old towel hamper in a locker room.*

*What the fuck have they been eating?*

*I can smell that one's breath from here.*

*At least they are not talking.*

"Aydin, I think you understand the problem."

Interrupting BV, Phil pointed to the security guard closest to the window.

"That sun is mighty, and it's as windy as a sack full of farts. You, pull that chain and close the blinds. The sun bouncing off that melting snow is going to pierce our brains if we don't keep it out."

Feeling confused and insulted, the security guard looked to his boss. BV dismissively waved for the guard to comply.

The security guard closed the blinds, creating random slits of sunbeams. The conference room became enveloped in an eerie aura.

*He's not so smart.*
*Allowing us to close the blinds was a mistake.*

"BV, I understand, but how is it my problem? Your bosses want the AI. The Chinese want it. The Brits. The Americans. The Iranians. Hell, even the Frogs want it. But I have not yet understood the problem."

"The problem is simple. You took one-hundred million Euros from the Chinese, and they want something for their money. I don't want you to give it to them. I will provide you with one-hundred million Euros. You pay back the Chinese, and I get the code."

"Two-hundred million."

"I am not going to allow you to extort one-hundred million Euros from me. I might be willing to discuss a finder's fee. But be cautious, Aydin."

"My apologies, I misspoke. I took two-hundred million from the Chinese."

The Cro-Magnon's face cracked for the first time.

*Another mistake.*
*BV is not in the loop and is unaware of how much is at stake.*
*He doesn't know how big the game is.*
*He's a middleman and a lot lower in the chain than I expected.*
*Don't get excited.*
*Relax, keep talking.*
*We are outgunned.*

"Plus, the Chinese don't want their money. They want my code."

"Your code?"

*Another mistake.*
*Strike three.*
*Someone up the food chain is manipulating this guy.*
*I hope Phil understood.*
*Of course, Phil understands.*
*Play it smart.*

"BV, why don't you tell me what you are doing here, sitting in my conference room, chatting?"

*Ah fuck, I can be stupid.*
*Of course, it is simple.*

*BV is trying to impress someone higher up his food chain.*

*Well informed but missing too many details.*

*I'll bet the dumbfuck's visit is not sanctioned.*


"Aydin, I am here for the code. You can deal with double-crossing the Chinese and stealing their money."

*"Aydin?"*

The Russians were surprised by the conference room speaking.

"Yes, Azima."

*"Should I allow the gentlemen in the lobby to access the internal network?"*

"No. Please initiate protocol alpha-one-five."

*"Please confirm protocol alpha-one-five."*

"Confirming protocol alpha-one-five, green."

*"Confirmed, protocol alpha-one-five."*

Allison's quizzical look amused Phil.

BV sat stone-faced while the Russian guards look worried. Aydin's grin forced BV to speak first.

"I am not intimidated by your toys."


*Yep, just another meathead getting by on intimidation.*


"My toys are the best in the world, and you know it, or you would not be sitting here. Your boys in the lobby are locked out. I turned this whole office into a Faraday cage. Do you know what a Faraday cage is?"

BV was unimpressed. His guards more visibly nervous by the minute. The one on the left tapped his earpiece before issuing one word.

"Tishina."

BV did not flinch at the Russian word for silence. He knows what a Faraday cage is.

*Wow, it stinks in here.*
*These guys are some kind of funky monkeys.*
*Phil's not great either.*
*Allison is ...*

Aydin looked over his shoulder as both a query to Allison's status and a signal.

*She is so fucking effortless.*
*How does she do it?*
*I'm going to buy her a heart monitor.*
*I bet her heart rate never gets above seventy.*

BV barks, interrupting Aydin's pleasant thoughts.

"Enough of this. Kindness in business is always a mistake. Kurok."

The Russian word *kurok* translates to *trigger*. It was the order for the security to pull weapons. They pulled their pistols but laid them on the table, resting their hands on the grips, when Allison's Walther pointed across the table to the guard on BV's left. With a press of his knee on the release, an M4 arced down from the panel next to Phil. Ignoring the automatic weapon, Phil pointed his Colt 1911 at the guard on BV's right.

*Everyone is so fucking stupid.*
*Maybe I'm shit for brains too.*
*Oh well, let's get this over.*
*Civilian life will kill me.*
*Perhaps today is the day.*

"BV, choose your words carefully."
BV continued his bravado.
"Your toy guns do not worry me. You cannot survive the encounter. Everyone in this room will die if you start shooting."
Aydin's voice did not waver.
"Azima?"
*"Yes, Aydin?"*
"What is the status of alpha-zero-one?"
*"I received confirmation; alpha-zero-one complete. KTF is en route for the cleanup."*
"Thank you, Azima."
*"My pleasure."*

*Fuck, it stinks.*
*Did that guy shit his pants?*
*I should shoot him for how bad he smells.*
*Look, even BV smells it.*
*Ha!*

*Stupid fuckers.*

"You are down two men already. If we do not reach an agreement, right fucking now, everyone not from the USofA is going to die."

Aydin didn't have to give the order. BV obliged by reaching for the Glock under his shoulder.

Allison and Phil did not hesitate. The guards each took a round in the forehead. The soft bullets dissipated in their skulls. Brains and blood splattered the walls. Aydin pulled his Glock 29 from the holder on the underside of the table. When the conference room door opened, Aydin put down the attacker from less than two feet away.

Turning his pistol back to BV, Aydin was mildly surprised to find the Russian smiling. BV gently removed his hand from under his shoulder and put both palms on the table.

Through the glass door, the last guard saw his boss give up. The security guard decided it was time to leave but made the mistake of opening the office door. The sniper did not err. The spent .308 round stopped when it hit the reinforced receptionist's desk. Blood and brains spewed over the terrazzo.

"Azima?"

*"Yes, Aydin?"*

"Turn the exhaust fans on, get this smoke and stench out of here."

*"Exhaust fans on."*

Everyone heard the air begin to move and recycle.

"Mister Trammell, you know me as Borya Vikentiy Goncharov, but my real name is Gavriil Misha Solovev."

"Ah, shit-fuck."

"I see you know who I am."

"I knew who you are in the parking lot. I did not shoot you because this was a test. You want something. I am listening. Do not give me a reason to shoot you."

"You are correct. This is a test I thought you would fail, but which you passed easily. In the mission orders I received, they underestimated your intelligence. I don't want your damned code. We have ways of finding people. You are on your own with the Chinese. For now, we can leave it as it is. In a few days, I will send word. We have a deal for you.

"Now, please tell your sniper I am coming out."

"Azima?"

*"Yes, Aydin?"*

"Rescind code alpha-zero-one."

*"Please confirm. Rescind code alpha-zero-one."*

"Confirming, rescind code alpha-zero-one, white."

*"Stand by."*

*I want simple.*
*What the hell happened to simple?*
*Allison!*

*Her mission orders must have a clue.*

*Fucking Allison.*

*They don't trust her, but they still give her a secondary target.*

*Why?*

*What do I get?*

*I get the shit sammich made from the dog's dinner.*

*I get dead people and shit sammiches.*


*"Code, alpha-zero-one, rescinded."*

"Thank you, Azima."

*"My pleasure."*


The Russian didn't bother to ask permission. He dug in the pocket of the dead guard on his right, pulling out the key fob for his sedan. Standing, he began to exit. Before he was through the conference room door, Aydin stopped him with a question.

"Is this going to be another Ramaqubah?"

Turning, smiling widely, the Russian spy almost chuckled.

"No, Aydin, this will be much more fun."

BV turned and left the office.

Mumbling and grumbling, Phil grabbed the M4, picked up his spend .45 shell, and waited for Aydin to stand so he could exit. Allison found her spent casing and hesitantly asked.

"Phil?"

"He's Drakon."

"Did you say dragon?"

"No, *Drakon*, but it is the Russian word for Dragon."

"Okay, so who is Drakon."

Phil looked from Allison to Aydin, who was standing up from finding his spent shell under the table.

*She is not going to like this.*

"That motherfucker, Allison, is the only high-value target Phil and I missed. Six years, we never failed. Not once, except for the shit pile that was sitting in that chair."

# Smoke and Mirrors

*Too many options create chaos.*

**Trammel House, 19:30, Warming**

Aydin never bothered to ask Phil when and how he learned to cook. He figured asking him would jinx it.

*Leave a sleeping dog lay.*

Allison never bothered to learn to cook well, and Aydin can't boil an egg. She loved Phil's cooking because he always seemed to prepare something healthy. Healthy annoyed Aydin, but she loved it. Today, baked halibut with baked rosemary-garlic fries. Finishing their dinner, Allison returned to the day's events. She cut to the chase.

"If that guy, *Drakon,* is so bad, why did you let him walk? What did he do?"

Phil began collecting dishes. He is staying as far from the conversation as possible. Aydin appears calm, sipping his Fat Ale, but his mind screams and wanders to bad memories.

*Calm down.*
*Relax.*
*You can figure this out.*
 *How much do I tell her?*
*Where's the line?*

*Bullet points.*
*Keep it high-level.*
*Her imagination will fill in the gaps.*
*That's it, high-level.*

Aydin's mind goes to his time in the desert.

Allison has known Aydin for nearly two decades. Across the table, she sees the face of the boy she saw as a kid. She waits because she instinctively knows he is mentally somewhere else.

### Hillside, Overlooking Ramaqubah, Sep 2008, Late Afternoon, Too Damned Hot

Aydin, Phil, a Special Forces Captain, and two British Support Team Commandos are belly down. The fire team is peering over the crest of a ridge at a small hamlet. Not on any map, the two-dozen buildings are named: Ramaqubah.

"Captain, is that the place? That building on the right? Aren't we a little lite for a building that size?"

"Sergeant, it's just a whorehouse and drug distribution warehouse. The first floor, the ground floor to you Brits, and part of the second floor is the whorehouse. The rest of the second floor is drug manufacturing and distribution. The third floor is drug storage and office space. Target is supposed to be in the office all day, every day."

Aydin is glassing everywhere and finds the recommended perch.

*Ah, fuck snacks.*

*This target is no dummy.*

*The dirty laundry hanging on the lines blocks the only perch with eyes into the third floor.*

"Captain, the recommended FFP's line of sight is blocked. Options?"

"Sergeant Trammel, you're supposed to be the whizzbang, blow 'em up, insurgent. You tell me, is there another final firing position?"

Aydin knew looking at the captain would give away his thoughts, so he continued glassing the hamlet.

*Fuck you, your silver bars, and your smart-assed attitude.*

"Captain, we can put the RPGs through the south windows from the two-floor building. That one, the building one block directly south of the target. The problem with that is, we won't have eyes-on to confirm the target is inside."

"Everyone, is that our only option?"

Each team member reviewed the available firing locations.

The Brit name Davies offered an option.

"Recon to the recommended FFP, cut the laundry lines?"

Aydin killed the idea.

"There are seven laundry lines attached to

three buildings on one side, two on the other, and multiple floors. We could cut them, but it will take too long. This guy is no dummy."

Phil's buttery Southern accent left no doubt there was only one option.

"Sergeant Trammell and I will recon down to the new FFP. Sergeants Smyth and Danvers will take up positions on our flanks and cover our ingress and egress. Captain, you will stay here, keep glassing, and let us know if more bogeys show up.

"I estimate seventeen minutes to the alternate FFP and another fourteen to exfiltrate.

"Captain, call in the evac for thirty minutes from the go command."

Confirming the plan, Aydin reached across and fist-bumped his friend. The Captain was happy he had a new plan to put in his AAR.

"I think we have a plan. Objections? None?

"Seventeen minutes to FFP. Fourteen from the fire command to extraction."

The four commandos didn't speak. With a focus only found in those willingly stepping into lethal danger, they slid over the crest and headed to complete the mission. Aydin's mind wandered on the way to the alternate FFP.

*Three more classes and I'll have a master's in computer science.*

*Just short of sixteen months to DROS.*

*I think Phil has a year left on his undergraduate*

*and eighteen months to DROS.*

*Colorado.*

*I liked it there.*

*Colorado Springs is beautiful, but the Denver Technical Center will have more jobs.*

*Pops retired there, someplace called Lone Tree.*

*Allison graduated from CU Boulder a few years ago.*

*The last letter…*

*Is an email a letter?*

*Email is not the same as holding something in your hands.*

*Ah, damn, I get it now.*

*Pops handwrites letters because he knows what it means to touch and feel something family-held.*

*Allison.*

*I wonder what she is doing now.*

Phil's slight movement of his hand halted Aydin and refocused his attention on the present.

Keying his mic in a whisper, Phil requested an update.

"Captain, are you seeing this?"

"Confirming, stand fast."

Phil looked one hundred meters to his left. Sergeant Smyth held up a tight fist. Looking right, at eighty meters, Sergeant Danvers did the same. Phil responded to the Captain while Aydin continued to glass the target.

"Confirmed, stand fast."

Phil whispered to Aydin.

"This smells bad enough to gag a maggot. Aydin, it is about to get a whole shit pile full of cattywampus. Somebody has eyes on us."

Aydin didn't take his eyes off the target building and the whores running into the street. Seeing people in lab coats following the whores out of the building, Aydin mentally processed the scene.

*Who are those people?*
*Lab coats?*
*Those are the drug makers.*
*Everyone is running out of the building.*

Aydin keyed his mic.

"Captain, abort criteria met. Somebody has eyes on us. Recommend recall and exfil."

"Sergeant, you will complete the mission."

Ignoring the captain, Aydin moved his field glasses from the street to the target windows.

Seeing the wisp of smoke, he screamed into his mic.

"ABORT! ABORT! ABORT! GO NOW!"

The forward commandos didn't have to be told twice. They began an exfil maneuver, with overlapping covering fire. A running firefight to the exfil LZ, they dove into the waiting chopper. The chopper is lifting before the commandos stop sliding on the deck. Sitting up, the Brits are returning a suppressing fire as the helicopter gains altitude.

Moving laterally, away from the LZ, the chopper pilot levels out. The fire team looks up to the Captain, who is already strapped in.

"Sergeant Trammell, I will have your ass for blowing my mission. What were you ..."

The Captain's tirade was cut off when the chopper lurched and rocked from the concussion wave. The pilot spun the helicopter around, gaining more altitude. Against the setting sun, the commandos watched the expanding mushroom cloud. Below the rising dust ball, half the hamlet had crumbled. The target building was a crater.

As the team looked to Aydin, he glared at the Captain and screamed over the din.

"Ammonium nitrate."

Sergeant Smyth hollered over the wind noise.

"How did you know?"

Aydin felt compelled to holler back and let the Captain know he made the right call.

"Ammonium nitrate is stable unless heated. It's nothing but fucking fertilizer. But bake it, and it goes boom. Delayed detonation is easy. Put the heat source next to a container of the stuff, let it get hot, and it all goes up.

"I saw the smoke from the delayed detonator. That fucker knew we were coming."

For saving their lives, Sergeant Smyth, Sergeant Danvers, and Phil fist-bumped Aydin.

**_Trammel House, 19:55, Clear and Colder_**

Allison knew Aydin was mentally somewhere else. She sat on the sofa, quietly waiting. Eventually, he returned to the living room and the woman he loved but didn't fully trust. After rechecking his texts, Aydin continued.

**Me**: Status?

**KTF**: Delay in glass transport. ETA to complete: 04:30.

"I let Drakon walk because the Service designates him as 'hands-off.'"

"What does that mean? Where did he come from? Who makes that kind of evil?"

"It means the pile of shit works for all sides, and all sides protect him. What sucks is everyone knows he killed a bunch of people in a place called Ramaqubah.

"They all know he ran a heroin trade and probably still does.

"Drakon was a Russian military adviser and was not *made*. He is truly evil, and no one wants to stop him."

"Aydin, Hon, I can't believe someone that bad would be designated hands-off."

"From the drug profits, he pays off the corrupt, including some Americans and Brits. But mostly, he pays the Russian Oligarchs. For the legit handlers, he trades information. He has a *lot* of information.

"Everyone leaves him alone."

Allison put down her wine glass. Considered, then asked.

"Do you think Drakon works with Radojko Vujić?"

Aydin started laughing, giving Allison the answer she feared.

### Trammel House, 06:20, Raining Hard

After the morning exercise, Phil's breakfast was lean and high protein. Aydin noticed.

"Phil, is there something you want to say?

Allison's eyebrows peaked at the tart question so early in the morning. Phil closed the stove gas before sitting and speaking.

"Something is not adding up. Out of the blue, Drakon shows up. Twelve years and now he is here? That is *not* a coincidence. He didn't care we off'd is security. Aydin, you know I am not going anywhere, but if you know something, now is the time to tell me."

With a nod to Allison, Phil closed his concern.

"It is time to tell *us* whatever it is you know about this cluster fuck."

Sipping his coffee, looking at Phil, unblinking, Aydin considered the request.

*They are not going to like the objective.*
*Someone extremely high up the food chain is*

*dangling a carrot for me to chase.*

*Fuck it.*

*This donkey will get the carrot and break the damned whip that keeps whacking me across the face.*

"I am in the dark too. There are too many unknowns. We will talk at the office. I need a secure connection."

Allison and Phil shrugged and began piling their dishes for the cleaners. Phil's comment closed the topic.

"You can drip butter on your boots, but that don't make them biscuits. We're as lost as last year's Easter egg."

### Mid-Morning, DTC, Whipping Rain

The trio stood in the lobby, removing their outer garments, looking around for signs of yesterday's skirmish. Laying their coats and jackets on the receptionist's desk, they moved to the conference room.

Allison was first to speak.

"Too bad we can't open the doors. It smells like paint and plaster in here."

Phil grunted and stepped toward his usual location. Allison decided, putting her back to the windows was probably a bad idea. She sat on the corner, to Aydin's right. Facing the windows, Aydin fired up his PC. While the machine booted, he removed the coffees from the cardboard carrier, pushing Allison's latte right and Phil's black coffee left. They thanked him with a nod and focused on their PCs, leaving him to his research. They knew Aydin would get to their answer soon enough.

"Azima?"

*"Yes, Aydin?"*

"Run the air recyclers. Run them until I tell you to turn them off."

The group heard the air handling kick on high.

*"The air recyclers will run until midnight unless stopped sooner."*

Aydin ignored the AI's response.

*Let's see if I can confirm the hypothesis.*

## Early-Afternoon, DTC, Easing Rain

Aydin had not spoken for hours. When he did, Allison and Phil were not surprised.

"Phil, how about some lunch?"

Allison didn't allow Phil to answer.

"*Not* burritos."

Standing, Phil walked along the window side of the conference room.

"I'm so hungry my belly thinks my throat's been cut."

Before he turned to leave the room, he stopped, looked out, then quickly turned back.

"We have visitors. The blue Ford parked one row over."

The trio all reached to touch their weapons.

Aydin didn't look up from his PC.

"They are Drakon's people, making sure we know they know where we are at any time. Stop over and ask if they want a burrito."

"Allison said no burritos."

"I heard. What are you going to bring back?"

Phil snorted and walked away.

Allison and Aydin watch through the window as Phil walked to the blue Ford, chatted briefly, then returned to his Silverado.

"He's bringing back burritos?"

"Yes, Allison, the taqueria is close, safe, and they are tasty."

Twenty-six minutes later, Phil's Silverado pulled into the parking slot in front of the conference room. Phil stepped out with two bags of Mexican goodness. Walking to the surveillance, he handed the smaller bag to the driver.

After leaving his coat in the lobby, he set the large bag in front of Allison.

She pulled two burritos marked chicken, three more labeled pork. Sliding the chicken to Aydin and the pork to Phil, she distributed the three unsweetened iced teas, several pink packets of sweetness then looked at the bottom of the bag.

In the clear plastic container was a fresh-looking chicken salad. Allison smiled at Phil, who returned the thank you with a question.

"Has wonder boy here decided to give us the

information, or should we just eat and nap? No? Damn. By-the-way, the boys in the car wanted me to thank you for their promotions."

Aydin grumbled.

*Okay, I think I have it, but damn.*
*How are we going to pull this off and not get dead?*
*Rain then snow.*
*Now it is raining again.*
*What is wrong with this place.*
*Fucking global warming, that's what.*

Grabbing a burrito, pulling back the foil, Aydin sat back and smiled. After a couple of bites, he decided to shock his unshakable friends. When he finally spoke, he did not disappoint. The information was not what Allison and Phil hoped for in a response.

# Reality Sucks

Phil finally felt it is time to start talking. Aydin and Allison parsed his ADD style of communications.

"Aydin, did anyone ever tell you, never kick a cow turd on a hot day? Every day is a hot day for our little group. Did anyone else notice Drakon was not nervous, but his guys were stinking up the place with their sweat? That Drakon fellow was never sweet-looking, but he didn't look that bad in the intel photos.

"It looks like Drakon fell out of the ugly tree and mashed his face to every branch on the way down. I wonder why *those* guys were nervous?

"Are those new blinds? Did they replace that wall? They replaced the sheetrock on that wall. No wonder it stinks like paint in here. Wait, the windows are a different color. Aydin?"

"It was Pops' idea. These four panels, the two panels in my office, and the door are double-paned, level eight, ballistic glass."

"Sweet. Of course, if someone pulls out a .50-cal, we'd be screwed, but sweet."

*A .50-cal is the problem?*

*If some dangerous fuck-nuts decides to take us out, they won't use a .50-cal.*

*The glass is for the meatheads too stupid to know it is ballistic glass.*

*Screw it.*

*We need to get going.*

*Get this over and get back to simple.*
*I miss simple.*

"Someone in our food chain has compromised The Service. I have an idea but no proof. No proof yet. He, or she, or maybe a fucking committee, is trying to deflect the source of the leakage and is pointing at Allison."

Dumbfounded, Allison sat in silence.

Phil grunted and kept eating.

*These two are tough as nails.*
*Okay, let's see how far they are willing to go to pull our asses out of this woodchipper.*

"Allison's mission is to contact Radojko Vujić. The objective is to make contact and see where it goes. Thin and vague for a counter-intelligence operation, but that's all there is to her mission."

Aydin stopped, waiting.

Allison continued with the next spork full of green rabbit food and shrugged an affirmative nod. Aydin considered and continued.

*She knows this is a bad deal.*
*She knows someone is setting her up.*
*She talked to Pops!*

"Did you talk to Pops?"

With a mouthful of garden mulch, Allison

pointed her plastic utensil at Aydin in the affirmative.

"Azima."

*"Yes, Aydin?"*

"Please initiate protocol alpha-one-three."

*"Protocol alpha-one-three is active."*

"Why is protocol one-three active?"

*"Protocol alpha-one-three is a sub-function of protocol alpha-one-five."*

Nodding, Aydin realized he did not deactivate the protocol alpha-one-five.

"Great, leave everything as it is. Thank you, Azima."

*"My pleasure."*

*That is a happy accident, locking this place down overnight.*

*I have to be more careful.*

*Here we go.*

*Let's see if they balk.*

"Our mission is to steal the Russian AI for facial recognition. But that is a diversion. No one wants that shitty software. It is a ploy to force the Chinese to act.

"The Chinese want my code and will be coming around, probably soon. We have two fronts to fight, the Chinese and the Russians. There are three huge gaps.

"The first gap: The Russians know my code won't help their AI. They want something else and turned over the rock Drakon was hiding under to point him at us. It is a counter-psych move. They know we are still pissed he outmaneuvered us at Ramaqubah. He was sent to get under my skin. It worked.

"They likely promised to pull him in out of the cold if he gets my code. Fuck them. Drakon receives one in the forehead when I see him again.

"The second hole is the Chinese and their goal. The Service doesn't think my core code is their primary objective. The Service believes the Russians and the Chinese are using the facial recognition core as a cover."

Phil put down his iced tea and muttered.

"It's the auto-ranging and target acquisition software?"

"Correcto-Mundo."

The gaps in Phil's understanding closed.

"That is why we had to pull it out of the safe on the Ptarmigan property. Allison, did you know it was in the safe?"

Allison chomped the last spork full of lawn clippings before responding.

"I knew there were flash drives. I did not know what they contained or that they are not even flash drives."

Aydin smiled and sipped tea, peeled the foil from the second burrito before resuming alternating the story with eating.

*They are going to love this part.*

"Phil, you are supposed to ask: Aydin, where

did you get the idea?"

Phil obliged.

"Hey Brain, on our way to world domination, where did you get the idea for the automated fire control?"

"Aliens, Pinky. The movie Aliens."

Closing the lid on the empty salad container, Allison snorted. She was also starting to connect the dots mentally.

Phil nodded approval before Aydin continued.

*Here goes.*

*Let's see if I can tie the background information to the three of us getting out of this cluster-fuck.*

"All the technology required for automated ranging and target acquisition exists. Several small companies have tried to put it all together but failed in several areas.

"First, triangulation for targeting is simple. Armies have been doing that since they started throwing rocks at each other. Binocular humans can range and adjust in milliseconds. Optics, even laser optics, struggle to confirm targeting on a small scale. Red dots are good, but the human behind the trigger is usually at risk.

"We have all seen the videos of laser-guided missiles hitting the human-controlled crosshairs from eight-hundred miles. But that is either preprogrammed mapping or the ordinance is tracking the reflection of a human-controlled high-powered laser.

"Drones are close to full autonomy, but no one trusts the AI to make independent decisions. Human operators fly the drones and initiate weapons fire from a desk at Nellis.

"On a small scale, it is much harder to do. What I did with the software is what the Russians and Chinese want. I figured out how to perform automated targeting at the ground level, without human intervention."

Phil's intentional slurping the last of his iced tea forced Aydin to stop and listen.

"You did all this while you had me working on refining the Azima code?"

"Yes."

"Brain, is there something I am missing?"

"Pinky, what if we combine the enhanced facial recognition with the never-fail target acquisition? "

Allison spat a mouthful of tea onto the conference room table. While she wiped up the mess, her questions are cautious.

"What does Radojko Vujić have to do with this?"

"As far as I can tell, nothing."

"Nothing? That means... What does that mean?" Phil interrupted.

"Aydin, you said three gaps. What is the third gap?"

"Allison's question *is* the third hole in this labyrinth of false flag objectives. Whoever is behind the opening of the backdoor to The Service is planning to use Allison's contact with Radojko Vujić as proof she is the traitor."

*Look at them.*
*They see it.*
*Good.*
*Let's see if they get the same cold shiver I can't shake.*

"What if, hear me out, what if *we* are the targets in a long-game of revenge?"

*They seem focused.*
*Keep going.*

"When we tracked down and were about to take out Drakon, in Ramaqubah, he knew we were coming. We know now that he was shipping anywhere between three and five million Euros worth of opium per month out of the building he blew up. A lot of that money was getting kicked upstairs on both sides. According to the intel reports, it took almost a year to return to full production because of the crop cycles.

"Drakon and his backers lost a minimum of thirty-six million and maybe as much as sixty-million. Tens of millions of Euros in private, untaxed, untraceable personal income, poof, gone.

"Someone has spent twelve years planning to get back at us for Ramaqubah. That someone works for The Service. The plan is for Phil and me to go down for something and point at Allison for contact with the Chinese and Radojko Vujić."

Stunned and silent, Allison and Phil contemplated the information, looking for holes in Aydin's summary. Aydin waited, thinking and checking his text messages.

*They get it.*
*We have three fights: the Chinese, the Russians, and someone deep in the Service.*

**Me**: Contact request, no trace, Sgt Danvers.

Looking up, Aydin expected the next question. "What's next, boss?"

Phil asked the question, but Aydin checked his phone then looked at Allison with his response.

**KTF**: Confirmed, contact request. No trace, Sgt Danvers.

"First, Allison is not going to contact Radojko Vujić. Whatever you do, no more freelancing. Everything, and I mean *everything* you do, will go through me. If we do not control every step, you will be burned, and neither Pops nor I will be able to pull your ass out of the fire. Freelancing eroded trust in your loyalty, play by the book, and get your trust back."

Choked up and unable to speak, Allison nodded in agreement.

*Holy shit, she took that harder than I expected. Damn.*
*Pops will be proud of us.*

Turning to Phil, Aydin closed the topic for the day.

"If this is a long game to get back at us, the worst place to be is on the defensive. We are flipping this around and going on offense. While we wait for a couple of things to happen, our first target is Drakon."

Phil nodded and asked.

"How?"

"He is at the Four Seasons in Denver."

"Brain, killing someone in the lobby of a five-star hotel is bad Juju."

"Pinky, we'll get him to come to us."

Allison was feeling the tension.

"What happens when we off Drakon? What do we gain?"

Aydin's dark side almost erupted. He caught himself.

*That might be the best question she could have asked.*

*Fuck, slow down, don't be a wiseass because you are ten steps ahead.*

*This is Misses Pasternack's fifth-grade class.*

*While she is teaching multiplication and division,*

*I am doing geometry problems because I am bored.*

*Let them catch up and be kind.*

"Excellent question, seriously. Offing Drakon gives us one thing we don't have now. It will flush his contact with The Service. We will be able to confirm the traitor."

# Create Reality



Allison used the house phone to call Drakon's room and asked him to come to the lobby to meet. Understanding she would not be alone, Drakon agreed.

Of course, his bodyguards appeared first, scanned the entire lobby. Nodded to Phil, and Aydin, before reporting the all-clear to their boss.

Drakon walked off the elevator, unphased and not fearing any harm. He sat across from Aydin, in a pseudo conversation pit hotels like in their lobbies. Allison to his left and Phil to his right.

Aydin noted four of Drakon's security in the lobby. Two are standing outside on either side of the revolving door. Two more are hovering near the elevators. Phil's gentle tapping of his finger on the arm of the chair confirmed Aydin's count.

*Drakon is afraid.*
*Something is bugging him to have so much security on display.*
*They are staying away from the windows.*
*Idiots.*
*It's not like we'd shoot up this charming place.*
*Stupid.*
*They are all stupid.*
*The show of force is a weakness.*

*But why?*
*What is he afraid of?*

Drakon did not miss a beat. His cocky nature emerged immediately.

"Shall we move to the restaurant for some dinner while we talk business?"

Sticking to the plan, Aydin responded.

"No, we do not plan to be here long. I didn't shoot you because we have a common enemy. Misha, may I call you Misha?"

The raised eyebrow told Aydin that Drakon was mildly surprised at the request. To poke fun, Drakon responded with the accent of his childhood.

"Da."

"Misha, someone offered you something to pull me into the light. They offered to put you back in business, in the opium trade, if you could get something from me."

Drakon sat stone-still, waiting.

"They masked the real demand in the crap about the AI and the Chinese. We know the Russians don't want the enhanced code. It will take them five years to integrate into that garbage they call AI.

"That leaves us The Brits and the Service. The Brits are buried right now. They are focused on keeping away the wolves from the Brexit disaster. They are not interested in something that does not help sustain their economy.

"The Service. The Americans. Maybe. But, here

is the rub, Misha. The Americans only have to ask, and I would give it to them.

"Here we are. Someone dug you up, pointed you at me, and gave you a bunch of bullshit as a premise to pull me into the light. What I don't understand is why now? If they give you your opium fiefdom back, what is in it for them? Money? No, it can't be just the money. Something else is in play.

"Misha, you must know, they are not going to put you back in business. Whoever is on the throne in this game is going to burn us all."

Drakon's face did not crack or change in any perceptible way. He turned to Allison, nodded in the negative before turning to Phil, and repeating the gesture. Landing his eyes back on Aydin, Drakon spoke softly. His question an agreement.

"What is it you propose?"

"Request a meeting, demand a face-to-face. Insist you meet in the open, on the patio at the Saguaro restaurant. You can find it. Set the meeting, then text me."

Aydin flipped his business card onto the table.

Drakon looked at the card, then back to Aydin.

"It seems I am the key to your plan. What's in it for me?"

Phil started to move, but Aydin's gentle lift of his hand stopped his friend from doing something stupid. Realizing the power dynamic shifted in his favor, Aydin pressed the conversation.

"You get my promise not to shoot you in the

face the next time I see you."

"Those are bold, harsh words for someone who is asking for help."

"Harsh? True. Who gives a fuck? You are going to help us pull your contact into the light. If you don't, whoever is pulling strings is going to get us all killed. You included, and you know it."

"If I agree to your plan, I am going to need something more. My guys will think I have gone soft if there is not something for me on the back-end."

"I'll give you a copy of the Chinese AI. Your boys back at the Technology Directorate will love you. The Russian AI program will leap five years ahead."

Thinking, nodding, the stocky criminal understood the value of the offer. He'd give Mother Russia something of value, and he'd get to come in out of the cold.

"Agreed."

No one bothered to shake hands, which was okay with Aydin.

*I am not touching that slimy fucker.*

Walking away, flanked by Allison and Phil, Aydin checks his phone.

**KTF**: Contact request, confirmed. Arrival ETA 16 hours.

The trio is walking along 14th street, Phil with one eye to the rear, wondering aloud.

"Drakon's contact in the Service is highly placed, but you told him to meet the contact at the Saguaro restaurant. That means the contact is here in Denver or will be soon. *That* means you know or have a good idea of who the contact is and where they are located."

Aydin heard Phil but did not respond. Turning right, on to Larimar street, Allison smiled.

"Ocean Prime?"

Aydin winked, said nothing, and kept walking. Phil resumed his monologue.

"Drakon probably does not know the contact's identity but figured Aydin knows who it is and how to contact him or her. Also, they are close enough to meet soon. That meant, Drakon understood you have more information than him. *That* means you have an advantage with information and strategy that he didn't like."

Reaching the entrance to Ocean Prime, stopping on the sidewalk, the trio looks around for tails or any sign of bogeys. Phil completed his summary assessment.

"It looks like you are a couple of steps ahead in this game. What I want to know is simple."

Allison smiled, appreciating something mildly profound was about to come out of Phil. Aydin tilted his head with a curious grin.

"You picked this place for dinner because Allison likes the fish, and they make a mean steak. Right?"

Beaming and patting his friend on the shoulder, the trio entered the restaurant.

# A New Reality

*Family is what you make it.*

**Early Afternoon, DTC, Blustery**

Through the conference room's ballistic glass window, Aydin watched Phil and his Silverado return from the burrito run. Checking his phone, he received the message he expected. The good news did not improve his dank mood.

**KTF**: Contact arrival confirmed.

**Pops**: Contac secured and confirmed. Be safe.

*This is going to be ugly.*

*The very fucking, over the top, no coming back, type of ugliness.*

*Drakon could walk, but I need to expose the threat.*

*I am going to make that shit pile dead on general principles alone.*

*Someone has to pay, and it is not going to be Allison, Phil, or me.*

*No fucking way.*

*Pops.*

*Pops knows.*
*He must know.*
*What if he doesn't know?*
*Did I get him out of retirement to help me, just to run face-first into this cluster fuck of ugliness?*

Phil's setting the chicken burritos, and iced tea on the conference room table broke Aydin's thoughts. Allison pulled her salad toward her, looked at Aydin, and asked gently.

"Are you okay?"

*She knows.*
*Allison always knows when I am worried.*
*She has always known.*
*Yep, this is a very fucking, over-the-top, no coming back type of ugliness.*

"I'm good."
"Liar."

Aydin's sideways glance was halted when his phone vibrated.

**Unknown**: Meeting set: 19:45.

Pulling back the foil wrapper, staring at his phone, Aydin decided to update his friends and change the subject.

"Drakon is meeting with the contact at 19:45.

151

Did you see the shooting in Hong Kong?"

Allison and Phil looked at each other, confused. Aydin harrumphed but helped.

"I'll email the link."

It took longer for Aydin to cut-and-paste the URL into an email than it did for the email to appear in their inboxes. Both kept eating while opening the link and reading the news article. They followed the embedded links to additional news articles and too many photos of dead people. Dead people on the sidewalk, the street, in the gutter, and a green-space park.

Phil has a burrito in his left hand, Allison, a spork in her Right. Both have stopped eating. After several seconds, they both look to Aydin for an explanation.

*They don't yet see the obvious because the articles say a crime war has started.*

*The big crime bosses have left Hong Kong to escape the communist rulers.*

*There is no crime war.*

*The murders are a trial-run by the communists.*

"Look closely at the crime scenes."

His friends turn back to their PCs and swipe left and right, alternating browser tabs through the few images of dead people. Both noticed the uniqueness at the same time, but Allison spoke first.

"Cameras."

"Lots of cameras."

Efficiently, Aydin brought his friends closer to his worry.

"Correct. These weren't murders. They were assassinations. The guy in the Fila sweatsuit was on his morning run through the park. He is a dissident who funds anti-communist propaganda campaigns. Those are his bodyguards next to him. So much for paid security.

"The guy in the blue sweater, who was sitting at the café, drinking coffee and eating scones."

Allison switched browser tabs, checked, then confirmed.

"The older guy on the sidewalk outside the café? Is that his wife lying next to him? Who are the other people?"

"That is his wife. He was a professor of Political Science at Lingnan University. He lectured on free markets, free elections, and the evils of totalitarian rule.

"The other guy, at the café, was a professor at The Hong Kong Polytechnic University. That is his wife lying in the gutter. He wrote a paper titled: The Evils of Ubiquitous Surveillance.

"He and the Poly-Sci professor had been friends from their days as undergrads in the eighties."

Pausing, Aydin let his friends process the information. Phil understood immediately.

"They can never have it. That dog won't hunt. Whatever you do, we need to keep the fire control software secure. I do not want to live the rest of my life knowing something I helped create is being used to assassinate people because they think differently."

Allison fully understood the implications, thanks to Phil's statement.

"If they had the fire control software, what would it take to implement? I mean, it can't be used everywhere. Can it?"

Allison immediately understood her question put Aydin, mentally, somewhere black and cold.

*I am starting to understand. J. Robert Oppenheimer and the Bhagavad Gita: 'Now I am become Death, the destroyer of worlds.'*

Aydin broke his funk to respond.

"They need three laser-equipped cameras, line-of-sight to the target zone, and some way to hide the weapons. Or, they need two cameras and someone with the third reference point processor. Like what I did in the warehouse."

Aydin paused but continued before it became uncomfortable.

"Remember, the rifles, or whatever, do not have to be near the target zone or the target cameras. They just need a line-of-sight to the target zone.

"With the newest ballistics and advance flash/noise suppression, no one will know where the shots originated. Theoretically, with my core code, and targeting software, the AI could locate and eliminate any designated objective that wanders into the targeting zone."

Allison wondered if her face was as pale as Phil's. Aydin changed the subject back to the immediate threat.

"There is only one egress from Saguaro. We'll take three cars. If it goes tits up, we may need to extract Drakon. Allison with your Rover, Phil, with your Silverado, you both can four-wheel it across the landscaping if it goes bad and the egress is blocked.

"I'll park the Benz in the restaurant lot. Allison, you park up on the hill in the adjacent lot, facing Saguaro. Phil, across the side street, in the hotel parking lot. The hotel is on the high ground. Make sure we own it.

"Let's go over this a couple of times. Phil, I need your input. Can we get out of this when it goes down?"

Phil's jovial nature is absent.

"Are we going to get any support?"

"Yes. Can you get us out?

"I'll get us out."

"Allison, this is going to get very ugly. I know you think you are tough, but tonight will be a new level of terrible. Because of the civilians, this could get nasty, and if it does, if we make a mistake, there is no way out.

"We'll end up in Leavenworth, making little rocks out of big rocks, with nine-pound hammers."

"I'm good. Tell me what I need to do."

*Will she feel the same after?*

"Phil?"

"Google Maps says you have it right. Aydin will cover the up-close in the parking lot directly in front of the restaurant. Allison on the right flank, east, just above the level of the restaurant. My FFP will be the high ground across the side street, south of the target zone. I estimate the target range at 85-120 meters. The egress is west of the FFP. To the north, we are blind behind the restaurant.

"Drakon will position his people in the same defensive pattern. Two inside. Two outside. Two as a backup. They will be a problem if the shooting starts. What's your plan for Drakon's people?"

"You just said you'd get us out. How?"

"If the shooting starts, a bunch of dead Russians is the only way out.

*There is going to be a lot of shooting.*

**19:37, Saguaro Restaurant, Clear, Moonless**

"Phil?"

"I got eyes-on. Drakon is at a table one row off the outside fence, two tables west of the gate. The glass on top of the half-wall is a problem. I make six bogeys. The two you see, standing around. Two, in the black SUV, three parking slots north of Allison. The others are behind you, two rows over and six slots south in the black sedan. If he has any more inside, I got no eyes."

"Confirmed, stand by."

<br>

**Me**: Ready one. Status?

<br>

*This is about to become complicated.*
*Allison thinks she is tough, but she is going to have to be fierce.*

<br>

**Pops**: Confirmed. Ready two. Ready three. Be safe.

<br>

*If this goes off the rails, Allison and Phil can egress.*
*Phil knows how to go dark.*
*He'll take Allison with him.*
*If it goes off the rails, I will put a bullet in that fucker's forehead.*

<br>

**Me**: Confirmed, ready one. Request, option two on stand-by: DTC, ETA 20:30.

<br>

*The contact is late.*

*Ah damn, I should have known.*

*The contact has been at the bar, waiting to see if it is a trap.*

"Allison, Phil, be cool. I am going to bring our support online."

Aydin pressed a spinning red icon first. The local camera surveillance began to malfunction within a half-mile radius of the restaurant. He pulled two green images across the small screen and dropped them on the open comms channel's image.

Pops and Davies hear the chirp of the connection in their TCAPS. Pops on the hotel's second floor is in a corner room, Davies one floor directly above. Silenced weapons on tripods, they are deep inside, away from the open windows.

"Pops, status?"

"Five-by-five."

"Davies?"

"Peaches and cream, mate."

*The next voice I hear will be Allison.*

"Aydin?"

"Yes?"

"Is there something you want to tell me?"

"Not at this time. Stand by. Confirmed. Contact just sat across from Drakon."

"Here's the play. Davies, as planned, you have target one. Pops, the guard who is standing east of the main door. Phil, the guard on the sidewalk to the west.

"Phil and Pops, the guys North of Allison, are going to see their buddies drop. They'll need attention.

"If we do this, we'll be moving before the guys behind me react."

"Phil?"

"Affirmative."

"Pops?"

"Good to go."

"Davies?"

"Right as rain."

"Allison?"

"I need a drink."

"Davies, when ready."

From the middle-level hotel's third-floor corner room, Sergeant Davies' line-of-sight to the target was perfect. The .308 round would clear the glass windbreak by several centimeters.

The team heard the Brit's tone and did not question his resolve.

"On fire."

"Three.

"Two.

"One.

"Fire."

Drakon's head exploded. Two seconds later, the bodyguards standing outside Saguaro dropped to the concrete.

### *20:05, Saguaro Restaurant, Clear, Moonless*

The contact sprinted from the patio, through the side gate, and stopped cold. Wearing a baseball cap, CU sweatshirt, jeans, and new Nike sneakers, the contact is prepared to run. Aydin is standing in the parking lot, pointing a pistol. Instead of shooting, he pointed up the small hill where Allison flashed her headlights.

Turning and jogging toward the small hill, the contact saw two men jump out of an SUV. Their pistols are drawn, they begin running toward Aydin and the restaurant. Both men were blown off their feet. Pops, from the second floor of the hotel. Phil from behind the driver door of his Silverado.

The contact sprinted up the hill and climbed into Allison's Rover.

Davies and Phil covered Aydin for good measure, waiting for the last two guards to step out of their vehicle. The guards died crouching behind the parked cars.

Everyone egressed. Only Phil and Aydin noticed the cleaner's van pulling into the parking lot. Allison turned, saw her new passenger pointing a pistol, laughed, and said two words.

"Hello, mom."

### *20:27, DTC, Clear, Moonless*

The comms between the vehicles remained open, but no one spoke during the trip from Lone Tree, north on I-25, to the DTC. Allison and Moms rode the 22 minutes in uncomfortable silence.

The trio pulled into the parking lot forty seconds apart. When Phil's Silverado made the final turn into the designated parking spot, two cleaner vans roared in. Diagonally positioning to cover the three vehicles, the cleaners were ready for a jailbreak.

Moms jumped out of the Rover and began to sprint away from the office complex. A masked cleaner jumped from the almost stopped van, dashed, and brought down Moms with a taser.

A second masked cleaner joined the first, picking up Moms and dropping her on the van's floor.

Allison watched her mother in a daze in her passenger-side mirror, kick and fight the bigger, stronger men. Allison felt no remorse. She watched the zip ties get doubled on her mother's wrists and wrapped around her ankles. Allison watched until the van door slid closed as the third cleaner was pinning the zip ties on her mother's wrists to the wall of the van.

# Staying Alive is a Game

*Trammell House, 06:22, Overcast*

## Breaking News

We are continuing our live coverage of the mass shooting in Lone Tree. Our on-site reporter, Miranda LaLonde, has been on the scene overnight. Miranda?

Thank you, Crystal. As you can see over my shoulder, the Lone Tree police, the Douglas County Sheriff, the State Police, and the FBI are still scouring the scene for clues.

Sources tell me this was a sophisticated Russian Mob hit. Competing forces are in a power struggle for control of the opium trade in the United States.

No longer confined to the coasts, the influence of international organized crime extends to America's heartland.

Crystal, back to you.

Stay tuned to KRDN for additional details.

Aydin reached across the counter, grabbed the remote, and pressed the mute button. Allison was pale, not eating, but not crying.

"How did you know?"

*Allison knows it all now.*
*Tell her the truth.*
*Be calm.*
*Even.*
*Relax.*
*Breathe.*

"I didn't. Pops did."

Phil peeled a half dozen mandarins, setting them on a plate for everyone. Aydin has separated the wedges and meticulously removed the pith from each small wedge.

Phil silently slid a cold glass of pineapple and mango juice toward Davies and nodded toward Allison. Davies continued to push the glass along. Pineapple and mango juice, her favorite. She nodded thanks, sipped, and continued.

Aydin slid the cleaned mandarin wedges along and pointed to Allison.

*She hates the pith.*

Davies repeated the process with the mandarin wedges. He stopped the small plate of fruit next to

Allison's glass of nectar. Aydin watched until Allison looked at him and tilted her head with a meek smile.

*Since she was a little girl, she has hated pith.*

"Of course, Pops knew. What did you do?"

"I didn't believe him, but he insisted. So, I began looking for proof. Finding the evidence was easier than I expected. Moms has been running counter-ops for at least twenty years. She was the one who tipped Drakon at Ramaqubah. What she didn't realize was a hard-core player was watching. All these years, Pops was watching. Moms' attempt to flip you was out of bounds. Pops will miss Moms, but he can't lose you.

"Allison, Moms has been manipulating you all your life. She wanted to turn you so you could take over running her counter-ops. That is why she talked you into the disaster with Tran. But …"

Allison cut off her husband, looked up from staring at the tangerine-colored sweetness, and smiled.

"You and pops have been playing the long-game for … how many years?"

*Phil and Davies don't even know.*

Smiling at his friends, Aydin confirmed Allison's assumption.

"Since we got burned in the desert, almost

killed, and Drakon walked."

Looking from Phil to Davies, Allison continued, looking at her husband and life-long friend. She fully understood the game.

"Moms wanted you dead because she knew you could, eventually, trace it all back to her. That is why she grew to hate you. Wow, did she hate you!"

She stopped talking, her face becoming paler.

"She thought of me as a tool. She wanted me to take over, but if I got killed, so what."

*She gets it.*
*Maybe she is tougher than I thought?*
*Phil was right.*
*Allison does have a good heart.*
*Sometimes not the best decision making but a good heart.*

Allison's phone vibrated. Swiping the screen and looking at her phone, tears appeared for the first time.

> **Dad**: All good here. Dinner, bring Phil. I have someone for him to meet. Love, you, Dad.

The men did not ask about the text. They changed the subject. Phil's jovial nature is re-emerging.

"Aydin, I thought you said you weren't going to

kill Drakon the next time you saw him?

"I didn't kill him. Davies did."

Shaking his head in mock disgust, Phil continues with a question for Davies.

"Too bad about Smyth."

"Yeah, bloody 'ell, who knew his misses had it in her. She blew his bollocks into the mattress with a shotgun while his girlfriend watched. He bled out in the ambulance. Allison is different. I *know* she would shoot you in the bollocks. There'll be no fookin around on this lass."

Allison nodded in agreement. The laughter quickly faded. Davies continued.

"It has been twelve years, and it felt like yesterday. The driver will be here in an hour. My flight is at 13:00. I wish I could stay longer, but I hear there is a beach in our future?"

### Pop's House, 17:52, Bright Spring Day

Sitting at the formal dining table, Allison remained keenly focused on making dinner a good time. Aydin on her right, with Pops on her left, at the head of the table. Across from Aydin, Phil. Between Pops and Phil, Miranda LaLonde.

Pops' filled the wine glasses, told Google Home to turn off the ballgame, and turn on the Outlaw Country music channel. Turning up the volume before he spoke, he made sure everyone was attentive. A man of action and not words, Pops was Pops.

"Miranda?"

Putting her hand on Phil's forearm, receiving raised eyebrows, Miranda asked Aydin a question.

"Tell me about the targeting algorithm. How did you overcome the variability in the spatial distance?"

# Shiny Lies

## Storm Front...

*"Once you've lived the inside-out world of espionage, you never shed it. It's a mentality, a double standard of existence."*

*John le Carre*

### DTC Conference Room, Mid-Morning, Warm and Sunny

Monday, after the Sunday dinner with Pops, Allison, Aydin, a Phil are in their usual places, in the conference room. Their morning coffees and lattes dry. Allison is in a mental fog, looking at her PC but not seeing the text. Phil is reading about internet privacy and authoritarian rulers. Aydin is finishing his After-Action Report, the AAR, and thinking about being gullible.

*I am swearing too much.*
*The stress is making me swear.*
*I am too young to feel this old.*
*At least it is warm.*
*The new protective glass alters the light.*
*It has a lite amber hue.*
*But it is warm, and I can still feel the sun's ultraviolet rays heating the tabletop.*
*The thigh doesn't ache so much when it is warm.*

*I should have seen the reality.*

*I could have connected the dots at least two years ago.*

*I should have seen it when I was twelve.*

*Moms has been playing us since we were kids.*

*What twelve-year-old thinks about their parents being spies?*

*It did cross my mind a couple of times.*

*I should have paid attention to my intuition.*

*That's Phil's secret.*

*He never misses or ignores his instinct.*

*He pays attention and believes the voices in his head.*

*Allision knew.*

*She told me about overhearing her parents talking to my parents.*

*In the fort, we built in the forest, behind the base housing.*

*Allison said she heard something about changing who lives with whom.*

*Spies and swingers?*

*I bet it was my mom who instigated it.*

*Mom was a throw-back to the sixties.*

*I miss her.*

*She loved life.*

*Fucking cancer.*

*Our parents were spies, and now we are spies.*

*It's a family tradition.*

*Ah, fuck snacks.*

*Now I have Hank Junior's song in my head.*

*I could ask Pops, but I'll ask Dad.*
*Dad will know.*

Phil steps out to the head, returns, and waits for Aydin's attention. Phil surprises Aydin and Allison with his inquiry.

"I've been reading some interesting items."

Snorting, Aydin looks back to his PC with a snarky comment.

"Was it painful?"

Ignoring the barb, Phil continues.

"I've been reading about the Cold War and all of the counter-espionage. Back in the day, everyone spied on everyone else. That TV show, The Americans, had it right about the end of the Cold War. But you guys had something different. Your two families tied together for decades. Two families were stationed on the same bases for more than twenty years. Something is unusual about the arrangements. How did your families get into the web of black-ops and counter-intelligence?"

Sitting back, looking first to Allison, then to Phil, Aydin espies Allison's eyebrow twitch. His mental darkness rumbles before he contemplates his response.

*What the fuck?*
*Can he read my mind?*
*Na, stop that stupid shit.*
*No one can read minds.*

*Phil's been researching and probably made the correct leap.*

*Fuck it.*

*I'll let Allison answer first.*

*I need to stop swearing.*

*Fuck it, who cares.*


Turning to Allison, Aydin winks and waits. She knows Aydin is struggling and obliges in a soft tone.

"You can ask Pops or Dad, but we'll get the same answer they have been giving to Aydin and me for twenty years. 'It is a coincidence, based on our AFSC.' Their Air Force Specialty Code is now labeled 14NX and is generically listed as *Field Intelligence*.

"I know they were recruited individually on their college campuses. They met in Basic Training at Lackland air base in San Antonio, TX. I think they paired up in Monterey, at the language school.

"The area along the California coast was so expensive, the four of them decided to share a two-bedroom apartment. I heard Aydin's mom once say their time in Monterey was the best of her life. She loved California.

"Before they graduated from language school, they made a pact. They would get married, in a double wedding, and then never request re-training to a new AFSC. The recruiters picked their candidates well. Our parents *wanted* to be spies.

"They used their free-wheeling, bohemian lifestyle as a mask. All over the world. Florennes Air

Base in Belgium. Ramstein, in Germany. Beale in California. Plattsburg in upstate New York. A perfect place for spies. We spent a lot of time in Montreal because of the Russian Embassy. Schriever airbase and that little fucking dot, Falcon Air Station in Colorado.

"There are also the times we lived as civilians. Paris, Sterling and Reston Virginia, Croydon in England.

"Plus, one of them went TDY regularly. The Temporary Duty assignments never stopped. One of them was always gone, and we never knew where or when they would come back.

"Security Police would knock on the door. The SPs would show whoever they asked for the orders. The person going TDY would put on a uniform, grab their B4 bag, kiss and hug us, then leave with the SPs.

"I think our mothers were better at language skills. Dad was good at planning and running the missions. Pops was the muscle. I remember the day he came home from sniper school. Moms took him right upstairs and locked their bedroom door.

"I know there are two families. One is my family, with Moms and Pops. I know there is Aydin's family, Mom, and Dad. As a kid, I thought of us as one family.

"How did our families get into counter-intelligence? The short answer is, Phil, they were recruited in college, loved the spy life, and never wanted out."

Allison stopped speaking. She understands, Aydin does not like to be reminded of their teen years. The erratic schooling, few friends, and limited guidance. Aydin was too smart, by half, at a young age.

Phil nodded a silent thank you before he and Allison turned to Aydin.

*Ah, fuck snacks.*
*I guess it is about time Allison knew the truth.*

"All of that is true and more. Our parents were as close to being hippies as you could be and still be in the military.

"The language skills were the key to their success. There was the occasional assassination. I know of at least four. But that is all another front. They cultivated the cover of Bohemian Air Force couples with high-level security clearances. They were not hiding. No, sorry, they were hiding in plain sight.

"All four could have easily joined MENSA. All four had a knack for something we now take for granted. Back then, it was almost unheard of, nor its value understood.

"Our parents were some of the first computer hackers."

Turning to Allison, seeing her frown, Aydin waited.

*She knows I hate talking about our childhood.*

Allison's sweet grin preceded her comment.

"So many things make sense now. I never understood why we always had to have chicken wire covering the garage or workshop. Everywhere we lived, Pops and Dad created an electronic security room.

"Mom and Moms were always *going out*. They were the seduction. Pops and Dad were the protection. Wow, what a life.

"Too bad Moms had to screw it all up."

The conversation died, with everyone sitting in silence until Allison perked up.

"So, Phil, tell us about Miranda LaLonde."

Shifting nervously in his chair, Phil refused to look up.

"There's nothing to tell. You know Miranda said she would come by tomorrow."

"That is not what I meant."

Shrugging, Phil admitted to his friends.

"We are going out on Friday, after her ten o'clock news segment."

Allison, seeing Aydin smiling at his friend's discomfort, gave her the confidence to pester Phil with some of the fun he likes to deliver.

"Miranda and Phil, sitting in a tree…"

Aydin opens a couple of tabs in his browser when thoughts turn back to the present.

*Let's see who Miranda LeLonde is and why does Pops know her?*

# Pixie Dust

*"I don't always see the light, but I, sure enough, feel the heat."*

*Ray Wylie Hubbard*

*Fast Left Hand*

### DTC Conference Room, Noon, Warm and Sunny

Allison and Aydin are waiting for Phil to return with lunch. Miranda is scheduled to arrive at one o'clock. Annoying to Aydin, Allison is persistently driving the conversation.

"I don't know about her. She seems to know a lot more than I would expect. If Pops knows her, she is a spy. Or a spy in training. If she is who she says she is and not a spy, why isn't she a reporter in DC or New York, or Paris, or anywhere there might be something important to keep an eye on? This is Colorado, for fuck's sake."

"Allison, we have been over this. Cheyenne Mountain? Falcon Air Station. Rocky Flats used to be here. There is classified high-tech here in the DTC and out in Boulder. The Space Command is here.

"My guess is, she is here to keep an eye on something, and Pops probably is a mentor."

"You guess, or you know."

When Aydin refused to answer, Allison pressed the topic.

"Do you think she works for The Service?"

Again, Aydin refused to answer. Annoyed, Allison grunted and barked as Phil walked in.

"I'll ask her myself."

"Ask who, what?"

"I am going to ask your new girlfriend a couple of questions. What a spy is doing with a face on TV every day, and why does she live in Colorado?'

Putting Allison's salad and sweet tea down, moving to Aydin with chicken burritos and unsweetened iced tea, Phil sat.

"She is not my girlfriend. One *planned* date does not make a girlfriend."

"I saw her at dinner and you two on the porch. She *wants* to be your girlfriend."

Peeling the foil from one of his pork burritos, he decided to ignore the statement. Aydin's mind is running the possibilities.

*What does Phil say… 'Slap my willy and call me silly.'*

*I found two references for Miranda Marie LaLonde.*

*The first died of influenza in 1918.*

*She was 12 years old.*

*The second died at 102, two years ago.*

*The dead girl is the clue.*

*Phil's new girlfriend is hiding something.*

*Her BIO on the KRDN site says she is a 2012 graduate of Northwestern's Medill School of Journalism.*

*But there is no record of a Miranda LaLonde attending.*

*Time to ask for some help.*
*Today, play it cool.*
*Gather intel, see where she leads.*

Seeing Aydin pick up his phone and begin to send a text, Allison and Phil eat quietly.

**Me**: Need background deep dive. Target: Miranda Marie LaLonde. DOB est: 1994.

**KTF**: Deep dive. Confirmed.

The trio finishes their lunch and watches Miranda pull in and park her BMW to the main door's left. Miranda is wearing a lite blue, paisley dress and dark blue pumps on the late spring day. As she is walking in, Aydin's gloomy thoughts return.

*She is showing off for us, wearing an on-air outfit.*
*She plans to be here for a few hours.*
*Talk to us, then head to the station.*
*Did she lighten her hair?*

Miranda lets herself in, turns, and walks into

the conference room. Smiling to Allison and Phil, setting her purse on the table, she sits across from Aydin.

Aydin reaches up, drags the purse over, dumps the contents on the table, and begins to massage the subtle leather, looking for hidden compartments. Satisfied, there are no recording devices. Aydin places everything back in the purse and slides it back across the table.

With a flat tone to hide her mild annoyance, Miranda responded to the invasion.

"I could have the recorder in my bra."

"Phil?"

"No way. She'd slap me faster than green grass through a goose. You do it."

Miranda winked at Phil before she turned back to Aydin. She pulled down the front of her dress's neckline, showing she didn't wear a bra. Aydin did not flinch.

"There are no longer any expectations of privacy."

Allison was smiling.

"I like her. Let's see if we can keep her alive. For Phil."

Turing to Allison, nodding, Miranda continued her soft assault.

"It smells like an Ensenada taco stand in here."

"That's because they only eat burritos. Maybe you can talk Phil into diversifying our lunch options."

"I'll see what I can do, but no promises. Phil

and me, we're fixin' to pass a good time."

Tilting her head to Phil, Miranda turned back to Aydin and waited.

*I heard it.*
*She is from the deep south.*
*Was that a slip or intentional?*
*The slight twang.*
*Intentional.*
*She is testing, probing.*
*She wants to know if I did my homework.*

"Miranda Marie LaLonde died in 1918. She is buried on the Fò Miranda ranch outside Thibodaux, Louisiana. What's a good girl from the deep south running away from or running to?"

"Excellent, Aydin. I grew up in Lafourche Parish, Louisiana."

The brunette stopped, waiting. The game was on, and she loved the game. Aydin considered before obliging.

*She is smart and well trained.*
*Why do I feel like I know her?*

"You have been at KRDN for eight months. Before that, you were at some station in Washington state that doesn't seem to exist. Your last address is listed in Richland, Washington. The Hanford nuclear production complex was decommissioned before you

181

were born. The decomm and super fund cleanup are on-going.

"Someone was using the lax decomm and the cleanup work to steal spent fuel rods. Several countries can turn spent fuel rods into low-grade fissionable material.

"I had to look hard, but I found it. Two Iranians were picked up in Kennewick and detained. A week later, you were here in Colorado, smiling at the KRDN cameras."

Aydin stopped, mulling.

*She has not flinched.*
*It is all true.*
*Now it is time to poke hard.*

"You were recruited from the LSU campus. No one ever thought the cheerleader, majoring in political science, was odd. Cheerleaders are communications majors, so they can grow up to be talking heads on the local news. No one considered a cheerleader as someone wanting to be a spy. What is someone with your background as a cheerleader turned talking head doing in the spy game?"

*There!*
*Her eyebrow twitched, and she blinked.*
*Good guess.*
*Why do I feel like I know her?*

"They told me your ability to research is outstanding. They underestimate you."

Phil chimed, followed by Allison.

"That's our Aydin. Always piddlin' around, learning things."

"Yeah, but our Aydin usually doesn't tell us the details until dead people are lying around."

With a deadpan face, Miranda continued.

"Did you take it all the way?"

"I did."

"Are you going to share with Allison and Phil?"

"Not yet."

"Why not?"

"Because I don't believe it."

"You don't believe it?"

"No."

"You don't believe it because you don't want it to be true. Or you don't believe it because you want it to be true?"

*She's good.*
*I'll make her say it.*

"What do you think?"

"I think you are playing games. Games, which I was told you don't play. No matter. Let's talk about the paper titled: The Evils of Ubiquitous Surveillance."

*Ding. Ding. Ding.*
*Pops did this.*

*He knows.*
*Dad must know also.*
*Allison is going to freak out.*

"Do you have to be at the station?"

"No. My regular shift is Wednesday through Sunday."

*Did she dress up for Phil, or is she making a point?*

"Screw it. Follow us to the house. Phil will grill. We'll have a nice dinner and talk about anything that comes to mind."

"What about The Evils of Ubiquitous Surveillance and your new toys?"

"Yeah, we can talk about those too."

# Lost the Labyrinth

***Early-Evening, Trammell House, Slight Chill***

The pool heater is creating tiny wisps of steam over the Tahoe Blue hue of the pool. The four sit on the deck, watching across the fire pit at the tendrils of mist rising in random patterns. Phil grilled steaks and potatoes for Aydin and Phil. Salmon with roasted veggies for Allison and Miranda.

They are enjoying drinks, Fat Ale beer for the boys, red wine for the girls. Allison and Phil sit quietly when Miranda begins to open up to Aydin's questions.

"Nice house. Big for two people. Do you ever get lost on the way to the pisser? Spy work pays well."

"Well enough."

"One hundred million Euros from the Chinese is *well enough?*"

*She is intelligent and well-informed but inexperienced.*

"Two hundred million."

Tipping her glass in respect at the amount, Miranda continues.

"Others can do what you did with the targeting software. You just happened to be first. Coupling your advanced recognition algorithms with the targeting software is dangerous.

"Some might say you intend to destabilize the

global power dynamic."

*Ah, fuck snacks.*
*I missed it.*
*I totally fucking missed it.*
*She's here for me!*
*She must work for The Service, and someone doesn't trust me.*
*But ...*
*What is that?*

Turning to his left, Aydin looks across the fire pit toward Phil. Tapping the little finger of his left hand, Miranda and Allison could not see the subtle signal on the outside of the deck chair. Phil understood.

"I'll be right back. Too many beers."

The trio watched Phil step into the house. Aydin continued.

"What does a cheerleader do with a poly-sci degree?"

"If you know I was a cheerleader, you must know my real name."

"I do, but I don't believe it."

"Don't or won't?"

"Don't. You were seventeen when you entered LSU. There was no Miranda LaLonde before 2001. Therefore, someone got to you in high school. You graduated early, slipped away, and came back as Miranda. LSU was passing a good time for you. Your face is everywhere on social media. It is an excellent cover. Overt and obvious."

Aydin stopped talking when Phil returned. Walking around the fire pit, Phil stood with his back to the hillside. Facing Aydin, lifting his right hand to his chest, the former commando held out two fingers.

Allison understood the message. Miranda saw the faces turn dismal and understood the message. To hide her mouth, she leaned forward, like she was playing the fire.

"I didn't bring them. They are not with me. What do we do?"

Phil responded.

"I lit up KTF. Miranda, do what we tell you, exactly what we tell you when we tell you."

Miranda nodded affirmatively.

Phil stepped over, pulled another Fat Ale from the refrigerator, and poured himself a tall Jamison.

Before he got back to his seat, handing the beer to Aydin, the whisper was clear.

"Stay down. Get inside. Move fast."

As he turned to sit, Phill threw the Jamison on the fire pit. The erupting fireball was the cover they needed. The four scrambled from the patio into the house.

The first bullet shattered the double-pained glass of the slider. The second bullet went through Miranda's left shoulder, fragmenting her clavicle.

Aydin pointed to Allison, then to Miranda, then the couch. Allison grabbed Miranda, drug her behind the couch, and pressed the throw blanket on the wound to stop the bleeding.

Phil and Aydin took up defensive positions, an overlapping field of fire, through the now empty slider. Their M4s preposition by Phil during his bathroom break.

"Phil?"

"One is up on the hill, the same as two weeks ago. The other is closer. I think he is on the Pederson's porch."

"Fuck."

"Yeah, fuck. I like the Pedersons. If they killed the Pederson's, I am going to enjoy fucking these guys up. Help is on the way. I really have to pee."

Miranda chuckled. Aydin remained cool.

"Azima?"

*"Yes, Aydin?"*

"What is the ETA for KTF?"

*"Stand by."*

Pulling down a kitchen hand towel, Allison is tying it around Miranda's shoulder when she asked about privacy.

"You told me to return the Alexa. You made me return it because you were working on Azima. When were you going to tell me you installed her IN OUR HOME?"

"Uh … Umm … Now."

Miranda looked up to Allison, smiled, and poked.

"Men, cain't live with them, and you cain't shoot

`em."

*I heard it again.*
*I know that voice.*
*Why do I think I have seen her before?*

A sniper's round hit the couch, but the reinforced backplate stopped the bullet.

*I need to do something about that hill.*
*If these fuckers hurt the Pederson's, I am going to give them pain.*

*"Aydin?"*
"Yes, Azima?"
*"KTF indicates one sniper is down, but they are unable to locate the second sniper."*
"Tell them to check the deck of the house to our northwest."
*"Stand by."*
Phil's tone is almost cheerful.
"Hey, Pinky?"
"Yeah, Brain?"
"I have an idea."
"Is it a good idea? Because most of your ideas, Brain, result in dead people."
Aydin's face cracks the slightest snarky smile.
"It is not my fault people want to steal good ideas."
"What's your idea, Brain?"

"*Aydin?*"

"Yes, Azima?"

"*KTF says the second sniper is confirmed but no line of sight. He suggests you draw the sniper out.*"

Looking around, considering the options, Aydin halts his gaze on Allison. Her eyes are narrow and intense.

"Allison?"

"Miranda is in a bad way."

"Understood."

Phil and Aydin looked at each other, and without words, they played roshambo. Phil always exaggerates his third fist swing, giving Aydin just enough time to catch Phil's choice of rock, paper, or scissors. Aydin is not paying close enough attention to Phil's choice. Phil's response was falsely bright and cheery.

"I win!"

Allison barked.

"Wait!"

She crawled to through the kitchen, to the panty, pulled open the vault door, and pulled down a tactical vest.

Reaching Miranda, she squatted on her haunches, readying herself. In one move, she stood, threw the vest to Phil, then dove to the carpet next to Miranda.

The sniper's round grazed her left shoulder.

"I'm good."

Miranda's dark humor oozed.

"Good thing we are right-handed."

Ignoring the banter, Aydin was uncertain.

*Phil is not going to make it.*

"Pinky?"

"Yeah, Brain?"

"This side of the fire pit is your best option."

"My thinking also."

"I said to the rabbit, are you going to make it?"

Phil's response to Aydin quoting a Ray Wylie Hubbard song is the next line.

"Well, I got to."

Phil grabbed a throw-pillow of the chair, then duck-walked along the wall, to the edge of the slider. Reaching the open space that used to be a patio slider, he held up the throw-pillow.

The sniper's round hit the pillow, dead center.

"This guy is good. He's well-hidden and slicker than owl shit. I need a distraction."

Allison barked again.

"Wait!

"This furniture. The couch and the two chairs. They have reinforced back panels under the leather. Push the chair to the door, hide behind the chair, and shoot over the top."

Aydin is nodding agreement but is not happy with the suggestion.

*She's thinking but doesn't realize that it is*

*foolish.*

*This guy will put one in your forehead when you look over the barrier.*

*This feels like the desert without the heat.*

"We can use the chair to buy time. Phil, I am going to push it to you. We are going to push it onto the patio. Make it look like we are setting up a defensive perimeter. Maybe we can draw him out for KTF's guy."

"Understood. It is going to be painful."

Aydin's response is monotone.

"What's a little ground glass in your knees?"

"Aydin, hurry up. I can't stop the bleeding. Miranda's in trouble."

Miranda gave Allison a weak thumbs-up.

Pushing the chair forward resulted in two bullets hitting the chair. When Aydin reached the door, Phil rolled in behind the chair. Looking down at Aydin's knees, Phil couldn't resist.

"You're bleeding."

Aydin didn't miss the Predator reference.

"I ain't got time to bleed."

They pushed the chair onto the patio. Heads down, they heard and felt the next round hitting the hardened plate.

The bullets stopped.

*"Aydin?"*

"Yes, Azima?"

*"KTF reports all clear. Ambulance ETA four*

*minutes."*

"Thank you, Azima."

*"My pleasure."*

Phil and Aydin jump up and run to the women. Allison is on her knees, pressing on Miranda's shoulder. Blood from Allison's shoulder wound is running down her left arm.

Miranda looks up, smiles at Phil before turning her head to Aydin.

"Have you figured it out?"

Miranda's voice is gravelly. Aydin hears the connection and connects the dots.

*I knew she looked familiar.*

"I think so."

"Took you long enough."

Aydin's retort was in Phil's accent.

"I've been busier than a cat covering crap on a marble floor."

"Yeah, and the Chinese are coming."

The lights of the ambulance bouncing through the window told them it was time to move. Phil opened the front door just in time for the paramedics to race inside. The medics had Miranda on the gurney, and in the ambulance, in under four minutes. Phil hollered before they close the ambulance door.

"Are you taking her to Sky Ridge?"

"Yes."

*"Aydin?"*

"Yes, Azima?"

*"KTF reports the snipers were independent. Cleanup crew in-bound. ETA, 24 minutes."*

"Thank you, Azima."

*"My pleasure."*

"Azima?"

*"Yes, Aydin?"*

"Tell KTF to check on the Pedersons."

*"Will do."*

Allison and Phil looked at each other, shrugged when Allison mouthed the word *independent*. She looked to Aydin, staring through the open space, across the pool, over the pool house, at the back of the Pederson house. Aydin understood something Pops said when he was sixteen.

*'Aydin, life is never what you expect. Always remember to expect the unexpected.'*

That memory led him to a memory from his father.

*'Son, there are surprises around every corner. Everyone and I mean everyone, is looking for an edge. Remember that.'*

"One of the snipers was here for Miranda. The other for me."

# Smoke and Mirrors

### *Early-Morning, Trammell House, Slight Chill*

The trio is sipping their coffee at the breakfast bar. The lite breakfast Phil prepared is uneaten. Allison is staring into space with unfocused eyes. Phil is sitting, looking at his phone for any news related to a shooting in an affluent neighborhood. Aydin is staring at the clear Visqueen covering the slider. His thoughts are spinning through possibilities.

*There is more to this than the facial recognition code and fire control integration.*

*Someone is pulling strings to get me to stop.*

*Why?*

*The Service ordered us to contact the Chinese.*

*That is legit, a classic counter-espionage preemptive strike.*

*Moms sent Drakon at us.*

*Classic revenge.*

*But why now?*

*Why try to hurt us now?*

*Moms knows something is about to happen.*

*Does Allison miss her mother?*

*Probably not.*

*They didn't talk much.*

*Maybe she'll miss her at Christmas.*

*What is about to happen?*

*Why take us out before it happens?*

*What does someone not want us to do?*
*Two snipers.*
*One headshot for me and one for Miranda.*
*What does she know?*
*Did they fix her shoulder?*
*The Sky Ridge emergency room doesn't see two GSW in a year.*
*In three weeks, they have seen a half-dozen.*
*A local talking-head coming in with a shoulder shattered by a bullet will stuff the rumor mill.*

"Azima?"
"*Good morning, Aydin.*"
"Request an update from KTF on Miranda."
"*Requesting update, stand by.*"

*Miranda is the key.*
*Allison is going to freak out.*
*How can I prove it?*
*What did my dad say...*
*Oh yeah: 'There is nothing wrong with being the black sheep of the family.'*
*Was he talking about himself?*
*Was he talking about me?*
*NO!*
*I got it!*

"*Aydin, I have the update from KTF.*"
"Please, continue."
"*Miranda's gunshot wound was reported as an*

*accidental discharge. A reconstructive orthopedic surgeon was brought in. She rebuilt Miranda's scapula and clavicle. KTF assigned a 24-hour security detail."*

"Do we know when Miranda will be out of intensive care?"

*"Yes, Miranda is scheduled to be moved to a private room later today. The recommended visiting hours are 05:00 to 17:00 Monday-Friday and 08:00 to 17:00 on Saturday and Sunday."*

"Were you able to collate the other information request I forwarded yesterday?"

*"Yes, the information is in your inbox, with the standard decrypt password."*

"Thank you, Azima."

*"My pleasure."*

Aydin reads the email on his phone then returns to staring at the Visqueen covered slider.

Allison had seen Aydin like this when they were in high school. At fifteen, he didn't know what he wanted from life. At sixteen, he was fixated on becoming a Pararescueman. He wanted to be a Para-Jumper, a PJ, and wear the Maroon Beret. At seventeen, he wanted to be a sniper. At eighteen, college, then sniper school.

For eight years, she waited for him. He never understood she is lost without him.

Eventually, he turned from staring at the plastic covering to find Phil and Allison looking at him. He met the unanswered request.

"Miranda Marie LaLonde is not her real name.

She was born in October of 1990 at the Marine Corps Support Facility in New Orleans, Louisiana. Her adoptive parents are a retired Air Force Two Star and his wife."

Pausing, Aydin seems unfocused.

*Why those people?*
*The General was a Lieutenant, fresh out of the Academy when they adopt a baby girl?*
*How is the General connected?*

"Azima?"
*"Yes, Aydin?"*
"A message for KTF: Request a detailed background check, General Bryan, with a Y, Michael Cole, Retired, and his wife, Marina Dawn Cole."
*"Stand by."*

*Why those two, what did they have or need in 1990 that led them to adopt a baby girl?*

*"KTF confirms background check."*
"Thank you, Azima."
*"My pleasure."*

Allison spoke for the first time.
"Why do you thank a machine?"
Phil brightened at Allison's question, expecting Aydin's response.
"The phrase, Thank you, Azima..."

*"Yes, Aydin?"*

"Nothing at this time, Thank you, Azima."

*"My pleasure."*

"As I was saying, that phrase and her name are triggers. Saying her name initiates a session, and the thank-you phrase terminates the session."

Allison nodded agreement but pressed.

"Is it just me, or does Az… Does she change the tone of the responses? Does she possess tonal have inflection?"

"She does. It is advanced heuristics. But …"

*Holy fucking shit-snacks.*
*That's it!*
*I'm not the black sheep, nor is Allison.*
*It is all a front.*
*The Chinese.*
*The Russians.*
*It is all misdirection.*

Aydin turned to Allison, put down his coffee, picked up a lemon-raspberry scone, and waited. After a long, tense few seconds, Allison bit.

"What?"

"Did Moms ever say anything to you about artificial intelligence? Not the facial recognition stuff, but real, thinking for itself, sentient artificial intelligence?"

Phil's head is bobbing in understanding.

Allison eyed Phil's unconscious movement. She

searched her memory.

"Not that I can remember."

"Did she ever say anything to you about one day knowing the true history of our families?"

Allison's face brightened with the metaphorical lightbulb going off.

"Yes, she told me one day I would know everything about what our parents did."

Aydin finished his scone, sipped his coffee, and stared at his wife.

*Should I tell her now?*
*No, I'll let Miranda tell her.*

# Black Sheep

*"Aw, it was not a place for law-abiding citizens."*
*Ray Wylie Hubbard*
*Mother Blues*

**Trammel House, 19:30, Warming**

Friday evening, Aydin and Allison have brought Miranda to their home to recuperate. Dispatching Phil to Miranda's apartment, he has returned with several changes of clothes and toiletries. In the guest bedroom, Miranda is propped up on too many pillows. Phil is mothering like a hen.

Standing at the foot of the bed, Aydin and Allison are waiting for Phil to stop flittering before asking questions. Allison went first.

"What will happen to your on-air segments. Won't you be missed?"

"I called in and told them I'd be back in a couple of weeks. The air-head Kaley will cover. I'll spend a month of Sundays covering for her."

Looking around, she continues.

"This is very nice of you. This bedroom might be bigger than my apartment. But, Aydin, you didn't bring me here to show off your fancy home or because you feel guilty that I got shot. Does she know?"

"No, not yet. First, why did you get shot?"

"It's a long story."

Stepping over to the settee, Aydin flopped

down and responded.

"I have time."

Allison filled the other settee as Phil perched on the edge of the king-sized bed.

"Believe it or not, he was a former boyfriend. He and I were in the same class at Quantico. Sniper school. We were the best shots. When I broke it off, he made threats. I reported the threats, and he was booted from the program. His father is, was, a Senator who disowned him for failing. In their family, no one crashes. The guy you took down vowed if he couldn't have me, no one could have me.

"It sounds like a county song, but it is the truth. Some people never learn to accept rejection. Lesson learned, be careful who you piss off. A jealous, trained sniper is a dangerous son of a bitch.

"What about you? Do people shoot at you for target practice?"

*She knows.*

*Who does she work for, and what is her mission?"*

"Until you showed up, I was looking in the wrong places. Thank you for giving me the correct direction."

Miranda shuffled herself, punched and pillow, and turned back with a crooked smile to mask the contortion of pain.

"You would have figured it out eventually."

"Maybe not. I didn't care to look that deeply. Those things don't interest me."

Allison and Phil looked at each other with slightly tilted heads. They silently agreed to remain quiet.

"They interest you now."

"Yes, they do and thank you for that. Until a few days ago, I did not understand how you fit into the big picture. But that was an error also. You are not really in the game."

Miranda nodded and sipped the bendy straw to retrieve the mango-pineapple juice Phil had set on the nightstand. Aydin continued.

"You are not in the game, but someone pointed you at our game for a reason. Should I tell them, or should I leave that for you?"

"Oh, I'll tell them, but first, a few questions?"

*She thinks I don't know what she is doing or why.*

*She is probing, assessing.*

*I knew I recognized her.*

*Now I see it as plain as day.*

*This will be good.*

"Fire away."

"Do you and Allison think your parents guided you to, and trained you for, the counter-espionage game?"

"I won't speak for Allison, but I believe she will

agree. Looking back, I see all the clues. The subtle ways of looking at things. Yes, I believe we were groomed."

Allison looked from her husband to Miranda.

"I did not see it until college. Looking back, I didn't *want* to see the manipulation. Yes, it is all there, and we are here because of our parents."

"Do you think your aptitude for advanced computer software has anything to do with your childhood?"

Aydin's forehead wrinkled before he responded.

"We are all products of our environment."

"Yes, but do you think your environment was constructed to foster your high IQ?"

"Does it matter?"

"Of course, it does. Allison, also. Did you ever wonder why, in school, everything was easy for you?"

Squinting, Allison wondered where the questions were leading. What did Miranda expect to achieve?

"I wondered now and then. Less so in college. Why?"

"You and Aydin are not unique. There are others. All four of your parents loved the spy game. Allison, everyone except you refers to your father as Pops. He especially loves the game. Aydin, your father, is called Dad, and he loved the games within games. I am sorry about your mother."

Aydin nodded thanks. Miranda continued.

"But your mother, Allison, the game is her life.

Well, the game *was* her life. She is out of the game now, even if they ever set her free."

Allison, Phil, and Aydin sat, staring at the woman they did not know but who knew their life's history.

"Don't worry, Phil, I got nothing on you before the time you and Aydin became a deadly force in the desert."

Miranda cracked a smile, shifted her position, and asked.

"Do you want to tell them, or should I?"

Aydin opened his mouth to answer, but Phil intercepted.

"She's just like Aydin. It is starting to make my ass itch that you two have all the details while we sit here and root, knuckle deep, for crusty snot.

"I'm tolerant by nature, but I'm growing cantankerous. When I get cantankerous, me-n-someone is gonna mix."

Phil stopped, looked around, and waited. Allison and Miranda burst into guffaws. Aydin held up a palm in surrender.

"Phil, you have known me for a dozen years. You know I would not hold back from you. Until a few days ago, I was still trying to figure out the undercurrent of this cluster fuck.

"Hell, we got shot at less on a mission in the desert than we have in the past three weeks. Someone wants what we have, and Miranda is the key."

Turning from Aydin to Miranda, Phil raised an eyebrow. She nodded with a wide grin.

"You all know I was adopted. You know I grew up in Lafourche Parish, Louisiana. What you don't know is why. Lafourche Parish, Louisiana, is as far from everything as possible in the United States. Well, as far a reasonable, and not freeze your ass in Wyoming or Maine.

"Until I was recruited, I did not understand why my parents chose to live outside Thibodeaux. My father was from Ohio, and my mother from Arizona. We have no family in Louisiana.

"They weren't hiding. Not exactly. By design, they were under the radar.

"The first thing I learned was to drop the southern accent. I was lucky. Neither of my parents had a southern accent. Mine was learned in school.

"What does this all mean? Why am I here? Why is Aydin elusive and vague? The last one first: Your parents, all four of them, trained Aydin to be evasive and vague. It is his nature.

"Why am I here? It may not seem like it, but I am here to help. I was also groomed but for a different objective."

Miranda's summary is interrupted by Aydin's phone vibrating. Pulling the phone from his pocket, the group hears the request.

*"Aydin?"*

"Yes, Azima?"

*"KTF has filed the preliminary report on the background check you requested."*

"I will check the report in a few minutes. Thank you, Azima."

*"My pleasure."*

Aydin pointed his phone at Miranda, indicating she should continue, before returning it to his pocket.

"Different objective. My parents groomed me, and then The Service completed training of a sweet southern girl in domestic counter-intelligence."

Flipping on her deep southern accent, Miranda summarized and waited.

"No one suspects a sweet southern girl of anything. They rightly expect she's pretty as a pumpkin but half as smart."

Aydin broke the silence.

"You or me?"

"You, it's in the report you just received."

Pulling out his phone, placing it on the small table between the settees, Aydin looked up and focused on Miranda.

"Azima?"

*"Yes, Aydin?"*

"Is there a summary of the report I requested?"

*"Yes."*

"Please read the summary."

*"Summary of, background review of General Bryan Michael Cole, Retired. General Cole married Marina Dawn Cole, née Ptovin, in September of 1990. The Coles adopted one child in October of 1990. As of*

*this date, all are alive and residing within the United States.*

*"General Cole's entire career was within the AFOSI. The Air Force Office of Special Investigations.*

*"After establishing permanent residence in Lafourche Parish, Louisiana, in 1990, the General, a Lieutenant at the time, accepted numerous unaccompanied assignments until his retirement in 2016.*

*"Numerous postings in a 33-year career are highlighted by two assignments to the Pentagon and four postings to USAFE. The United States Air Force Command, Europe.*

*"Shall I continue?"*

"No, that will be enough. Thank you…"

Miranda barked and immediately grabbed at the sharp pain in her repaired shoulder.

"Wait!"

Looking up, rubbing her shoulder, she spoke softly.

"Ask her if the report has the name of the adopted child."

Miranda's smirk returned Aydin's grin. Allison rubbed the goosebumps on her forearms. Her right hand checking the bandage on her shoulder had not come loose. Phil skeptically eyed the wounded women. Aydin's tone was even.

"You are a smart girl. This way, neither of us has to say it."

Miranda responded.

"Pretty as a pumpkin but half as smart."

"Azima?"

*"Yes, Aydin?"*

"Is there reference to the adopted child in the initial report? Is there a name of the child?"

*"Scanning stand by. Yes, there is a section titled: Adoption Summary."*

"Read the section title Adoption Summary."

*"Adoption Summary, In July of 1990, Lieutenant Cole requested and was granted permission to adopt a child. An exception was issued due to the sensitive nature of Lieutenant Cole's responsibilities and the duty classification of the birth parents. The Secretary of the Air Force approved the adoption.*

*"The adoption was completed on October 14th, 1990, the day of the child's birth. The child was Christened Katherine Elizabeth Cole."*

Miranda filled the silence.

"Damn. Ask her if there is any reference to the natural parents."

"You asked her."

"Azima?"

*"Yes, Miranda."*

Stunned, Miranda continued.

"How do you know my name?"

*"I derived your name from the interactive conversations."*

Her face twisted in thought, Miranda continued.

"Is there any reference to the names of the

adopted child's natural parents in the summary report?"

"*Scanning. No.*"

"Thank you, Azima."

"*My pleasure. Aydin, is there anything else?*"

"No, thank you, Azima."

"*My pleasure.*"


To sow confusion, Aydin is grinning like the Cheshire Cat. He dumped the topic on Miranda.

"Tag, you're it."

Miranda snipped at Aydin before turning to Allison.

"You'd be happy if you had good sense. Allison, what was your mother's maiden name?"

"What? Uh. Cole, I think. What the fuck?"

"My birth father's name was Michael Matthew Trammel."

Aydin is unphased by the revelation, and Allison is a touch shocked but remains controlled. Phil is enjoying the soap-opera aspect of his friend's lives. Miranda sees her comment did not get the reaction she expected and continues to educate Allison with the information she thinks Aydin already knows.

"My birth mother's name was Katherine Marie Cole. My name is Katherine Elizabeth Cole.

"My adoptive father was your mother's younger brother. I bet you never knew she had a brother. She has two brothers. Katherine is for your mother. Elizabeth is for Aydin's mother."

Miranda stopped, letting the stunning news linger before turning to Aydin.

*She's good.*
*That was smooth.*

Aydin acquiesced to Miranda, then turned to Allison.

"Miranda, or Kat as she was known before LSU, is our half-sister."

# The Reality of Family

***Miranda's Apartment, 09:30, Overcast***

The Thursday following the revelation, Aydin has sent Phil on errands. He left Allison alone with Miranda, with his instructions to get Miranda to talk about her life. Quietly, Aydin instructed Azima to surveil Miranda 24-7.

Stating he was going to the office, Aydin has let himself into Maranda's apartment.

*Something is not adding up.*
*There are too many coincidences.*
*No pictures.*
*She has no pictures?*
*She is not planning to stay.*
*This looks like rental furniture.*
*This is not adding up.*
*Get what I came for and get the hell out.*

Pulling out several plastic bags, sterile swabs, and putting on surgical gloves, Aydin begins collecting samples.

*Lipstick, check.*
*The drinking glass with her lip marks, check.*
*Her hair in the sink and caught in the shower* drain.
*Check.*

*That dirty wine glass I saw on the coffee table.*
*She's either messy, or she left those lips on that wineglass deliberately.*
*The bed?*

Unmade, pulling back the duvet revealed several small, discolored spots. Using the specialized swabs, Aydin collected four samples from the bed.

*That should be enough.*

Looking around one last time, Aydin sees a vent cover screw is not tightened down.

*That vent is too high for Miranda to reach.*
*The counter?*
*Yes, there, scuff marks.*
*She stands on the counter, leans around, and opens the vent.*

Putting the dirty wine glass on the counter, Aydin pulled over the cheap coffee table. Using his Swiss Army Escape and Invasion pocketknife, Aydin unscrews the vent. Reaching inside, he pulls out a flash drive.

*What is she hiding?*
*It was a little obvious.*
*No one trained in counterespionage would leave a screw loose unless they want it to be found.*

Replacing the vent cover, leaving the screw as he found it, putting the coffee table back on the carpet dents, returning the dirty wine glass, ended his search.

*Something is not adding up.*
*There are too many coincidences.*
*We are wrapped in the middle of a long game.*
*That is the only answer.*
*This is some part of the long game, and Miranda is a new player.*
*She probably doesn't know this is a long game.*

## DTC Conference Room, Late-Morning, Overcast

One-on-one, Aydin and Phil are discussing Miranda. Allison and Miranda are headed toward the office with lunch. Phil is unpacking a Dell laptop he purchased at Aydin's direction.

"Phil, KTF won't use 23andMe. He'll send someone to that guy in Florida who built the genome database. We'll know something in a few days."

"I get it. That's what this PC is for, the flash drive. You want to isolate whatever is on that thumb storage from the network."

"Here, boot from this."

Aydin slid a blue thumb drive, with the logo of a penguin, along the table. Phil catches it without looking up. Inserting the thumb drive, then powering on the PC, Phil chooses the alternate boot option. The

Linux operating system command prompt appears.

"We're up."

Aydin slides the flash drive he took from Miranda's apartment. Phil inserts Miranda's storage stick and begins scanning. Aydin continues his work while Phil scours the device for clues. After several minutes, Phil reports.

"It's her private data. Photos, PDFs of important documents, her will, diplomas."

"Look at the photos."

Phil wrinkled his forehead at the odd request but began reviewing the more than a thousand photos. After several minutes, Phil found something interesting.

"This folder of photos is odd. They are pictures of a park. Looking at the buildings in the background, a park somewhere in Eastern Europe or Russia."

Aydin slid a third thumb storage to Phil.

"Copy Miranda's flash, all of it. Use this. It will make a duplicate image of the drive on the PC's hard drive, and then it will prompt you to decrypt the photos."

Phil didn't think twice. He loaded up the software. When prompted, he pointed the decrypt software to the folder with the unusual images.

"Aydin, how did you know? Where did you get the decryption software? This is not good. I am here for you. You know that. If you want me not to see her, I'll stop, but I need to know more. Aydin, you have to give me more. I feel like you are trying to take on everything by yourself. You can't take this on by yourself."

*He wants to help.*
*Phil can't help me.*
*Not really.*
*But maybe.*
*Something is not adding up.*
*This can't be a long game carried over from the cold war.*
*It is not a new cold war.*
*Maybe it is a new cold war.*
*Ah, fuck snacks.*
*Why do they want me dead?*
*Not everyone fancies me dead.*
*What did Miranda say? 'Do you think your environment was constructed to foster your high IQ?' 'In school, everything was easy for you?'*
*She is implying Allison and I were groomed for this.*
*A long game.*
*A generational long game.*
*She said: 'You and Aydin are not unique.' That means there are others, or she thinks there are others.*
*What is the endgame?*
*The advanced AI?*
*The Targeting Software?*
*The combination of the two?*
*Ah, fuck snacks.*

*What am I missing?*

Aydin's thoughts are interrupted by Allison and Miranda plopping lunch onto the conference room table. Seeing the women enter, Phil palmed the flash drives and closed the new PC. He is beaming because he is perpetually hungry, Phil chimes.

"It smells so good if I put it on top of my head, my tongue would beat my brains out trying to get to it."

Aydin refused to look up at the comment. Allison rolled her eyes and began distributing plastic utensils.

Miranda glowed and gave it right back.

"Look at him. He's grinnin' like a possum eatin' a sweet tater."

Ignoring it all, Aydin peeled the foil off one of his chicken burritos and began eating. Miranda kissed Phil on the forehead, sat with her back to the window, close to Phil, opened her salad container, and waited.

Miranda underestimated Aydin. He would not speak, forcing her to give in.

"You missed the pin camera in the viewport of my front door. Did you find what you were looking to retrieve?"

"I didn't miss the camera, and I found what I wanted."

"Did you open it?"

"I did."

"Do you know what it means?"

"I do."

"What are you going to do about it?"

"Nothing. Phil, give her back the flash drive."

Phil hands Miranda the flash drive Aydin took from her apartment.

"You are not going to do anything. You are going to wait. You are going to wait for what?

"I'll wait until we know who wants me dead. Someone wants me dead because I can piece it all together."

Allison and Phil watched the two verbally spar. Alternating between bites of salmon salad and sweet tea, Miranda continued to eat with one arm. The smell of salmon irritating Phil's sense of smell and psyche for what is real food. After sipping, she waited for Aydin to look at her but continued the conversation when he refused to look up.

"They don't want you dead for what is on the flash drive."

"Correct."

"Do you know who they are and why they want you dead?"

"Not who, but why."

"What are you going to do about it?"

"Nothing."

Annoying Phil and ignored by Aydin, the aroma of Allison's lunch of fish mingled with Miranda's. Miranda's simple response to Aydin's question was a little too quick to be believed.

"Nothing?"

"Correct, nothing."

"That seems a little naïve."

Ratcheting up the tension, Aydin and Miranda are now eyeing each other. Phil turned to Allision and interrupted.

"What did you do to my burritos?"

"Guacamole, it was Miranda's idea."

Without looking at Phil, Miranda inserted her reasoning.

"It's good for you."

"Yeah, well, it tasted like the south end of a northbound goat."

Undeterred by the diversion, Miranda persisted.

"I was saying, that seems a little naïve."

Aydin slightly shook his head in the negative. He returned to his PC before responding.

"They will come to us. We need to stay alive long enough to know who is at the top of the food chain. Moms was taking direction from someone. We need to know who that someone is and their endgame."

### Trammel House, 19:30, Rain Starting

Phil insisted on the dinner he prepared is eaten at the formal table. Allison made Aydin and Phil put on clean shirts with collars. Miranda was quiet but smiling throughout the meal.

Phil poured the last of the second bottle of wine, sat, and asked a question.

"Aydin, I am a little confused about something.

May I ask you about your family? Your families?"

Allison put her hand on Aydin's forearm, smiled, and nodded okay. Aydin agreed.

"Sure."

"You and Allison refer to Aydin's parents as *Mom* and *Dad*."

"Correct."

"Allison's parents are *Moms* and *Pops*."

"Correct."

"Were they always stationed together?"

"No, well, sort of. There were times when I think they were assigned to different duty stations, but I think they worked it for Allison and me to remain together. There were two or three times when Allison stayed with us while Moms and Pops were TDY. One or two times, I stayed them while Mom and Dad were TDY."

Phil joins the conversation.

"Did you think it was odd that your friends kept coming and going, but you two, your families, stayed in the same places?"

Allison notices Miranda is focused on Phil. She realizes Miranda is searching for information or confirmation of her knowledge.

Aydin's head is bobbing with a realization.

"Phil, you may be on to something. Allison, do you remember Robert and Chrissy in Bentwaters?"

"Yeah. They bragged about doing it all the time. Everyone knew they were lying."

"Do you remember what Chrissy said?"

"No."

"She said she and Robert first did it when they were stationed at Ramstein. Robert said, no, it was at Lakenheath the first time."

Pausing, Allison realized the connection.

"They were like us."

"Yes, I think they were. Also, Matt and Kristy at Plattsburgh."

"Weren't they older?"

"Yes, by a couple of years. I had advanced Trig with Kristy. She said it was nice to speak to someone other than Matt."

Aydin stopped, considered, then looked to Miranda. Ending the evening, Miranda closed the discussion and left no doubt about her intentions. Putting her hand on Phil's forearm, she answered Aydin's gaze.

"I'll move out of the guest bedroom to the guest house. Assuming Phil is okay with a roommate."

Phil's retort was straight from his eighteen-year-old self.

"I'm too poor to paint and too proud to whitewash. I accept the good when it falls on my head."

### Trammel House, 04:30, Raining

*"Aydin?"*

"Azima, why are you waking me?"

*"Miranda is attempting to leave."*

"Let her. Let me know if her phone goes

221

offline."

"*Will do.*"

Thank you, Azima.

"*My pleasure.*

### Trammel House, 06:30, Raining

Miranda has returned from her early morning outing. The four are eating a lite, high-protein breakfast. Phil's dry comment slides by without comment.

"If we get through today, it'll be two weeks with no one shooting at us. No one shooting at us for two whole weeks is time for a party."

Waiting, getting nothing, Phil does not give up.

"Fuck you guys. We are going to dinner, and I am picking the place."

Aydin gives in.

"Allison, take Miranda to Park Meadows, pick up a couple of agreeable outfits. Phil and I will head to the office. Meet back here at 16:00. We'll clean up, then head out to one of the dives Phil adores."

Allison and Miranda fist-bumped

### DTC Conference Room, Late-Morning, Clearing

"*Aydin?*"

"Yes, Azima?

"*The DNA results are available.*"

"Already?"

"*I do not understand that question.*"

"It is a query confirming the results were returned much earlier than expected."

*"I understand. I will incorporate that into my processing protocols."*

"Please, forward the results to Phil and me."

*"Done."*

"Thank you, Azima."

*"My pleasure."*

Aydin and Phil read the 18-page report twice before Phil speaks.

"Miranda had sex with that young, weekend sports anchor. She should have washed her sheets."

"That is what you are focused on?"

"No, but it is interesting. Girls have needs, and who better than a young jock."

"Whatever. What about the part describing Miranda's parents?"

"Well, there is that. Do you think she knows?"

"My take is it is 50-50, she knows. I lean toward she doesn't. The question is, how do we tie it back to Moms?"

### Dive Restaurant Patio, Early Evening, Warming

The four are seated on the patio at the Barrier Bar & Grill. The Barrier Bar & Grill's patio abuts a nice restaurant's outdoor seating, a cornerstone of the downtown revitalization. The jeans Aydin and Phil are wearing fit the décor at the dive. The women are overdressed. The floral summer dresses are a tad too lite for the evening. Phil notices.

"The women are perky enough to cut glass."

Miranda and Allison ignore Phil. Determined to make the best of it, Allison vetoes dinner by calling an audible.

"Phil, we are having drinks here and going next door for dinner. That place is nice. Plus, it will be warmer inside."

Crestfallen, Phil agrees.

"Okay, I'll make sure they have a table."

While the trio waits for Phil's return, Miranda opens up with an observation.

"That same car has gone by at least three times."

Allison has made the same observation.

"Three times on Main Street and once around on Victorian Drive, turning left on to Main. Aydin?"

With his back to Main Street, Aydin asks.

"Allison?"

"At least two in an emerald green Chevy Tahoe."

Aydin does not hesitate. He and Phil have pistols under their jackets, and the women have Allison's .380 caliber mouse pistols strapped to their inner left thighs.

"Let's go."

The three meet Phil on the sidewalk. He confirms they have a table. Taking an inside window booth, the men sit on the inside of the booth, next to the window. Aydin updates Phil.

"Emerald green Chevy Tahoe."

"Roger that."

Finishing their dinner, waiting for the desert to share, Allison heads to the restroom.

On her way, through the window, she sees the emerald Green Tahoe parked on the street, beyond the rear parking lot. Stepping through the side door onto the side patio, one of the men from the green Tahoe has his back to Allison. He is closing the metal gate when she sees the pistol in his waistband.

When he turns, seeing Allison, he reaches for his pistol. Allison is already pointing her small Walther and puts the assailant down without a word. Looking at the pistol, Allison is surprised at the small caliber's effectiveness at a short-range.

When they hear the pistol, Aydin, Phil, and Miranda, form a perimeter defense. Allison steps back into the restaurant. People inside are beginning to rush out. The patrons of the Barrier Bar & Grill take the gunshot in stride. Allison's update is calm and focused.

"One down, I don't know where the other is. My bet is he is on the sidewalk to the west."

Miranda may be a spy, but she is not used to being shot at and is looking to Aydin for advice.

"A pincer move. Phil and Allison, out the back, around the block, come in from the west. Miranda and I will wait, say 40 seconds?"

Allison and Phil do not hesitate. They race out the back, down the short ally, around the buildings, up the side street, and arrive at Main Street's sidewalk.

Aydin points, indicating Miranda goes east, onto the side patio, and covers the sidewalk from the building's corner.

Seeing Miranda arrive at the corner and giving thumbs up in the window, Aydin steps forward to look through the westernmost window.

The window shattered, but the round is redirected.

*That asshat doesn't understand deflection.*

Hearing two more shots, Aydin stepped onto the sidewalk. The second assailant is lying over the short metal fence separating the sidewalk from the outside dining area. Allison and Phil are walking up when the fourth and fifth shots are heard.

Aydin turns around, and they see Miranda face down on the concrete. Rushing to her, they catch sight of the green Tahoe between the buildings, screeching away down the backstreet. Reaching down, Aydin finds a pulse. Looking up to Phil, he nods to the tables.

Phil grabs the clean table napkins and begins to apply pressure, stemming the bleeding.

Aydin takes command.

"We wait for the police. This was self-defense. It is on the cameras. When the cops arrive, put down your weapons and put your hands up."

## *WB, Lincoln Ave, Oh-Dark-Thirty, Bright Moon*

Phil's pressure on the wounds saved Miranda's life. She was taken to Parker Adventist Hospital. Allison, Phil, and Aydin were transported to the Parker police station, interrogated for hours, then released. They walked the mile and a half from the station back to Aydin's parked Mercedes.

Allison's waited for the solitude of the car. Her tone is gentle.

"They came for her. If they were after us, why run off after they thought they killed Miranda? They did not confirm the kill, which is classic inexperience, or the shooter is pussy and afraid. Someone must have hired locals to take her out.

"I guess this confirms her pissed-off boyfriend story was bullshit. Everything that comes out of her mouth is bullshit. It is all shiny lies. Can we ever believe what she says?"

Aydin remained silent. Allison knew her man was somewhere else mentally.

*They don't want her talking to me.*
*Why not?*
*There is a connection I am missing.*
*The key must be in the DNA tests.*
*Maybe.*
*Ah, fuck snacks.*
*What do we do now?*
*What the fuck am I missing?*

*Every time I think I have it, something else points me in a new direction.*

*The connection must be obvious, but I can't find the son-of-bitch.*

*Fuck. Fuck. Fuck.*

*Calm.*

*Breathe.*

Phil is disappointed and breaks the silence.

"Two weeks. We couldn't make it two weeks?"

# Family Ties

### *Early-Afternoon, Parker Adventist Hospital, Warm*

Allison, Phil, and Aydin are standing at the end of the single-person hospital room. They are listening to the surgeon talk to Miranda.

"Whoever fixed your shoulder did an excellent job. This time, you were shot twice, just below the shoulder. One went through with not much damage. The second, or first, pierced the top of your left lung. I closed it all up, cleaned everything, and you should recover. You were lucky. They used low-velocity rounds. If they have been high-velocity, you would have lost your lung to the congealing effect.

"You'll be here for a few days while we monitor your breathing. I am sure your friends can take care of you when you are discharged."

The surgeon didn't wait for a response or a thank you. He walked out of the room without making eye contact.

The trio stepped up to the bed, Allison and Aydin, on one side. Phil, on the other side, after closing the blinds, blocking the view from the hallway. Aydin opened the interrogation.

"Where did you go yesterday morning?"

"To my apartment. The decrypt code is the expiration label on yogurt."

"We don't need the decryption code. Try again."

"I didn't know you didn't need the decryption

code. If you have seen the pictures, you know the details of the message."

"I know what they say. We'll come back to that. Your mother is Katherine Marie Cole. Do you know who your father is?"

Miranda turned her head, looking toward the window and the cloudless sky above the blinds. Aydin remained focused on the questions. He continued to press the topic.

"You know who your father is, and it is not my father. My father is a good man. He and my mother were faithful to each other. Your mother, Moms, not so much. If you know who your father is, you know we killed him."

"I know."

"Why are they trying to kill you?"

"Because I know who my mother worked for and why. She and the guy you know as Gavriil Misha Solovev are my birth parents."

"You said, *know as*, what don't I know?"

"Gavriil Misha Solovev's real name is Michael Anthony Ptovin. He is the younger brother of my adoptive mother, Marina Dawn Cole. Their parents were Russian immigrants who fled religious persecution. They settled in Arizona. My father was recruited, and his training began when he was twelve.

"He could pass for native Russian and be used by all sides to spy on everyone. But something went wrong. He started playing for himself. He and my mother met when she was assigned to bring him in after he went rogue.

"Instead, he talked her into flipping."

Allison interrupted.

"That is when she came home, shot. He shot her to cover not killing him or bringing him in."

"Correct. Ptovin cut a deal on both sides. The Russians left him alone because of his American connections. The Americans left him alone because of the secret he kept."

Aydin is connecting dots but still has gaps.

*There is another player.*

*There has to be someone between Ptovin, Moms, and their handler at The Service.*

"I am sorry we killed your father."

"Don't be. I didn't know him, and from what I do know, he deserved it. My mother and father are kindly retirees, living in Louisiana."

Aydin nodded and continued

"Now, you have the secret, and the secret wants you dead."

Miranda forced a smile.

"Correct. One of the little secrets I have that I will share is this: They want you more than they want me. Do you know why?"

For a long while, Aydin was silent, thinking.

*She's right.*

*They want me, and I don't know why.*

*She is stringing this out.*

*She wants something to happen.*

*She is waiting for something to happen.*

*What is she waiting for, and why is she delaying?*

*The advanced AI and the target software are false flag operations.*

*It has to be something else, but what?*


"Phil, you can stay. I'll send a car for you. Allison and I are going to head home."

Without another word, Allison and Aydin leave the hospital.

### WB, Lincoln Ave, Afternoon, Warm

"Azima?"

*"Yes, Aydin?"*

"Send a text to Kermit, pick up Phil at Parker Adventist Hospital, 16:00."

*"Text sent. Shall I report when I receive a reply?"*

"No. That will be all. Thank you, Azima."

*"My Pleasure."*

"Aydin, what is going on? I trust you. Phil trusts you. But you are hurting, and I can't help unless you talk to me."


*I can't catch a break.*

*Not one fucking break.*

*Allison is not going to like this.*

232

*She will think I am interrogating her.*
*Oh well, no sugar-coated bullshit.*
*What did Allison say? 'No shiny lies."*
*Oh well, she asked.*


"Did Moms ever mention anything to you about working behind the iron curtain?"

"Not that I can remember. Why?"

"Did she ever talk to you about sexpionage?"

"If you think what I think sexpionage is, maybe."

"It is what you think it is, and *maybe*?"

"Well, a couple of times, when she and my father would fight. After the fights, when I was about twelve, she'd talk to me about women doing things to be successful. Of course, she told a twelve-year-old girl, men would do just about anything for a pretty woman."

"Was she grooming you to be like her?"

Allison hesitated.

"Yes, I see it now. I suppose I always knew it, but we all choose to ignore the hard parts of being a child."

Allison is looking out the passenger side window, thoughtful before she continues.

"Honey Pot. Honey. She called it honey or candy. Ah fuck. Now I know where I got that phrase. Sorry, I won't use that term anymore."

"I don't mind. I like your candy."

Allison's smile was half-hearted.

"She traded sex for information. Drakon, flipped her. No wonder Pops doesn't give a shit about her being hauled away. It was Pops who put you on to her, right?"

"Yes."

"Good for him. I need a drink. Do you think it is warm enough for a swim?"

"The pool is heated."

"That's not what I meant. We'll be alone for a couple of hours."

Aydin smiled but remained focused on the road.

"Aydin, what does Miranda know?"

"She knows who in the Service is manipulating all of this, and she knows why they want me dead."

"Are you sure?"

"I am sure about the mole in the Service, not about why they want me dead."

Allison's comment left no doubt in Aydin's mind.

"We'll kill the mole."

Pulling into the garage, Allison was stripping out of her jeans before Aydin stopped the car. Naked before she opened the door, she was not shy.

"You get the drinks, and I'll be in the warm water."

# Everything Is In The Cloud

*"Some get spiritual 'cause they see the light and some*
*'cause they feel the heat."*

*Ray Wylie Hubbard*

*Conversation With the Devil*

### DTC Conference Room, Mid-Morning, Hot

Allison is at the Trammell house, tending to Miranda, who is back in the guest bedroom. Phil is griping, Aydin is ignoring him.

"Aydin, it has been a week. We can't keep coming here and getting nothing done. We have the money in the Swiss account. Let's take some of it, find a beach, far away, and figure this out somewhere else."

*He is antsy, so am I.*
*He knows they are going to come at me again. I can get Miranda to talk.*
*If I can get her to talk, I can close the gaps.*
*He sweats when he is nervous.*
*I can smell it, like in the desert.*
*I need to do something.*

"Did you find anything else in the photos or on Miranda's flash drive?"

"No. Just that one message about her father, mother, their history, and the threat to kill her if her mother gave her any names. Judging by her getting shot twice in two weeks, she must know the identities."

"I am going to get Miranda to talk."

*"Aydin?"*

"Yes, Azima?"

*"You have an urgent call from a number originating in Washington State."*

"How do you know it is urgent?"

*"It is the third call in less than five minutes. The second call left a short voice mail, which I examined. From the voicemail, I determined the urgency criteria were met."*

"Put it through. Thank you, Azima."

*"My Pleasure."*


Aydin pressed the speaker button, connecting the call before the first ring ended.

"Fírinne software, how may I help you?"

*"You can't help me, but I can help you."*

Shocked, Phil and Aydin look at each other. Phil mouths the word 'Moms?'

"I doubt you can help me. Did your handler work it so you could call?"

*"You need my help. If you don't listen, they will kill you, Allison, Kat, and Phil. Everyone dies."*

"She prefers Miranda."

*"Her name is Kat. Forget that for now. Listen to me. Taking out Drakon was a mistake. It put a hole in the supply chain. The money stopped. Sponsors need*

*to get paid, or people start dying."*

"Katherine, I am not interested in listening to your threats."

*"Katherine? What happened to Moms? Never mind, listen to me, turn over Kat, and everyone else walks."*

"No."

Aydin is scrolling his computer, looking through lists of data.

*There, got you.*

*"Aydin, be reasonable."*

"No, Miranda is under my protection. Next, you are going to threaten me again. Don't bother. Katherine, you made a mistake. I know you are in a secure facility in Aurora. I have the caller ID for the cell phone you are using."

The line disconnected. Aydin looked at Phil, spun his PC around for Phil to read, then smiled. He commented while Phil read.

"I think Miranda is going to be surprised by the news."

"Aydin, wasn't Captain Arnold, the guy on the Ramaqubah mission, from Washington State?"

"Yes."

"Isn't that weekend sports anchor named Arnold from Washington State?"

"I dunno, is his name Arnold?"

"It is, and he is from Washington State. Our

little Miranda was planning to get to dad through the son."

*Phil got it before I did.*
*I should have listened when he whined about the DNA results.*
*She was tracing Dad through the son.*
*Why does Miranda want to off Captain Arnold?*
*Aw, fuck snacks.*
*Of course, the mission in Ramaqubah was supposed to fail but not destroy opium production.*
*Fuck. Fuck. Fuck.*
*Captain Arnold didn't want an alternate FFP.*
*He probably didn't know Drakon would blow up the whole town.*
*Captain fuck-nuts didn't plan on Drakon trying to kill him and us.*
*Aw, fuck snacks.*
*Drakon was jealous.*
*Fucking Moms.*
*Everyone was fucking Moms.*

"Phil, that fuck-nuts Arnold is Moms' handler."

"Does Pops know?"

"I don't think so. He would have told me. Arnold is coming after us because of Ramaqubah. We fucked up his retirement plan."

"Arnold has access to Moms. Aydin, if Arnold has Moms in Aurora, Miranda and Allison are in danger."

Aydin was moving before Phil finished his statement. Phil grabbed the tactical gear from the hidden vault and met Aydin at his Mercedes. Tossing the tactical gear in the back seat, sliding into the front passenger seat, Phil hears Aydin yelling into the comms connection.

"No, Allison, right now. I don't care if you have to carry her. Get to the safe room. Tell her Arnold is coming, and it is not that weenie sports broadcaster."

*"Ah, fuck okay. The safe word is fuck snacks."*

"Got it."

Aydin smiled, cut the connection, and roared out of the parking lot.

### SB, I-25, Late Morning, Hot

"Azima?"

*"Yes, Aydin?"*

"Send a text Pops: Condition one-one-baker."

*"Please confirm, Text: Condition one-one-baker, send to Pops."*

"Confirming, Text: Condition one-one-baker, send to Pops. Eggshell white."

*"Authorization code confirmed. Sending."*

"Thank you, Azima."

*"My pleasure."*

Phil stared straight ahead, focused and intense, but asked anyway.

"Can we change that closure confirmation sequence? I am tired of hearing her say *my pleasure*."

Aydin ignored the question.

*Good, Phil's in mission mode.*

*Allison will go down swinging.*

*The office is between Aurora and the house, but he wouldn't do it himself, would he?*

*No, Just like in the desert, he'll show up after his people do the dirty work.*

*I'm going to kill that motherfucker on general principles.*

*Moms.*

*She allowed all this to happen.*

*No wonder Pops never talks to her.*

*Allison must be freaking out.*

*She met a sister she never knew she had.*

*She learned or confirmed what she knew about her mother.*

*Her mother was trying to turn her into an international criminal.*

*When that didn't work, Moms tried to kill her daughters.*

*I thought my family was fruitcake nutty.*


"What Phil?"

"I said, how do you want to play it?"

"I hadn't thought that far ahead. Do you have an idea?"

"The Pederson's place."

"That is Fucking-A brilliant!"

"Yep. The Pederson's are away. We come in from their deck. I'll go south, around to the sniper perch. When you make for the house, it'll draw out the sniper. I'll take out the sniper, then cover your flank.

"Pops will cover the front of the house from the end of the street."

"Agreed."


Seventeen minutes later, Aydin pulled into the Pederson's driveway. The duo snuck around the house, to the rear deck, and began the recon. Phil spoke first.

"I got nothing."

"Me neither."

"I guess you better be sweet on your feet getting to that slider?"

"I guess you better be sweet with the M4 on that sniper so I can get to the slider."

"Sixty seconds."

Phil fist-bumped his friend, then duck-walked to the end of the deck, down the three steps, and disappeared around the edge of the Pederson house.

Counting in his head, Aydin was reeling.


*One-thousand-seventeen.*

*One-thousand-eighteen.*

*This is so bad, but it will be over soon.*

*One-thousand-twenty-nine.*

*One-thousand-thirty.*

*There must be someone else.*

*Arnold and Moms know too much.*
*If we take out Arnold, who remains?*
*One-thousand-forty-two.*
*One-thousand-forty-three.*
*One-thousand-forty-four.*
*Someone close.*
*Very close.*
*Allison?*
*No, I'd feel it.*
*Pops?*
*Hell no.*
*Dad?*
*Maybe, but he's not close.*
*One-thousand-fifty-five.*
*One-thousand-fifty-six.*
*Fuck it.*
*Let's go.*

Aydin slipped off the deck, around the large hydrangea bush, and stopped at the fence. Popping up, their guess about a sniper was correct. Aydin heard the distinct sound of Phil's suppressed M4 firing one shot. He hopped over the fence, and in a hunched position, ran the ten yards to the back of the pool house. Squatting, rising slowly, looking in the lower corner of the window, he saw two armed men wearing tactical gear. Lowering with his back the wall of the pool house, the amora of hydrangea was overpowering.

Holding back a sneeze, he waited for Phil to

make eye contact. Phil was belly down on the deck when Aydin spied him.

Holding up two fingers and pointing to the pool house, Phil responded with two fingers.

Targeting his M4, Phil gave Aydin the thumbs up.

Grabbing a handful of the fertile soil, Aydin noticed the rich smell before tossing it against the window over his head.

The soil made a tinkling sound against the window before landing in his hair and on his shoulders. It was enough noise to draw one of the assailants to the window.

The glass shattered from Phil's bullet, also landing in Aydin's hair.

Looking up, Phil gave Aydin a hand across his eyes signal. Phil couldn't see the second attacker.

Leaning right, crawling, Aydin was happy the moist soil made no sound. Reaching the southwest corner of the small building, looking up and to his right, Aydin saw the shadow of a rifle muzzle. The rifle silhouette against the white door jam. Standing and squaring his tactical vest to the wall, he stepped back three steps. Aydin mentally calculated where the assailant was standing.

*He has to be in the shower stall.*
*Good thing it is plastic and not tile.*
*He must be back and to the right; otherwise, Phil could see him through the window.*

Turning his head, Aydin received the 'no eyes' signal from Phil.

*Well, here goes.*

Aydin spun on his suppressor before he unloaded five rounds, chest high, across what he thought was the width of the shower stall. Two bullets hit the assailant's vest, pushing him forward and into Phil's sightline.

Aydin watched the red mist expand through the open door and dissipate before stepping around and peering in.

Turing, Phil had arrived. Aydin walked the north side of the pool, Phil the south. Reaching either side of the slider, they both peeked in.

Allison and Miranda are zip-tied and sitting on the couch. Aydin could see Allison's eyes. She ignores him and turns to focus on the wall opposite the sofa. Blinking twice, she twisted her neck to relieve tension.

Aydin holds up a fist and steps back with his vest against the wall. Phil halts and steps back, putting his tactical vest against the wall.

Aydin holds up two fingers and points in the directions Allison indicated.

Phil shakes his head in the negative, pointed toward the wall. By extension, he pointed to Allison and Miranda, then mimed, slicing his throat.

Aydin nods agreement and gives a palm-up

signal. The *do you have any ideas* gesture.

Receiving a negative headshake from Phil, Aydin was convinced everyone he loved was about to die.

*All those missions in the desert, and it comes down to this.*

*They must know their guys are down.*

*For fuck's sake, if they look outside, they will see that one in the pool house.*

*What are they waiting for, Christmas?*

Aydin's thoughts are interrupted by the front doorbell. The shocked look from Phil confirmed he heard it also.

Aydin pointed for Phil to peek in because he would be able to see the front door. Phil leaned around as the bell rang a second time. One aggressor is standing behind Allison, the other about to open the door.

Phil held up a fist, followed by three fingers, spinning the digits in the air, then halted.

The front door opened. Pops is standing there.

Phil dropped a finger.

A short conversation while Pops is looking and pointing at a clipboard.

Phil dropped another finger. Aydin put his right hand on the slider handle.

Phil sees Pops throw up his hands and begins to turn away.

Phil closed his hand, then rushed forward. Before Phil moved one full step, Aydin had the slider open and the attacker behind Allison down. Arnold had answered the door but failed to turn fast enough. Phil's two 1911 rounds into Arnold's vest knocked him down and the air out of his body.

Phil cut the women loose while Aydin dragged Captain Arnold to the center of the room.

*This fucker is going to pay.*

Phil halted Aydin's thoughts of revenge.

"Doesn't this fucker work for Kermit?"

Handing his pistol to Allison, Aydin pointed to Arnold and stepped over to look at the dead attacker.

Before he could answer, Allison confirmed Phil's statement.

"He was in the van when my mother tried to run. He tied her to the wall of the van. We couldn't make it to the safe room. That fucker was already in the house when we started to move.

*There's a missing piece.*
*Kermit is going to go ballistic.*

The gentle knock on the front door turned everyone's head. Aydin spoke calmly.

"Miranda, let Pops in.

"Azima?"

*"Yes, Aydin?"*

"Code one, right fucking now."
*"Please confirm code one."*
"Confirming code one, Kermit The Frog."
*"Code one confirmed."*
"Give me the ETA when you have it."
*"Stand by."*

Aydin stepped back, taking back his pistol from Allison. As Allison was hugging Pops, Aydin waved the muzzle for Arnold to roll over. Phil handed wire ties to Miranda.

*"ETA, seven minutes."*
"Thank you, Azima."
*"My pleasure."*

Miranda tied Arnold's wrists. Then kicked him in the side as hard as she possibly could. Hitting the Velcro straps and not the body protection, she was sure several ribs cracked from the kick. Arnold rolled away from the boot onto his back.

The effort stung Miranda's wounds. She sat on the sofa. Phil stepped over and silently ask if he could help her. Miranda nodded to the pistol.

Phil reversed his grip, giving her the handle. Aydin watched, thinking.

*I can let her kill him, but we will lose so much information.*

*He knows the whole network.*

*I'll use Moms against him.*

*Aw, fuck snacks.*

Stepping over, Aydin looked down at Arnold, putting his back to Miranda and her pistol.

"Give me one reason I should not let her shoot you."

"I know why they are trying to kill you, and it is not what you think."

"You don't know what I think."

"It has nothing you did in the desert or after. You think you are so smart. You are a fucking moron."

*Son of a fucking motherfucking, piece of shit.*
*Calm.*
*Breathe.*

"I can get that information from Moms."

"No, you can't. Katherine doesn't know. I tried to keep her from trying to kill you, but when you blew up our retirement, she... Well, you know Katherine."

Allison stepped over and put her boot in the already cracked ribs. The pain caused Arnold to puke. Aydin's tone is calm and fierce.

"I didn't blow it up. You are a fucking moron. How is *your* retirement? Drakon and Moms were the dealers."

"Katherine came to me in the desert. She brought me into the game. She and I were going to cut out Drakon and take over the production."

"You mean Phil and I were going to take out

248

Drakon for you."

Arnold shrugged in agreement.

Pops spoke for the first time.

"Kermit's here."

The cleaners rushed in, led by Kermit. Seeing his guy lying on the floor in tactical gear, Kermit lost it and began stomping on the traitor's skull.

Pops and Phil rushed over to pull Kermit off the dead man.

Kermit looked around, nodded, then spoke.

"Everyone out, we got this. He stays. Our bosses will want to talk to him."

Kermit stopped and looked at Aydin for confirmation.

*Do I let him take Arnold?*
*Yes. If I can't trust Kermit, I can't trust anyone.*

Aydin nodded okay, then spoke.

"There's one up on the hill and two more in the pool house. How long?"

Kermit looked around before answering.

"We brought a replacement slider."

Pissed off beyond angry, Kermit shot out the perfectly good slider then responded.

"Four hours."

# A Family Tradition

**Trammell House, 06:52, Overcast**

## BREAKING NEWS

THE UNREST IN HONG KONG CONTINUES AS THE CHINESE GOVERNMENT CONTINUES ITS CRACKDOWN ON DISSIDENT PROTESTS.

THE NEW GOVERNMENT IS USING ITS UNIQUE FORM OF MARTIAL LAW. ALL GATHERINGS OF MORE THAN FOUR PEOPLE ARE BANNED. NO GROUPS OR GATHERINGS ARE PERMITTED AFTER SUNSET.

TWELVE PEOPLE WERE KILLED IN YESTERDAY'S CLASHES. DETAILS ARE EMERGING.

STAY TUNED TO KRDN FOR ADDITIONAL DETAILS.

Allison grabbed the remote control and muted the news broadcast. A week after the attack, the four began to resume their international espionage agents' average life.

Phil enjoyed nursing, Miranda. She enjoyed being nursed.

Allison did not speak of her mother but did open

up to Aydin about some painful memories triggered by Arnold's story.

Phil and Aydin interviewed six candidates for the receptionist position. Four had expired security clearances and were disqualified immediately. One resume had so many spelling errors, Aydin was convinced the candidate plagiarized it from the internet.

The last seemed qualified but did not want to work full-time but expected full-time pay and benefits.

Phil's whine was subdued.

"We are never going to find anyone."

"Azima?"

*"Yes, Aydin?"*

"Tell Kermit we want to interview another set of candidates for the receptionist position. specifically, we want former Air Force, AFSC 3F5X1, Administrative Assistant, or Army MOS 42L, Administrative Specialist, with an active security clearance."

*"Understood. Do you want confirmation?"*

"No, I trust you to deliver the message. Thank you, Azima."

*"My pleasure."*

Phil's dour mood lightened slightly.

"*My pleasure.* It's growing on me."


Aydin was having the most mentally challenging time with the recent events. He spent all day, every day, in the office doing two things:

Improving Azima's code and searching for the clue to confirm his theory. When he found it, he did not speak for two days.

Aydin's Master's thesis on the Actual versus Perceived Depth of AI is the clue he missed. Government, Corporations, and AI enthusiasts have been following him since his master's paper was published. Aydin's thesis, Actual versus Perceived Depth of AI, coupled with the paper The Evils of Ubiquitous Surveillance, created panic in the intelligence community.

Apply the shiny lie of autonomous targeting, and Government, Corporations, and AI enthusiasts will kill to own the technologies.

*People are shooting at me because they think I created sentient artificial intelligence.*

# Designer Shackles

## Life's Whimsey

*"The CIA's research program is described in a book called 'The Search for the Manchurian Candidate.'"*

*Ken Follett*

**Trammel House, 04:20, Clear**

*"Aydin?"*

"Azima, why are you waking me?"

*"The security camera designated Front Yard is reporting activity."*

The night light in the smoke detector kicked on when Aydin leapt from the bed. Allison looked up to see Aydin's finger over his lips, indicating she should not speak.

Allison's dreams always end with what might have happened. In her dreams, Aydin is dead, shot by the enforcer she hired in the Chinese deal. Someone she hired and trusted not to kill her husband. Shaking off the nightmare and hiding her frustration at the never-ending threats, she looked up to Aydin. Opening the hidden panel in the headboard, pulling out his Glock 29 is an indicator for Allison to do the same. She pulled her Walther PPK from her side of the headboard and rolled silently out of bed.

"Azima, wake Phil."

*"I will wake Phil."*

Aydin gave Allison a fist, meaning sit tight, then exited the bedroom. Peering through the edge of the main room's bay window, Aydin saw a dark figure dash back to a vehicle that sped away.

Phil's silent approach was expected. Aydin held up a fist. Phil peered out at the opposite edge of the large window. In a whisper, Aydin updated Phil.

"At least two. One was on the lawn, ran to a dark sedan, probably an old Chevy, and they left."

"Do you think it was kids looking for trouble?"

"At 04:20, what do you think?"

Phil accepts Aydin's premise it is not kids looking for trouble. His head is slowly turning in all directions, scanning for threats. Seeing no threats, he states the obvious when his undiagnosed ADD kicked in.

"You know, all the home-defense course recommendations say you should use a tactile shotgun for home defense. Pistols are too dangerous if you miss."

"We have known each other for over a decade, do we ever miss?"

Shaking his head at his silly question, Phil continued the surveillance.

"I think we need to take a look around."

"Where is Miranda?"

"In the kitchen, with Allison. They are ready to pull out the firepower if we need it."

"How do you want to play this?"

"I'll circle back, through the side gate, come in

from the south. You give me 30 seconds, and then you exit through the front door."

"Wait."

Aydin dashed to the kitchen, intent on pulling protective tactical gear from the hidden vault. Arriving in the kitchen, he found Allison and Miranda, each holding up a tactical vest. Taking his vest from Allison, he nodded toward Miranda, then Phil.

In the dark of the main room, vests straps pulled tight, and Velcro flaps closed, Aydin and Phil fist-bumped before Phil was through the slider. Aydin began counting down the 30 seconds.

*One-thousand-four.*
*One-thousand-five.*
*One-thousand-six.*
*Who the fuck is messing with us now?*
*One-thousand-eleven.*
*One-thousand-twelve.*
*A message.*
*This is a message.*
*What kind of message?*
*A message from whom?*
*Ah, fuck snacks.*
*Phil is right.*
*We need two weeks of calm.*
*One-thousand-twenty.*
*One-thousand-twenty-one.*
*That's long enough.*

Flipping off the power to the porch light prevented the motion sensor from activating the light. Cracking the front door, Aydin slipped out, staying in the shadows, waiting. Several seconds passed before he saw Phil's silhouette against the distant streetlight. Assessing Phil's clockwise direction of travel, Aydin moved to circle the property's front in the opposite direction.

After circling the property twice, finding nothing, Phil joined Aydin on the porch. Continuing to scan for threats, Phil pointed to the thin ray of the rising sun reflecting off the distant mountain peaks.

Stepping back into the house, they begin to pull off their vests before joining Allison and Miranda in the kitchen.

"Azima?"

*"Yes, Aydin?"*

"Send all the home security camera footage to my email."

*"Will do."*

"Thank you, Azima."

*"My pleasure.*

Miranda remained silent.

Allison began collecting the gear.

Phil closed the event.

"Breakfast at 06:30."

**Trammel House, 06:30, Clear**

The four decide to skip their regular morning

workout routines. They are in the kitchen, Phil cooking, the others sitting at the breakfast counter. The aromas of porridge, maple syrup, raspberries, and walnuts, mingle with the smell of rich coffee. A side dish of cracked peppercorn bacon is necessary to relieve the tension. Quiet and feeling better, the pressure is leaving their faces until Azima spoke.

"*Aydin?*"

"Yes, Azima?"

"*The security camera designated Front Yard is reporting activity.*"

The four moved silently, began to arm themselves when the flashing lights bounced off the stainless-steel appliances. Everyone looked at everyone else until an exasperated Phil grumbled.

"What the fuck now? Today is becoming a shit on the hoe handle kind of day."

Aydin's mind is all over the map as the four head to the front of the house.


*This can't be good.*
*Someone was nosing around at oh-dark-thirty.*
*Now cops?*
*What do the cops want?*
*What are the possibilities?*
*Does this have something to do with Miranda?*
*Probably.*
*What about Moms?*
*It could be Moms.*
*Why would it be Moms?*

*It never ends.*
*Every few days, another threat or surprise.*
*I wonder how Allison is doing.*
*I need to ask.*
*She hasn't spoken to Pops in a few days.*
*We need to see him.*
*Maybe later today.*
*What the fuck is that?*

Two police cruisers have stopped, front bumper to front bumper, directly in front of the Trammel house. The officers, one male and one female, are standing on the sidewalk, looking at the naked body of a woman lying face down on the lawn. Phil understood what he is looking at, his tone mildly curious.

"Brain?"

"Yeah, Pinky?"

"You don't think we missed the naked lady earlier, do you?"

"No, Pinky, there was not a dead naked lady on the lawn a couple of hours ago. Azima?"

*"Yes, Aydin?"*

"Back up the recordings. Everything, audio, and video, here at the house. Make duplicates of everything recorded until I tell you to stop."

*"Duplicate recording beginning now."*

**Trammel House, 09:30, Clear**

The Douglas County Coroner is signing off the

ambulance crew's paperwork to transport the body to the morgue. Heading into the house, the coroner finds Aydin, Allison, and Miranda sitting at the breakfast bar. She counts a total of seven Sherriff, State Police, and representatives from the District Attorney's Office standing around in the kitchen.

Phil is feeding everyone and ensuring their coffee cups do not run dry.

Smiling at Aydin, accepting the offered coffee, the coroner begins the summary close to the investigation.

"She has not been dead long. Based on standard algor mortis tables and the cool morning, she has been deceased for a couple of hours. There are needle tracks on her feet. It looks like an overdose. Toxicology will confirm the OD. Fingerprints say she is Katherine Marie Kearney neé Cole. Mrs. Trammel, is she your mother?

"Yes."

# Lies of Commission

**Trammel House, 09:35, Clear**

"Misses Trammel, you are calm for someone who just saw her mother lying dead on the lawn."

"We were estranged, and she was not living at home with my father. We seldom spoke and have not spoken for several days. I, we, expected something like this might happen to her."

"I understand. Did your mother have a drug problem?"

"I do not know, but nothing surprises me about my mother."

The coroner looked up from the digital pad, eyed Allison, then looked back down.

"It looks like whoever she was with dumped her for you to find."

The coroner turned over the questioning using the slightest point of her chin toward the Detective from the Sherriff's office.

"Misses Trammel, is there anything you can tell us about where your mother has been and possibly, with whom she was with over the past few days?"

"No. I said, we have not spoken for a few days. Moms never told us where she was going. When she was living at home, she never told us when she would be back."

Everyone turned to see two tall men, wearing black suits and black ties, let themselves into the

Trammel house.

Holding up a badge, the closest announced their presence.

"I am Agent Cooper, and he is Agent Durant. We are from the Air Force Office of Special Investigations. When the coroner has completed her investigation, Lieutenant Colonel Cole's body will be remanded to the Air Force for burial.

"Detective Gerrard, the cause of death is an accidental heroin overdose. Lieutenant Colonel Kearney's body will be respected. Any questions?"

Everyone looked to everyone else until all eyes returned to Agent Cooper. Confirming he had everyone's attention, Agent Cooper pointed to the recording device then mimed slashing his throat.

The district attorney's office representative picked up his device, clicked off the recording, and stuck it in his pocket. Agent Cooper looked around and asked.

"Anyone else?"

The female deputy sheriff clicked off her body camera.

Agent Cooper looked around a second time and asked.

"Anyone else?"

Agent Cooper spoke after receiving a negative headshake from everyone.

"Lieutenant Colonel Kearney was a patriot who, under the pressure of her duties, lost her way. People in her role, even in retirement, are monitored. We believe we know where Lieutenant Colonel Kearney was and who she was with prior to her death. Detective, when we confirm their location, we will provide you the details of their identities and locations.

"Until then, this matter is closed.

"Any questions?"

Allison looked to Aydin, expecting something. Seeing his face, she understood he was somewhere else.

*This is a message from whoever Moms and Arnold rolled up to in this cluster-fuck of a mess.*

*Someone at the top of the food chain killed her because she could lead us to them.*

*But who, and why now?*

*What is the message?*

*Why are they afraid of me, afraid of us?*

*I keep looking. I keep firing, but I am missing a few bullets.*

*Something odd is going on, and I do not understand how it all fits and points back to me.*

*Oh, fuck.*

*No, this is not a message for me, or Allison, or Phil.*

*Miranda.*

"What was that agent Cooper?"

"Mister Trammell, am I boring you?"

"No, not at all. Was there a question?"

Pointing to the business card he had tossed on the counter, Agent Cooper's tone had grown terser.

"Yes, Mister Trammell, I request you contact me if you learn anything or experience any other unusual activity."

"Sure, will do."

Grunting their reluctant acceptance of Aydin's false sincerity, the Air Force Agents leave without another word. The coroner tossed her business card next to the Agent's card and departed. Everyone not living at the Trammel house left in a line, except homicide detective Gerrard.

When the front door closed, he turned to Aydin, not Allison, before confirming his position.

"She accidentally OD'd. Her drug buddies dumped her on your lawn. Those Air Force Zoomies are not going to tell us anything. They never do. Unless you can produce who she was hanging with, that is how this ends. Is there anything you want to add?"

*The detective wants this to go away and add one more closed case to his numbers.*

*He did not like the Air Force special agents sticking their noses in his business.*

*He knows we have protection.*

*We'll make this go away for him.*

"No, nothing to add."

"Good."

The detective departed without another word. Phil stepped over to the bay windows to look at the mountains and noticed the female patrolwoman's cruiser was still parked on the street.

Stepping to the front door, Phil opened it to the patrolwoman standing on the porch. Her dark hair is pulled tight, and her face is expressionless. The thick tactical vest under her uniform hides her thin frame. Phil waved her inside. She declined with a shake of her head, then spoke.

"The other patrolman, Danvers, there is no way he could have arrived before me when the jogger called it in. This is my area to patrol. His patrol area is on the east side of the county. Why did the jogger call it in and not knock on the door?

"From the jogger's home, to here and back, is over twenty-three miles. Who *jogs* a marathon up in these hills? Whoever called it in gave a false ID, claiming to be out for a morning jog."

The patrolwoman went quiet and stared at Phil until he spoke.

"Thank you for the information. My recommendation to you is to write your report and forget about this when you sign the report. There are players involved well above our paygrade, and nothing good will come from poking around."

The patrolwoman scowled and walked away. Phil waited for her cruiser to crest the hill, out of sight. Closing the front door, Phil returns to the kitchen and begins collecting dirty coffee mugs.

"Aydin, did you hear the patrolwoman?"

"Yes, we heard. Azima?"

*"Yes, Aydin?"*

"Stop the duplicate recording."

*"All duplicate recordings stopped."*

"Put all the files on the secure server, remove all traces from the capture devices."

*"One moment, please.*

*"Files moved to the secure server, wipe complete."*

"Send a text to KTF. Background check for Douglas County Sherriff Deputy, Patrolman Danvers. First name unknown."

Miranda interrupted.

"Azima, wait. His first name is Jeremey."

Brow furled, Aydin asked.

"How do you know that?"

"I heard the Patrolwoman use his first name."

Nodding agreement, Aydin continued.

"Did you catch the patrolwoman's name?"

"Menendez. Juanita Menéndez."

"Azima, send a text to KTF. Background check for Douglas County Sherriff Deputies: Jeremey Danvers and Juanita Menéndez."

*"Sending the text to KTF. Is there anything else?"*

"No. Thank you, Azima."

*"My pleasure."*

**Trammel House, Master Bedroom, 11:45, Clear**

Allison has stepped out of the shower. She is wrapped in an oversized towel, drying her red hair with a second towel. Aydin is pulling on his boots when he realizes Allison is watching him.

"You don't have to come with us to the office. I know you think you are tough. Allison, you, and Miranda lost your mother today. Moms is gone. Do you want to talk about it?"

"No, not really. I kind of expected this to happen. Not the OD part. That is bullshit. She was not a junkie. They killed her because she probably threatened to expose them. Killing Drakon, exposing Arnold, you have taken out a big part of their supply chain.

"No, hon. I am okay. Did you talk to Pops?"

"I did when you were in the shower. He's taking it like you: He expected it. He said he would come by the office later to chat."

Aydin's thoughts are for his wife, and the sister-in-law he learned existed two weeks ago.

*Pops and Allison both expected Moms to end up dead.*

*Miranda never knew her mother.*

*What kind of family is that?*

*Miranda is not upset.*

*I understand.*

*Allison is taking it too well.*

*How did I miss the clues all these years?*

*People see what they want to see.*

*What do I do for Allison?*

"Allison, I am here when you want to talk."

The red-haired spy bent to kiss her man, then resumed drying.

"You go to the office. I will follow along with Miranda and a late lunch. Azima?"

*"Yes, Allison?"*

"Tell Miranda to meet me at my car in 30 minutes."

*"Message delivered. Confirmation received."*

"Thank you, Azima."

*"My Pleasure."*

"Allison, one more time. Phil and I spent months, years mentally preparing for the loss of loved ones. When my mother died, it still hurt more than I can tell you. I am here when you want to talk."

Eyeing Aydin in the fog-rimmed mirror, Allison stops pulling the brush through her hair and speaks to Aydin's reflection.

"Aydin, I love you. I still have Pops. Phil too. One day, I may feel the loss, but today ... Today, I am okay. This was coming, and everyone knew it. Now it is your job to figure out why they are coming at you. Because, Brain, you, I can't lose."

Understanding, without a word, Aydin walked away.

# Lies of Omission



Aydin and Phil are at their usual seats, heads-down, researching, and not speaking. Phil interrupts the silence.

"I'm hungry. Do you think the girls will be here soon?"

Aydin shrugged, non-committal.

*Maybe it is time for the beach.*
*Phil's two weeks without getting shot at is sounding Fuckin-A beautiful.*
*What about Allison?*
*When my mom died, it was hard, but that was different.*
*Fucking cancer.*
*Allison is right.*
*Everyone expected this for Moms.*
*I guess I will wait and not be a pest.*
*She will talk when she is ready.*
*Miranda.*
*What am I missing?*

Phil persists.

"What do you think happened this morning? They got spooked at 04:20 then circled back to dump the body?"

"No, I think the incidents are unrelated."

"Oh? Well, fuck me, that is not good."

"No, not good. Phil, someone is screwing with us. With me. Hard. The facial recognition core code is one piece, but it is at the bottom of the list. Next up on the list is the targeting software. Again, important, but not that big. Combining the two is third from the bottom. I can see a path to someone wanting to combine both and market the results.

"Moms, Drakon, and Arnold are next on the list. Someone is very pissed-off we cut-out their middlemen. Revenge can be a powerful motivation, but it still does not add up.

"The papers. My thesis: Actual versus Perceived Depth of AI caught fire. I did not know it was being read all over the world. Then there is the professor's article: The Evils of Ubiquitous Surveillance. Merged, the two papers created panic in the intelligence community. Together, the pieces are a scary future but still not at the top of the list.

"The top of the list is Miranda and her adoptive father, the General."

Aydin paused, unsure of the reality in his thoughts.

*It has to be right.*
*There is no other option.*
*Ah, fuck, there are always options.*
*But this one makes the most sense.*
*It has to make sense.*

"Phil, consider this idea. What if General Bryan Michael Cole was the Air Force's equivalent of a Handler for my parents and Allison's parents."

Phil's silence told Aydin he was considering and mentally trying to debunk the idea but found no path to counter the premise. Aydin expanded his theory.

"The problem I have is age. General Cole is younger and joined the Air Force several years after our parents."

Interrupting, Phil demanded a summary.

"Run it down for me again, starting at the top."

"First is Miranda, her adoptive father, the General, and why someone is trying to kill her.

"Next is the espionage/counter-espionage targeting my paper on AI and the professor's article on surveillance.

"Third, Moms, Drakon, Arnold, and whoever is at the top of the opium supply chain. Revenge is the motive."

"Finally, the code we created. Both the facial recognition and the targeting software."

Phil's response in a somber tone is unusual.

"Two and four are the same. What does anyone care about two articles if they can't apply the concepts?"

Aydin looking up, turning to Phil, was an acceptance of Phil's premise. Phil continued.

"That leaves one and three. One wants Miranda dead, and it looks like three wants you dead. They probably would like to see both of us deceased."

Phil's eyes grew wide with a realization.

"What if one and three are connected. Take the opium syndicate being pissed off, off the table for a moment. What if the espionage/counter-espionage theory and the advanced code we created are connected? What if someone wants it all?"

Phil stopped, turned, and watched Allison's Rover pull into the parking slot between Aydin's Mercedes and his Silverado.

His ADD emerging, Phil's mind flew to a new topic.

"That Silverado has seen better days."

"It's only three years old."

"Yeah, but look, the brush guard is bent, and the new Sierra's are sweet."

The two watched Allison and Miranda step between the cars toward the sidewalk. Looking past Phil's Silverado, Aydin spotted the vehicle from the first of this morning's surprises.

"They were followed."

Without a word, both were moving to the hidden vault for larger weapons. Allison and Miranda entered the small lobby to find Aydin and Phil pulling on tactical vests.

The women moved to stand behind the reinforced reception desk, setting the lunch on the desk and pulling their pistols from their purses.

Aydin's voice was mission mode.

"Allison, did you see that Chevy Caprice following you?"

"I thought I saw someone following us in an old beater car. They pulled off at Arapahoe Road, and we continued to Orchard Road. Where is it?"

"You pulled in from the north, and they came up from the south. There, beyond the grass, in the other parking lot. I think it was the car from this morning at 04:20."

"I did not see anyone tailing us, but maybe they pulled off knowing we were headed here."

Phil moved to the edge of the lobby, right of the main door, and summarized the situation.

"They have not sold that car in this country since the mid-nineties. It means it is a local or someone is trying to act like they are local. That food smells good. Aydin, how do you want to play this?"

"Can we get up on them before they drive away?"

"From here? Maybe. We will be exposed if they start shooting."

"Yeah, my thoughts also. What about this? You and I will leave in your Silverado. The girls will keep an eye on our friends while we drive around the building and coming in behind the Caprice.

"When we are behind the building, I'll climb through the sliding window and hide in the bed. You pull in behind the Caprice, pinning them, I'll pop-up, covering the area with my Glock."

Phil's affirmation did not receive the chuckle he expected.

"Might as well. You can't dance, and it is too

wet to plow."

Handing their M4s to the women, Aydin and Phil checked their pistols, confirmed reserve magazines, then exited the front door.

As soon as the building was between them and the Caprice, Aydin was through the sliding window and face down in the truck bed.

In the lobby, Miranda turned to Allison.

"They didn't ask, but I think we can help. Can you shoot that?"

Allison's look of disdain and repulsion at the question told Miranda what she needed to know: Allison is ready for a gunfight.

"Okay, here's what we will do. When Phil stops the pickup behind the Caprice, we will move to the space between the Mercedes and the Rover. I'll draw down on the Caprice with this M4. You cover my six."

"Understood. Won't that put Aydin and Phil in your line of fire."

"Yes. I don't miss."

Miranda ignored Allison's raised eyebrows. Keeping her eyes on the Caprice, Allison leaned the M4 she was holding in the corner and checked her pistol.

Both women moved to the door and peered out.

Phil's Silverado is making the final turn into the parking lot beyond the grass median. The Caprice issued a small puff of exhaust, indicating they started the engine. Before the Caprice rolled two feet, Phil was parked behind, broadside to the Caprice.

Aydin popped up, drew down, but failed to account for the Caprice ramming Phil's pickup. He toppled onto the massive trunk of the older car.

Phil was coming around the front of his pickup when the driver's window lowered. Fearing the worst, he dove to the ground and rolled under his Silverado.

Aydin rolled off the trunk lid, landing on his feet, his pistol pointed at the face in the right-side mirror.

The front passenger window lowered, allowing the occupant to extend empty hands. Aydin stepped to his right and barked.

"Phil, get up. Driver, lower the windows."

The closed windows began to lower. Three more sets of empty hands emerged from the open windows.

Aydin stepped two more paces to his right, covering both passenger doors. Phil mirrored Aydin's position on the driver's side, waiting for Aydin's next order.

"All of you, open the doors from the outside. Climb out and lay face down."

Four males complied. A female voice was heard.

"We are coming out too."

Phil tilted his head to Aydin, who shrugged and gave the command.

"One on each side. You in the front seat, come to me. You in the back, exit the driver's side."

The females complied.

Allison and Miranda walked up to positions in front of the Caprice, mirroring their partners.

Phil uttered disgust.

"Ah fuck, this one must have crapped his pants. The smell could gag a maggot. Boy, where have you been eating, off the gut wagon? They are just kids. You, driver, are there any weapons?"

"No, sir."

"Phil and Aydin repositioned to scan the car's interior. Both noticed the crumpled fast-food bags on the rear window deck and floorboards. The trash covers the car's interior with panties and unopened condoms on the dashboard. Phil was unable to resist.

"Following us around is not entertaining enough? Are you living in your car, or did you get bored?"

Aydin intercepted the interrogation.

"Never mind that, why are you watching us? What were you doing at my house this morning?"

It surprised Aydin when no one responded to his question. They are more disciplined than he expected.

*This is a serious crew.*

*They are a bunch of young, late teens or early twenties want-to-be hoodlums who are in too deep and are too inexperienced.*

*Her, she is looking around, evaluating escape options.*

*She must be their leader.*

Aydin stepped over and put the sole of his right boot on the heavy-set brunette's right hand. Beginning to press, he asked again.

"Why are you watching us? What were you doing at my house this morning?"

Turning her head to look up at the tall man, she gently scraped her chin on the asphalt. The brunette's response was calm and measured.

"A grand per day."

"From whom?"

"I don't know."

"How did you know who to follow? How do you get the money?"

"The dead woman. She came to us about a week ago. She said we'd get $500 a day to follow someone and report everywhere they went. I said $1000. She didn't flinch and paid us a week in advance."

"How do you report?"

"I leave a voice mail."

"Give me your phone. Unlocked."

Aydin released the brunette's hand, allowing her to rub away the grit from his boot. She reached into her back pocket, pulled out the phone. With two hands forward, she unlocked the phone and held it up.

Aydin grabbed the phone and began scrolling. It did not take long. After tapping the phone on his thigh, thinking, he handed back the phone and spoke loud enough for Allison, Miranda, and Phil to hear.

"Arnold's phone. How do you get paid?"

"PayPal."

"How did they find you?"

"The gig economy, how else?"

"How did you know about the dead woman?"

"Bobby was hiding in the flower garden, across the road, two doors up."

"How long was Bobby watching? Which one is Bobby?"

The male passenger, closest to Phil, raised his right hand at the wrist. Phil noticed.

"This one. Stinky."

Before he continued the interrogation, Aydin made a show of putting his pistol in his waistband. Allison, Miranda, and Phil made their weapons less obvious.

"Bobby, were you in the flower bed all morning?"

"Yes."

"You saw who placed the body on my lawn?"

"Yes."

"Well?"

"The cop."

"Which cop?"

"The female cop."

Before he asked, Aydin stepped back over and pressed on the Burnette's hand again.

"A couple more questions. What is your name?

"Kimber."

"Kimber, who were you told to watch?"

"Her."

Her left arm stretched at an odd angle, Kimber pointed to Miranda.

"What were you doing on my lawn?"

"We got bored. Deanna wanted to see your house."

*Fucking amateurs with no way to trace back the source of who hired them or who is paying.*

"Here's your final report. Target made us surveillance over. Pay through today."

"I got it."

"Kimber, what happens if I see you or your friends again?"

Training her neck to look up, she glared at Aydin.

"I like living. You won't see us again."

Aydin stepped away, circled, and stood next to Allison and Miranda. The four watched the six wanna-be detectives pile into the oversized land yacht. Receiving the thumbs up from Aydin, Phil drove away in his Silverado.

The trio stood and watched the Caprice begin to pull away. When Aydin caught Kimber's eye, she gave him the middle finger of her sore right hand.

In response, Aydin moved his shirt, exposing his Glock. Kimber pulled down her finger.

# Lies Beget Lies



"The food's cold."

Allison barked back.

"Phil, there is a microwave in your office."

"I know that, but it is not the same."

After zapping his burritos, Phil flopped into his customary seat in the conference room. Munching a burrito, he is staring at the dents along the passenger side of his formerly beloved Silverado.

Aydin is sitting, not eating, staring into space. Allison understands the moment. She left her husband alone. Turning to Miranda, Allison is done playing twenty questions.

"Miranda, enough of the bullshit. Enough of the cutie-pie southern charm. Enough of everything. It seems the only thing we have in common is we have the same birth mother. I don't believe that either, but I guess the DNA doesn't lie.

"Who are you, and why are the people who are after Aydin and Phil following you?"

"Hey, leave me out of this. It's all on Aydin."

Allison is not playing around.

"Shut up, Phil."

"Miranda, I am going to need some answers right fucking now or, using Phil's term, we are going to mix."

Miranda put down her spork, wiped her mouth,

sipped tea, and reacted.

"Everything I told you about our families is true."

"Bullshit. Until you tell me something I can believe, I am going to assume everything that comes out of your mouth is a lie."

"Believe what you want. We have the same birth mother. Your father is Pops, and mine was Michael Potvin."

"I don't care about that right now. What I want to know is: Who put those kids on us, and why? How are you linked to Arnold, and why were you going after him? What was your goal when you caught up to him?"

Aydin looked up from his PC and leaned back, listening. Phil finished off his first burrito, picked up the second burrito before, he too, leaned back and waited. The air in the conference room felt tight despite the air handling continuously turning over the 72-degree air. Seeing she is outnumbered, Miranda leans back and opens up.

"Arnold was the means to the end. We thought we could get to Arnold, and he would lead us to his handler. Aydin is right: Someone is pulling strings, and it was not Arnold or our mother. Someone very high up in The Service is the target. We don't know exactly who it is. Everything is compartmentalized, and the whole thing is on a need-to-know basis.

"In The Service, you know who you report to, whoever is one level up in your department. You know who reports to you, one level down. You may know the second level down. The whole organization is flat, maybe five levels in total.

"We were trying to figure out who was handling Arnold, and through Arnold, who was running our mother. We thought our mother was Arnold's handler, but something changed when he returned from the desert and was discharged.

"Something big changed, and it is not just Aydin figuring out the history and connections of Drakon, Arnold, and our mother. Someone, presumably the top-level handler, is afraid of something important being traced back to him or her."

Miranda turned her focus from Allison to Aydin.

"They *are* coming after Aydin's code, the facial recognition code, but the targeting software is the money maker. They told me in the mission brief: The targeting software is three-to-five years ahead of the next closest competitor.

"Your facial recognition will boost the best algorithms here, in the US, and in China. They don't have to kill you for the code. They could buy it. You could quickly get the NSA, DoD, DHS, CIA, FCC, DoI, and every other three-letter .gov to approve the export license. Every .mil wants better targeting.

"But you haven't applied because you don't want to sell it.

"So, what we have left is one question. How do we figure out who is at the top of the food chain, and what is their motivation?"

Lifting her spork, Miranda lifted her salad, then leaned back, emulating the other three's posture. Allison's severe tone has not lessened.

"*We.* You said *we,* several times. Who are *we?* Who do you work for, and why should I believe whatever you say?"

With a mouthful of salad, what Phil calls rabbit food, Miranda was clear enough to be understood.

"Azima?"

"*Yes, Miranda?*"

"Please request an ETA for Pops arrival."

"*Requesting ETA, stand by.*"

Miranda continued to munch green leaves. Phil's burritos are finished. Aydin's lunch is lying untouched. Allison's salad container is open, her plastic knife and fork at the ready.

"*Pops reports his ETA is twelve minutes.*"

"Thank you, Azima.

"*My pleasure.*"

Allison and Miranda finished eating their salads, and the four waited in silence. Allison could tell from Aydin's face. He is considering Miranda's story.


*She didn't say anything we didn't already know.*

*She is vague, but she made a mistake.*

*She is in the game much deeper than she wants us to know.*

*She guessed correctly.*

*I am not going to sell the code. I*

*f the feds want it, I will consider selling it but*

*maybe give the targeting code.*

*If the targeting code helps the guys on the ground, it is worth giving away.*

*Pops?*

*Miranda hinted at Pops knowing something, but what?*

*He tells me everything.*

*I think Pops tells me everything. Maybe he is holding back?*

*Aw, fuck snacks.*

*Pops and Allison are going to be emotional.*

*This is not good.*

*That's it!*

*Miranda wants the emotion of Pops and Allison to divert the conversation.*

*She is running out of lies.*

*Is she telling the truth about her role, or is she diverting?*

*She could be acting.*

*If what she said is true, the lies must be in what she didn't say.*

*We still don't know her real mission.*


Aydin refocused his eyes when a new Sierra pickup with shiny temporary tags pulled into the parking slot to the left of the main door. Phil ID'd Pops as the driver before turning to Aydin.

"A new pickup?"

"Yours is ready. Pick it up on the way home."

Phil just nodded and waited. Aydin retrieves

three new flash drives from the reception desk, then follows Pops into the conference room and sits.

Allison stood when Pops entered the conference room. The two embraced. Neither had tears. After a long moment, they stepped back. Pops pushed Allison's hair out of her face, then gently asked.

"Hon, are you okay?"

She is usually calm, even, and not excitable. Allison's tone is gloomy, even for her.

"Yes, dad, I am okay. We knew this was coming. I have known this was coming since I was a teenager. It hurts but not as much as I expected."

Hugging again, they hesitantly separated and sit. Pops looked to Aydin.

"Thanks for the truck."

"The least I can do. It is registered and insured by the business, don't wreck it."

"I don't plan on it. What about Phil? He won't live with those dents I saw pulling in."

"He gets one also."

Pops is grinning, and Phil is beaming with his response radiating southern charm.

"Happiness comes in waves, and I am surfing the high tide."

Pops chuckled at Phil's comment before turning back to Aydin and speaking with his head tilted toward Miranda.

"What lies has she been telling you today?"

"It is hard to tell. Miranda is very good at mixing the truth and the lies she wants you to believe."

"She was trained well."

"Yeah, there's that and the frequent use of the pronoun *we*. It is starting to feel like Miranda doesn't work for The Service. Not exactly. I can't figure out who would convince her to take on missions that have gotten her shot. Twice. Sniper school, who got her into Quantico?"

Aydin's brow raised, and his eyes got wide. Pops laughed aloud before responding.

"Took you long enough."

Aydin did not respond. Swapping out the flash drives he picked up, he is thinking through the possibilities.

*Miranda is like Allison and me.*
*She was trained to be who she is.*
*But we had each other.*
*She was alone.*
*She must be scared.*
*She has no option.*
*This is all she knows.*
*That is not true.*
*She could walk away.*
*Walk away to where or what?*
*Oh yeah, I remember why I know her!*

Refocusing, before Aydin could ask Pops for confirmation, Allison opened up.

"Look at him. You can see it in his face. Aydin

just made a connection and learned something. The question is: Will he tell us what he figured out, or do we have to wait for more dead people to learn what is going on in his little brain?"

Twisting his mouth before he spoke, annoyed at his wife's snarky comment, Aydin asked Allison a question.

"Do you remember the July 4th party at Barksdale? We were eleven, no twelve."

Pops banged the table, white teeth glowing, eyes sparkling, and pointed at Aydin.

Allison looked from Aydin to her father and back before the sideways twist of her lips emerged.

"We were eleven. Miranda was there, but she was called Kat. They were all there. Robert Walker and Chrissy Nelson. Matt Thomas and Kristy Lewis."

Dumbstruck with a realization, Allison turned to her father and continued.

"It was a reunion."

Pops' response is even and informative.

"It was a party to celebrate the end of The Program. They tried to keep The Program alive after the end of the Cold War. When the Berlin Wall came down, everyone knew it was over."

"What was over? What Program?"

"You won't find it in any news reports or Freedom of Information Requests. No smart-assed reporter will find anything by filing a FOIA request. Hell, The Program didn't have a name. We gave it a name. Albert gave it the name."

Hearing his father's given name refocused Aydin's attention.

"Dad?"

"Yes, your father, Albert, took over as the default leader of The Program. He was the leader until they stopped the funding. He loved the job. The missions, the training, the education, he loved all of it. Your mother, Penny, loved it in the beginning. She was the best with computer stuff. She was a hacker before the term existed. The computer stuff became too complicated, and we were ordered to focus on The Program. Eventually, she wanted to retire and live a quiet life.

"Albert never wanted it to end. Miranda, your father, your adoptive father, Bryan, wanted you to be part of The Program. The Program was being wound down when you became old enough to begin training. Bryan never gave up. He guided your education, got you admitted to Quantico, and the training."

Turning away from Miranda to Allison, Pops ripped the lid off Pandora's box.

"Bryan wanted Kat to be just like her older sister. Smart, tough, fearless. He changed her name to Miranda Marie LaLonde, created the false persona, and guided her into the business."

Astonished, Allison sat stone-still, waiting. Pops continued the briefing.

"Bryan missed an essential part of the equation. He did not understand something our predecessors learned in the early decades of the

Program."

Pops went quiet, staring, unblinking at Aydin. Aydin's mind is racing.

*He knows I know what is missing in Miranda's training.*
*I see it now.*
*I was so stupid.*
*It is so simple.*
*But why me?*
*What about the others?*
*Allison and I are the youngest, excluding Miranda.*
*What are the others doing now?*

"Pops, I will answer your question. I know Dad misses The Program. First, what are the others doing now? We know about Robert and Chrissy. Matt and Kristy. There must have been a dozen more, six more pairs at the July 4th party. Where are the others?"

Pops' voice is low and soft.

"Fourteen, seven pairs. Eight are dead. Four died by suicide. Two were killed in car accidents, which were probably suicides. One from a brain hemorrhage and one drowned trying to save a kid in a river.

"The other six have all gone on to full lives far away from The Program. They are disconnected from The Program and its history. None speak to anyone involved with The Program except their immediate families.

"You and Allison are the only pair who stayed together."

Allison's eyes are pleading with Aydin for help in understanding what Pops was saying. Aydin answered the unspoken plea.

"Dad named the Program Cliste agus Cróga. Translated from Irish, it means: Intelligent and Brave. We were destined to become intelligent and brave. What the original Program administrators and doctors learned was a hard lesson. Producing intelligent and brave *lone wolves* created a breeding ground for rogue actors. Pairing the subjects reduced the likelihood of one of the guinea pigs going rogue. They changed The Program and introduced the team concept."

Pausing, Aydin looked to Pops to fill in the gaps.

"Aydin, Allison, I can't tell you everything I know. Some of the rules I never learned. Aydin, your father will know more about the real objectives of The Program. I was a mission specialist. Albert ran our portion of The Program.

"It is not a coincidence Aydin, and Allison, now Miranda, hold on to information. They hold on, keeping it to themselves, sometimes, until it is too late. Their desires to hold information comes from The Program. The Program ended almost twenty years ago, but our families have been inside The Program for nearly four decades.

"We are reaping the consequences of decades

of deception."

The silence in the room is oppressive, but no one felt compelled to speak. Eventually, with a tone dripping in icy contempt, Aydin turned to Miranda.

"You know who killed Moms."

Miranda's training, a life of being groomed for these moments, failed her when the beads of sweat appeared on her forehead. Her voice cracked with fear when she responded.

"I do not, but I know who does know. We need to talk to Arnold."

Everyone watched Aydin stare at Miranda. The tension is increasing with every shallow breath.

*Miranda's lies are woven in threads of truth.*

*I don't think she knows how to tell the whole truth about anything.*

*She's telling the truth about not knowing who killed Moms.*

*She is lying about Arnold knowing.*

*Pointing us at Arnold is a diversion to buy time.*

*She is afraid of something.*

*She is afraid, and she is waiting.*

*What is she waiting for?*

*Fuck it.*

*Enough of this for today.*

"Dinner is on me. Allison, pick a place Pops will like."

Everyone packs up, readying to leave. Aydin

waits for Miranda to use the head before he slips the storage devices to Pops, Phil, and Allison.

"Put these in your cars. It will upgrade the comms and GPS."

Without a word, the trio palms their devices and begins exiting the conference room. Miranda joins the team and Aydin's demand for an early dinner.

# The Sad Reality

**Trammel House, 04:55, Clear**

"Aydin?"

"Azima, why are you waking me? The alarm is not due for another 35 minutes."

"*The security camera designated Entry is reporting activity.*"

"Is someone trying to break into the office?"

"*I am unable to determine the correct response to your question.*"

"Continue to record the activity. Wake me again if someone enters the office."

"*Monitoring and recording confirmed.*"

"Thank you, Azima."

"*My Pleasure.*"

Allison had not moved, did not roll over, but was listening and asked a question.

"She inferred, from your instructions to record the activity, that she should initiate *monitoring* and recording?"

"Yes."

"Isn't that like the next-level of AI?"

"Yes."

Allison issued a hum, acknowledging Aydin's response, and went back to sleep. Aydin could not sleep.

*Allison has figured out Azima is one of the keys*

*to this mess.*

*Today, we will get Miranda to open up, or she gets kicked to the curb.*

*Phil?*

*What will Phil do if I kick Miranda to the curb?*

*How do I protect the Azima code?*

### DTC, Office Parking Lot, 08:50, Cloudy

Aydin, Allison, and Phil pull into their usual parking slots. Phil has timed dropping Miranda at her apartment to arrive with Aydin and Allison at the office. The trio exit their vehicles and stand abreast on the sidewalk. They are staring at a vagrant sitting on the short sidewalk, his back against the office door.

Black boots, old jeans, a dark blue hoodie with the hood pulled tight over his face. The vagrant has soiled himself. The sidewalk is wet from the vagrant to the curb, and the stench is overpowering.

Phil steps up, hollers, and kicks the bottom of the vagrant's boot.

"Yo, get up! Time to move on."

The action of kicking the sole of the boot disrupts the vagrant's balance. He falls over onto his right shoulder. Phil doesn't miss a beat.

"I've seen dead, and this jamoke is dead."

Aydin pulls out his phone and dials 9-1-1.

### DTC, Office Parking Lot, 11:30, Dark Clouds

The Greenwood Village Coroner is signing off

the paperwork for the contracted ambulance crew to transport the body. Allison and Phil are in the conference room. They are listening to the conversation on the sidewalk that Azima is feeding into the overhead speakers. Handing back the clipboard to the ambulance driver, the coroner turns to Aydin.

"You know, coroners are a small community. My friend over in Douglas County told me about your mother-in-law. Now it seems you are familiar with Mister Arnold?"

"I know him. We served together on a mission in the desert."

"Do you know why he would mix alcohol with whatever killed him?"

"I have no idea. I know nothing about Arnold's activities."

"It looks like he has several broken ribs. Maybe the pain medication and alcohol created an overdose. Toxicology will confirm the cause of death. Do you know why he would park himself on your doorstep?"

"As I said, I don't know anything about Captain Arnold. Former captain."

Before the ambulance crew can close the doors, a large black Ford sedan pulls up and parks in a way that blocks the ambulance from leaving. Aydin shouts before the agents have closed their car doors.

"Agent Cooper, Agent Durant, it is nice to see you again."

Ignoring Aydin, Agent Cooper speaks to the

Coroner and the Greenwood Village Deputy Sherriff.

"I am Agent Cooper, and he is Agent Durant. We are from the Air Force Office of Special Investigations. When the coroner has completed her investigation, Major Arnold's body will be remanded to the Air Force for burial.

"Major Arnold was a patriot who, under the pressure of his duties, lost his way. People in his role, even in retirement, are monitored. We believe we know where Major Arnold was and who he was with before his death. Deputy, when we confirm their location, we will provide you the details of their identities and locations.

"Until then, this matter is closed."

Aydin jumped at the chance.

"Did you memorize that speech?"

Ignoring the intentional barb, Agent Cooper closed the discussion.

"Any questions?"

The agent looked at the Coroner and received a negative headshake. He handed her his card and eyed the ambulance crew. With a wave of his hand, he instructed the ambulance crew to close the door and be ready to leave.

Aydin, the coroner, and the deputy stood in silence as the agents left, followed by the contracted ambulance. The Coroner turned to Aydin.

"My friend told me the Men in Black showed up on Monday. I did not expect to see them here for a dead drunk. He's not a common dead drunk, is he?"

Aydin stared, silent, waiting until she spoke.

"Okay, this is the big leagues, and those are the heavy hitters. Do you know why someone left you the message of a dead guy on your stoop?"

"I have no idea. My guess is Arnold wanted to talk to me, decided to wait here, but overestimated the pain meds and alcohol."

Twisting her head, considering, the coroner decided not to press the topic.

"Unless toxicology comes up with something obvious, it is an OD on pain meds and alcohol."

Turning to the deputy, the coroner received a quick confirmation shrug. The coroner put a close to the discussion of dead drunks.

"Mister Trammell?"

"Yes?"

"Can I expect any more dead people in our little hamlet?"

"No."

Aydin turned on his heel, stepped over the stain, entered the office, and found his chair in the conference room. Aydin, Allison, and Phil listened to the deputy gripe.

"He knows why this guy was put here. He knows why his mother-in-law was dumped on his lawn. Men in black? What the fuck is that about? Sorry. Next thing you know, we'll have black helicopters buzzing around."

The coroner looked left, across the parking lot, above the trees, and pointed. The deputy followed her finger to a dark drone, hovering above the trees.

"Deputy, those are probably true statements. My advice to you is to write it up and forget about it."

The coroner walked toward her car. The deputy pulled down the yellow tape before he drove off in his cruiser.

Phil turned to Aydin.

"Azima?"

*"Yes, Aydin?"*

"Stop recording."

*"Recording stopped."*

"Send a message to KTF: Requesting power wash of the sidewalk."

*"Message sent. Also, the summary reports for the background checks you requested are available."*

"Forward the summary reports to Phil and me."

*"Forwarding, summary reports."*

"Thank you, Azima."

*"My pleasure."*

Phil decided it is time to ask the hard question.

"Aydin, is it time to cut Miranda loose?"

*Holy moly, Phil understands.*
*Miranda is going to get us all killed.*

"Phil, that's kind of harsh. Are you sure?"

"She is nice to have around and a rock star between the sheets. But something is off. She never seems to tell the truth. Everything is bent and twisted. Every time I think she is opening up, a verbal door closes, and we are back to the beginning.

"I am not talking about The Program and you guys. I am talking about everything she says is buried in layers of bullshit. When you can find them, nuggets of truth are the corn kernels jutting out of the cow pies. Nothing is ever straight with her."

Allison sat unmoving, listening. Aydin understood the significance of Phil's comment.

"I do not trust her, either. The unfortunate reality is not good. She is playing her game and does not seem to care if we get hurt while she manipulates us."

"Can you hack her phone?"

Aydin twisted his head from his PC to Phil in response to the question.

"Yes, I have considered it a couple of times. Do you think it will help?"

"Yes. Miranda uses her phone in the bathroom. She said it is texting with her college friends. I'm calling bullshit."

"What do you think she is doing?"

Phil turns, sees the rain beginning to wash over the cars, and considers his response.

"I think she is updating whoever killed Moms and Arnold. I think she is a mole."

"What do you think she is looking to find?"

"That is the question. You're the Brain, you tell me."

"Pinky, world domination is mired in uncertainty. I have no fucking clue what she wants.

But I know this, having her around is dangerous. We never travel together. Three cars. Allison, you always follow Phil or me. Phil, when is Miranda due back?"

"Miranda went into the office. She said she'd text me when she was on her way home."

"Home to our house or home to her apartment?"

"Our house."

"Good, let's set up the phone hack."

Looking up, Aydin sees tears welling in Allison's eyes. Rushing around the table, he pulls up a chair next to his wife.

"What's wrong?"

"You. You moron."

"Me?"

"Yeah, you and Phil."

Looking over to his long-time friend, Aydin's wide-eyed, confused face is mirrored by Phil.

"Us? What about us?"

"I almost got us killed with the Chinese. I get that it was a terrible idea. You have no reason to trust me, but here we are. Everything you two do is designed to keep us alive. Us. Me. The three of us.

"After the Chinese, I thought you and I were done. But here we are."

"Why are you crying? It is a good thing we are here for each other."

"I am crying because I am sad."

"Sad? About your mom?"

"Yes, Moms, but Miranda also."

"Miranda? Why her?"

"Because, all our lives, it has been you and me. If you think about it, you will know it is true. We never had any other friends. Me and you. Then you brought Phil back from the desert. With Phil, my friends, my real friends, increased by 100%.

"I thought, maybe, Miranda would expand our group. I am sad because she will never be part of our group."

Phil's eyes glazed over with moisture.

Aydin stared at his wife until the words came to him.

"Do not be sad at the thought of not having another friend. Be happy you have us."

Allison punched Aydin in the bicep.

"I am happy, you moron. I can be sad too. I can be both. Phil, what about lunch?"

# The Unexpected Reality



During the morning commute to the office, Aydin realizes he is being tailed. Allison is in her Rover, two cars back, and one lane right. The traffic is too heavy to determine if there is more than one tail.

"Azima?"

*"Yes, Aydin?"*

"Open a connection to Allison, Pops, and Phil."

*"Stand by."*

*What the fuck now. It never ends.*

*"Connection established."*

"Thank you, Azima."

*"My pleasure."*

"I got one following me. Allison, the blue Ford at your 11 o'clock."

"Confirmed, I've been watching them. Two people. I believe the black Ford on my six, one car back, is also tailing. At least two more occupants."

"Phil?"

"Yes, Aydin?"

"Have you dropped off Miranda?"

"Yes, and I have a tail also. A black Ford, with two in the front seats.

"Phil, after dinner, did Miranda text again last

night?"

Phil's tone is determined.

"Yes, sir."

Aydin's tone is fierce.

"Stand by. I have a plan."

*This is not good.*
*We are outnumbered and outgunned.*
*An ambush?*
*This is an ambush, and I don't have a plan.*
*The tails know we will converge at the office.*
*Don't go to the office!*

"Azima?"

*"Yes, Aydin?"*

"Connect us to Pops."

*"Connecting to Pops, stand by."*

"Thank you, Azima."

*"My pleasure."*

*Pops will do it. He loves this shit.*

*"Aydin?"*

"Pops, we are being followed. Three vehicles, six bogeys. We are going to circle back and head your way. Can you take out Allison's tail?"

"Of course, I can. This is not my first rodeo. It will dent your new truck, but I suppose that is why you put the reinforced guard on the front."

"We will come around, south on Oswego, then

west on Ridgegate. When we cross Cabela's drive, you can make your move."

"Cabela's drive, roger that. ETA four minutes."

"Allison?"

"Yes, Aydin?"

"Slow down, let me slip in before Oswego, then do not let them get between us."

"Understood."

"Phil, where are you??"

"Southbound I-25, about two minutes from the Lincoln offramp."

"Forget Lincoln, take Ridgegate and hurry. You should arrive at the intersection just as we are passing under I-25. You have four minutes."

"Roger, that. Ridgegate in four minutes."

Aydin pulls in front of Allison, his Mercedes smoothly accelerating to wedge into the small opening. The tail on Aydin falls behind the vehicle trailing Allison.

*If we time this right, Pops can get a two-for-one.*

*Phil will have to evade.*

"Pops?"

"Yes, Aydin?"

"It'll be me, then Allison, then two tails, followed by Phil and his tail. Take out the first vehicle and let the second broadside you."

"You know I am old, right?"

"Oh, *now* you are old? I'll keep that in mind next time we are about to be ambushed. Phil?"

"Got it, evade the old guy who missed the stoplight and took out two in the intersection."

Aydin's focus is evident.

"Allison, there is a remote parking lot on the south side of the Skyridge Hospital. Phil will deal with pops. His tail will come after me. We make for the parking lot. Drive across the scrub if you have to. In the lot, I'll pull left and flip a 180. You do the same to the right and stop at a 45-degree angle to me. We'll have them in a crossfire when they pull in."

Allison's voice was choked.

"Understood. Make a 180, 45 to you, draw down on the bad guy."

Aydin hears his wife's voice break.

*Allison is starting to feel the pressure of being a real spy.*

*Up to the mess with the Chinese, it was all fun and games.*

*Now...*

*Now, it is real, and she is struggling.*

*I need to help her.*

"We got this. Pops, ETA one minute."

"One minute."

"Phil, I need a sitrep when Pops engages. If the third bogey does not follow, I'll spin a 180 for support."

"Understood."

"Pops, 30 seconds."

Seeing Aydin's Mercedes approaching from the east to prevent any eastbound traffic from blocking his target, Pops begins slowly rolling into the intersection. Confirming the gun will not fly out of his reach on impact, he checks the strap on his pistol holder for the third time. Putting down the windows, he wants an easy escape route.

The impact was more damaging than Pops expected, but the airbags deploying was a relief. Hitting the first tail vehicle in a T-Bone, the impact shoved the smaller Ford onto the sidewalk.

The second tailing car, as expected, was unable to avoid Pops' Sierra and T-Boned Pops' passenger door and bed.

Pops is catching his breath, pulling out his K-Bar to slice the airbags and deflate them quickly. Dropping the K-bar on the passenger seat, Pops pulled his Colt 1911 and began a threat assessment. Their airbags obscured the occupants of the two tail vehicles.

Aydin wanted to scream but kept his voice even.

"Phil?"

"Two vehicles down, third is headed your way. Pops?"

"I'm good, no eyes on the bad guys."

Phil stopped his pickup at an angle to Pop's truck. Swinging around into the truck bed, Phil climbs onto the roof of his pickup. From the rooftop, he has the two vehicles covered. Pops looks over his left shoulder, up at Phil, and receives a thumbs up to move.

Before he is out of the pickup, Phil is firing. Pops bends over, and then duck walks around Phil's truck. Jumping into the truck bed, Pops draws down on the second vehicle.

"Phil, who are you shooting at?"

"The passenger from the first vehicle got frisky."

"Oh, okay. The driver of the first vehicle appears to be unconscious. Those two-look frightened."

"I think they are trying to figure a way out or to create a plan to take us out. They are too stupid to try the reverse gear. Plus, traffic is starting to back up. We need to get down before we are on the six o'clock news."

Pops and Phil put down their pistols and climb off Phil's pickup without taking their eyes from the two in the second vehicle. Phil circling left, Pops right, they see men in the tail vehicle have their hands on the dashboard.

Phil steps over to the guy he shot, turns, bends, and confirms bleeding from the hole through the upper right arm. The wound is not life-threatening. Phil looks into the vehicle to ensure the driver is unconscious. Surveying everything, he shrugs to Pops, who holsters his pistol and begins directing traffic.

Aydin's Mercedes effortlessly spun the tires, allowing Aydin to turn the heavy car a 180 and angle toward the remote parking lot entrance. Allison did not follow on the asphalt. She drove her Rover across the open field and stopped as Aydin instructed.

Allison and Aydin are out of their vehicles. Aydin crouching behind the driver's door. Allison, standing behind the driver door of the taller Rover.

The black Ford pulls into the remote lot, stops about 25 feet from the front of Allison and Aydin's cars. The driver and front passenger door open at the same time. Hands are visible from both sides of the vehicle. A man steps from the driver's seat and a woman from the front passenger seat.

Allison does not take her eyes from the Ford and the people but speaks softly to her Rover.

"Azima?"

*"Yes, Allison?"*

"Can Aydin hear me?"

Allison hears Aydin's low-volume response.

*"I can hear you."*

"Is that who I think it is?"

*"It is."*

The couple from the black Ford step around their open car doors. With hands high, they move to the front of the vehicle and stand side-by-side. The woman speaks.

"Hello, Allison. Hello, Aydin."

Allison looks across the windshield of her Rover, but Aydin does not look at her. She sees he is thinking.

*Miranda's texts.*
*She was calling for help.*
*She reached out to the only people she trusts: The General and Marina.*
*But why them?*
*Why not her handler?*
*Aw, fuck snacks.*
*The General is her handler.*
*He is the missing link.*

"Hello, misses Cole, General. Before we put down our weapons, tell me why you were tailing us? Who are your friends?"

Aydin is a bit surprised when the General defers to his wife for a response.

"They are some friends from an RV club to which we belong. They agreed to meet us here and help Miranda. Are our friends alive?"

"Phil?"

"*Yes, Aydin?*"

"Status please?"

"*One got frisky and took a bullet in the upper arm. He'll live. His driver is still out cold. The other two appeared to have peed their pants and refuse to move from the vehicle. The ambulance and authorities are on their way.*"

Aydin looked to Allison then back to the couple. Seeing her husband put down his weapon, Allison did the same. Both stepped to the front and stood between their vehicles. They maintained a twenty-foot gap between themselves and the Coles. Aydin's summary is also a demand.

"One of your friends took a bullet in the arm, and the driver is out cold. The other two are still in their car. Why are you here?"

Marina Cole continues to respond.

"We came to help Miranda. You knew her as Kat, but now you know her as Miranda. Allison, I presume you know she is your half-sister?"

Aydin intercedes.

"We can get to the family genealogy later. Right now, I want to know why you were tailing us?"

The General finally speaks.

"Because they are watching you, and we want to help keep you alive."

At the ending of his sentence, the General points east to a small black drone, hovering between their position and I25. The four watch the drone lower and begin to retreat. The drone flies into the open side door of a white delivery van parked on the southbound apron of I25. The sliding door closes, and the van pulls away.

Aydin races back to his car.

"Phil?"

*"Yes, Aydin?"*

"Can you make the GSW look like it came from

the accident?"

"*Stand by.*"

Phil steps over to the person he shot and scans the area. Spying a two-foot length of rebar, he quick steps over and picks it up. Returning, he looks down at his prone GSW victim.

"Sorry, this is going to hurt."

Phil turns his body, blocking the view of the GSW victim from the backed-up traffic. Before the victim can respond, Phil thrust the rebar through the hole created by the bullet. He shoved hard enough. A foot of the two-foot rod is buried in the ground.

Standing tall, looking down, Phil smiles when he issues the orders over the screams of the wounded man.

"You banged your head in the wreck. Stumbled, getting out of the car, fell backward, and landed on the rebar."

Phil stepped back to his truck.

"Aydin, accident confirmed."

"*Thank you.*"

Aydin and the others hear the ambulance and local police sirens arriving at the site of the accident.

"Are your friends smart enough to keep their mouths shut?"

Marina answers.

"Yes, they are all ex-military."

"Good. Do you know where my office is?"

"We do."

"Meet us there at 15:00."

Allison and Aydin return to their vehicles.

"Phil?"

"Yes, Aydin?"

"Is Pops okay?"

"Is Pops okay? He is telling the ambulance crew how to field-dress the wound. Yeah, Pops is okay."

"Do I need to come there and help with the police?"

"No need, we got this. Apparently, the traffic light cycled incorrectly. Lone Tree has been experiencing problems with the traffic lights in this area."

*What the fuck?*

*Where did that come from?*

*Who messed with the traffic lights?*

"Phil?"

*"Yes, Aydin?"*

"Can you explain?"

*"Not at the moment. I will meet you at the office."*

### DTC, Conference Room, 12:15, Lite Rain

Allison and Aydin waited silently for Phil to arrive with Pops. Phil insisted on arriving with lunch. Pops is almost cheerful in talking to Aydin.

"Sorry about your truck, but it was not my fault. The traffic lights cycled wrong."

*He loves this shit.*

*He will never give it up.*

*I wonder if he will still be happy after my question.*

"Phil, what did you do to the traffic lights?"

"I told Azima ..."

*"Yes, Phil?"*

"Never mind. Thank you, Azima."

*"My pleasure."*

"You have *got* to fix that. I was saying. I remembered you shut down the cameras across the road when we were at the Saguaro Restaurant. I asked your new toy if she could access the traffic lights. She said yes. It worked."

Aydin is practically bobbing with understanding. He stopped, turned serious, and resumed his questions for Pops.

"Did you know General Cole is Miranda's Handler?"

Pulling the foil off his carne asada burrito, Pops smiles around the first bite. He swallows before responding.

"Bryan is not Miranda's Handler."

*What the fuck?*

*Not the General?*

*Who?*

*Marina!*

*I am a dumb son of a bitch.*

*No wonder I missed the connection because I never thought to look.*

*I never looked because she was never in the game.*

*Not like our parents.*

*Of course, she was in the game with a low profile.*

*I need to be better.*


"Why didn't you tell me?"

"You never asked, and it never seemed important. It is important now."

"I'd say it is crucial. The General and Marina are a team."

Pops kept chewing but nodded yes.

"Do you know why someone is trying to kill Miranda?"

Pops swallowed, wiped his mouth, sipped his hot, black, dark-roast coffee, leaned back, and responded.

"She knows the network. All of it. Inside and outside of The Service. She got lucky and hacked a document repository. In the repository, she found a document with the entire network."


*Aw, fuck snacks.*

*We are targets now because they think she gave us the names in the network.*

*We have to kill whoever is at the top of the food chain and everyone between Miranda and the top.*

*Maybe we can go back to blowing up shit in the desert.*

"Pops, who is trying to kill Miranda?"

After another long sip of coffee that is too hot, Pops answered.

"I was not sure until today. The guy with the hole in his arm was the clue. I know him from a mission. Bryan and I went on back in the eighties. The guy with the hole was an SP sent to guard Miranda. He kept coming around whenever Bryan was on a mission. Kat was about ten when she walked in on Marina and the idiot."

Pops stopped, sipped, then continued.

"Bryan knows but does not care. Why he doesn't divorce her, I don't know. You asked: Who is trying to kill Miranda?"

"Marina.

"Miranda knows something about Marina and The Service that Marina wants to keep a secret. Marina wants her niece, her adoptive daughter, Miranda, dead to hide her past."

# The Reality of Family



The General and Marina arrive at exactly 15:00. The conference room chairs have been reconfigured for the visitors. At the far end of the table, Aydin and Pops are across from each other. Phil and Allison are sharing the end of the table.

Two chairs at the other end of the room are positioned on either side of the table. The General sits with his back to the door. Marina, on the other side of the table, next to the windows.

The General skipped pleasantries and introductions.

"Phil, I want to thank you for taking care of our daughter. She has nice things to say about you. I hope we will see you around for a long while."

Phil meekly nodded acceptance to the compliment. The General continued.

"Aydin and Allison, I am sure you have learned of The Program and how your parents were selected to participate. Skipping that for now, what we need to understand is who is trying to kill Miranda and you two."

The disgust in Aydin's voice is unmistakable.

"We are not skipping anything. The Program was shut down before you could get Miranda paired. You decided to continue the path and guided her to the life of a spy: Quantico and counterespionage. She had no choice. We had no choice. For us, it is not a complaint. For Miranda ... Did you stop to think about what it was doing to her?"

The General's tone is conciliatory.

"It was a different time. We were different people. That is not an excuse. It is a statement of fact."

Sharply, Allison interrupts her uncle.

"You have not asked about Moms, your sister. You have not asked about Marina's brother. Miranda's father. What is wrong with you two?"

It is Marina who answers the questions.

"In this life, you get used to people dying. Close people die. Dwelling on the dead is never good."

Allison waved a derisive dismissal at the older woman before leaning back and looking at Aydin, who resumes the questioning.

"General..."

"Call me Bryan."

"Bryan, you say you are here to help. Do you know who wants your daughter dead?"

"Not yet, but we will figure it out."

Pops could not control himself.

"Bryan, you are a fucking moron. I told you before, and you ignored me. All these years later, and here we are talking about the same damned thing. You damned-well know the answer, now man the fuck up and admit it."

General Cole looked to the table, back to his longtime friend, then turned to his wife of more than forty years with a one-word question.

"Why?"

Marina Dawn Cole, née Potvin, did not flinch. She slowly stood to leave.

"Azima?"

*"Yes, Aydin?"*

"Initiate protocol Alpha-Alpha-One."

*"Protocol Alpha-Alpha-One initiated."*

"Request protocol, *Alpha-Alpha-Two.*"

*"Protocol Alpha-Alpha-Two requires authentication."*

"Authentication for protocol, Alpha-Alpha-Two. Happy days are here again."

*"Protocol Alpha-Alpha-Two authenticated."*

"Thank you, Azima."

*"My pleasure."*

"Sit down, Misses Cole. This building is sealed. You will not be allowed to leave until I remove the seal."

Sitting, the older woman began to speak, her venom directed to Aydin.

"You killed my brother. Because of you, Katherine is dead. Because of you, James is dead."

"Who is James?"

"Don't play stupid young man, no one ever thought of you as stupid."

"Azima?"

*"Yes, Aydin?"*

"What is Major Arnold's full name?"

*"James Arthur Arnold, USAF, Retired."*

"Thank you, Azima."

*"My pleasure."*

Aydin noted the General's attention redoubled when he interacted with Azima.

"Misses Cole, the false indignation you are trying to express is not working. You are not leaving here until we have answers."

"Boy, you can't hold me. I will leave whenever I choose. Little girl, what are you smiling at?"

Allison grins throughout her response.

"Aydin has it figured out. I can tell by the look on his face. Usually, when I see that look, dead people follow. I am okay with making you dead."

The older woman remained still but turned her head from Allison to Aydin, who continued to consider the possibilities.

*Could it be?*
*Maybe.*
*Yes, I think so.*
*How do I ask?*
*Don't ask.*
*State it as fact.*

"Misses Cole, your brother Michael. The Soviets did not turn him. The Soviets turned you, and you turned him. You both became double agents."

In his peripheral vision, Aydin saw Pops' eyes light up.

*I got it right, and Pops learned something.*

"His name is not Michael. It is Mikhail."

*She is a deep agent.*
*A double agent married to an Air Force General.*
*Heads are going to roll if there are any heads left to roll.*

Aydin is wrenched away from his thoughts by Marina's curt and condescending question.

"Young man, are you listening to me?"

"No, was it important?"

"When we get back what Miranda has stolen, we will take care of you and everyone in this room."

"Yeah, not so much. Your death threats are meaningless. We are…"

Aydin looked over to the General, who is pointing a silver Sig Sauer at his wife. Lunging toward the General, Aydin was too late. The .380 caliber round entered the woman's left temple and exited her right ear. Stopped by the double-paned, level eight ballistic glass, the cordite and blood mist's odor followed the bullet.

"Azima?"

*"Yes, Aydin?*

"Request upgrade protocol, *Alpha-Alpha-Two to Alpha-Baker-Two.*

*"Protocol Alpha-Baker-Two requires authentication."*

"Authentication for protocol, Alpha-Baker-Two. Happy days have passed us by."

"*Protocol Alpha-Baker-Two authenticated.*"

"Initiate air-handling, level three."

"Air handling, level three initiated.

"Thank you, Azima."

"*My pleasure.*"

Gently taking the General's pistol, removing the magazine and the chambered round, Aydin placed everything on the table and waited for the General to speak.

"She deserved it, and I should have done it twenty years ago. This way, I can tell our friends back home, she died on vacation. Brandon, you were right all those years ago. I didn't want to see it then.

"Miranda is the one who changed my mind. She understood Marina was playing all sides. Marina got bad when you killed her brother. All she talked about was coming to Colorado to protect her baby.

"All bullshit. Marina wanted revenge for her brother and her only true love... She wanted Miranda out of the way because of the list."

"The list, do you know where she hid it?"

"Aydin, Miranda doesn't have the list. She never did. To protect me, she never denied having the list. Here."

The general reached into his breast pocket, pulled out a flash drive, and slid it down to Aydin. Looking up from the storage drive in his hand, Aydin noticed the change in the General's face.

"Bryan?"

"Aydin, I am sorry about your mother. She was a good person who is missed. Please, tell your father I said hello. He is one of the good ones.

"Allison, your mother was unique. What you don't know is she and Marina were lovers. They met when your mother was a college freshman. Now we know it was a planned meeting. Your mother had accepted the college scholarship tied to joining the Air Force. Their meeting and becoming lovers was the beginning of a long game for Marina to be Katherine's handler. Marina truly loved Katherine."

Turning to Pops, Bryan waited.

"Katherine told me it was over with Marina, but I never believed her. It was easier to stay married. I could have divorced Katherine, but then I would have had to look over my shoulder all the time. Katherine was a lot of things, and vindictive was at the top of her list. Allison, honey, I stayed with her for you. Through it all, it was you and me."

"I know that, dad. I always knew that."

Turning back to the General, everyone waited.

"Miranda has been lying to you all because she doesn't know what else to do. She is protecting me and does not know the names on the list I stole. Over the past few years, she has taken a few assignments from The Service, but I kept a close watch. I never let her take on anything too dangerous."

The General stopped speaking, watching the three white vans pull up.

"Azima?"

*"Yes, Aydin?*

"Release protocol, *Alpha-Alpha-One."*

*"Protocol Alpha-Alpha-One released."*

"Thank you, Azima."

*"My pleasure."*

"We need to get out of here and let Kermit's team do their thing. Bryan, come with us to the house for drinks and dinner. Miranda will be by later. Phil will make sure of it.

"Phil, run Pops up to his house.

"Pops, meet us at our house at seven.

"Phil, is that enough time to cook?"

"I'm not cooking. I am picking up a takeaway from Saguaro. General, how do you like your steak?"

"Call me Bryan and just this side of mooing."

Everyone began packing up to leave. Standing, waiting for everyone else, Phil spoke loudly to their backsides.

"Our conference room has more dead people than the county morgue. We might consider replacing the carpet with Terrazzo. It'll be easier for Kermit's crew to clean."

# The New Family Reality



Allison stayed home with Miranda, Bryan, and Pops. Aydin and Phil are in the office, with the plan to go over the list Bryan provided. Their goal is to determine who is running point on the orders to kill them. The blood-stained carpet replaced, no trace of the mist, the chair Marina was sitting in is gone.

Already into their second large coffee, Phil and Aydin use a new technique to examine the drive contents.

"Tell me again, Brain, how does this work?"

"It scans every sector of the drive, at the bit-level, and duplicates it in the tool. The tool then scans the bits for patterns. When it finds a pattern it recognizes, using the advanced heuristics, it begins a circular scan for additional patterns."

"Circular?"

"On a hard-disk drive, an HDD, one that spins, data is recorded linearly. One row of bits after the other. Billions, trillions, of bits all in neat little rows. On a solid-state drive, an SSD, which all flash drives are, data doesn't have to be arranged linearly. The flash technology is supposed to mirror an HDD, but it doesn't have to. The tool you have looks linearly and horizontally for patterns."

"Wouldn't the accuracy of the tool depend on

the seeding? What are the patterns you seeded the tool with, and what if you don't find anything?"

"Pinky, that is exactly the problem. Which is why we are loading it up to the secure server and giving it to Azima."

"What are you using for pattern seeds?"

"The names of the targets."

"Azima?"

*"Yes, Aydin?*

"Read the seed file addendum I sent this morning. Read section one."

*"Section one:*

*"Mikhail Anton Potvin,*

*"Marina Dawn Potvin,*

*"Katherine Marie Cole,*

*"Aydin Matthew Trammell,*

*"Brandon Michael Kearney,*

*"Penny McCormack,*

*"Penny Trammell,*

*"Albert Clark Trammell,*

*"Katherine Elizabeth Cole,*

*"Allison Beth Cole,*

*"Bryan Michael Cole."*

Phil understood but asked anyway.

"What about me?"

"Because I don't think you are on any list. Everyone on that list connects to The Program. Directly or tangentially, they are all connected. Don't feel slighted. Not being on a list is a good thing. Thank you, Azima."

*"My pleasure."*

Phil accepted the closure and pressed the submit button. The countdown clock appeared and kept rising until it reached: 04:56:54 and began counting down.

"Aydin, the timer says almost five hours to complete the scan.

"That sounds about right."

"What are we going to do while we wait?"

"I am going to catch up on email and read the resumes of the receptionist candidates. You are going to read the spec file I created and start writing the new algorithm I designed. It will close a few of the holes in Az... in the AI's empirical and exploratory analysis processing."

Phil's response is not half-hearted.

"Happy. Happy. Joy. Joy."

## DTC, Conference Room, 13:25, Clear and Warming

Aydin has returned with lunch. Setting the bags on the table, he updates Phil.

"I spoke to Allison. She says dinner will be ready at 18:30, and we better not be late."

While he is pulling his burritos out of the bag, Phil's question is expected by Aydin.

"With this new code, the AI will have the ability to make interpretive decisions. She already infers from context, but this new code will allow her to jump from one logic thread to another and back. Or merge two lines of linear analysis if the expected result is deemed targetable.

"Brain, this is some next-level voodoo magic."

"Yes, Pinky, it is. What's world domination without a little whimsy?"

"Whimsy? You know, people will kill you to get this code?"

"I know."

"Are you worried?"

"Worried about getting dead or about someone stealing the code?"

"Both."

"No and No."

"Why not?"

"Dead is not going to happen. We have too much to do to allow dead as a possibility. Plus, your girlfriend mentioned the beach to Allison, and now it looks like sand is in our future. Someone stealing the code is not going to happen because of the safeguards."

"What safeguards?"

"Azima?"

*"Yes, Aydin?*

"What is your protocol to prevent unauthorized access to you?"

*"There are three levels of threat mitigation.*

*"Level One: Verbal challenge for passcode authentication.*

*"Level Two: Voice authentication or retina scan.*

*"Level Three: Voice authentication, retina scan, and DNA validation."*

"Thank you, Azima."

*"My pleasure."*

"DNA? On-demand? How the hell will she do that?"

"That, Phil, is something you do not want to know. Seriously, on-demand DNA is the Holy-Grail of security authentication."

Phil waited, thinking it through before he spoke.

"No one wants facial recognition or targeting software badly enough to kill. They want the on-demand DNA. But, Aydin, I didn't know about it, and I help you with the code. How do they know about it?"

"That, Pinky, is the question I hope the list will answer."

*"Aydin?*

"Yes, Azima?"

*"The scan results are ready."*

"Send them to Phil and me."

*"Sending."*

Both began closing windows and browser tabs, waiting for the message to arrive. Both opened the link to the secure server, entered the password, and selected the file.

"Thank you, Azima."

*"My pleasure."*

"Aydin, may I ask you a personal question?"

*Phil has never used those words with me.*
*Something important is bugging him.*

"Sure, go ahead."

"About The Program, do you think there was more to it than creating smart spies?"

"How do you mean?"

"I mean, the psychological effects of growing up in an environment as you did must have had effects. You and Allison. Now, I see it in Miranda."

"See what?"

"Emotions. Or the lack of emotions. No, your emotions are highly controlled and managed, Moms is dead, and Allison is okay with the death of her mother? The General off'd his wife in this room, and no one flinched. The Service covers it all, and no one asks too many questions. But that is the tactical part. What about the emotional part? Are you guys okay?"

*How the fuck am I supposed to answer Phil's question?*

*I have no idea if I am okay.*

*I never learned to be okay.*

*I need to talk to Allison.*

*She will understand.*

"Phil, I am okay. Allison is okay. We have no choice to be okay. I know you are worried but trust me, we are okay. We learned to be okay. I am going to talk to Allison about Moms and her aunt.

"But, Phil, this is who we are and who we were trained to be in this life."

Phil's expression indicated a reluctant acceptance and understanding to stop the conversation. Both turned back to their PCs, and the comfortable silence only found between real friends.

Phil is reciting what they are reading for no other reason than he does not want silence.

"Section one of the list contains over 200 names.

"Section two is a list of 16 active covert operations with mission details.

"Section three is a list of 108 inactive covert operations with summary details.

"Aydin?"

"Yes, Phil?"

"Name number 189."

"Juanita Verónica Menéndez. Bobby was not lying about the female cop dumping Moms on the lawn. Now we know why the background checks did not turn up anything unusual."

Aydin's monotone is focused.

"Name number 137, he supposed to be dead. Look at name number 138. Numbers 137 and 138 are assigned to active mission number six. From the mission summary, I got a C-Note that says mission number six is titled: Aydin and Phil.

"The beach is going to have to wait. These guys are dangerous. Let's get up to the house. Tomorrow, before he leaves, we'll bring Bryan and Pops up to speed. We'll get my father on the line. He'll have some input. Whatever we do, no one goes anywhere alone."

Reaching for his phone, Aydin calls Allison, putting it on the speaker before she answers.

"Hey, hon."

"Allison, is everyone with you?"

"Yes, we are sitting on the deck."

"Put me on the speaker."

"Okay, you are on the speaker."

"Pops, Robert Walker, and Kristy Lewis are on the list."

"I thought Robert was dead."

"Apparently not."

"There's your hole in the food chain."

"Yes, sir, and it is a dangerous hole. Recommendation?"

"I got things here, you and Phil get back, and we will make a plan."

Aydin clicked off the phone. Exiting the office, under his breath, Aydin mumbled.

"Twelve o'clock. Elevated."

Phil glanced up to see the black drone above the trees on the parking lot's far side.

In the car, he and Phil were silent while Aydin drove out of the parking lot. Phil's head is on a swivel, looking for threats.

Aydin pressed the comms icon, connecting him again to Allison. She immediately started talking.

"You are on the speaker. If you are calling about the drone, Pops spotted it right after you hung up."

"Allison, this is not good. Do whatever Pops

says."

"Roger that."

The line went dead again.

"Brain?"

"Yeah, Pinky?"

"Two weeks. Can we set a goal to make it two full weeks with no one shooting at us or us shooting anyone?"

"Gee, Pinky, I don't know. World domination and all…"

Phil's head remained on the swivel, looking for threats. Aydin made sure never to be boxed in by the traffic. His eyes constantly rotated through his mirrors, looking for threats. Pops and Bryan are armed and waiting when Aydin and Phil pull into the garage.

Bryan summarizes the day.

"No wonder Miranda doesn't want to go home to Louisiana. It is never boring here in Colorado."

# Two Weeks of Calm

*Trammell House, 06:45, Clear*

## Breaking News

In today's market news, a local company is all the talk on Wall Street. A small, Colorado-based software development company is expected to be the next billion-dollar IPO.

You heard that right. An unknown little company, headquartered in the DTC, is being touted as the next Microsoft or Apple. The privately held company issued a press release yesterday. In the press release, the company, which is named Fírinne, Is claiming to have developed the next breakthrough in artificial intelligence.

The owner of the company, Andrew Matthew Trammell, was not available for comment. We reached his spokesperson, who told us Mister Trammell would be available for comment later today.

We'll stay on this Colorado First story.

NOW, THE WEATHER WITH STORMY.

Bryan, Pops, Phil, Miranda, Allison, and Aydin are at the breakfast bar, watching the television news. Phil is picking up the used breakfast dishes. Aydin pressed the mute button on the television's remote.

"Azima?"

*"Yes, Aydin?"*

"Did you talk to a reporter yesterday?"

*"No, under the protocol designated non-committal, I ignored the repeated requests."*

"Did you issue a press release under the company logo?"

*"I do not understand the question."*

"Did you send any emails regarding the work we do at Fírinne?"

*"No, I do not initiate communications without your direct approval."*

"Thank you, Azima."

*"My pleasure."*

*Someone is setting us up.*
*Putting this out there, shines a light on us.*
*Someone is creating chaos…*

"Aydin!"

Turning, Aydin looked at his wife.

"Stop that. Let us help you."

*Son of a bitch.*

"The press release is meant to intimidate us and make us vulnerable. People, lots of people, are going to be coming around. We need to stay away for a few days. Too many people around will lower our security profile."

Stopping, looking through the window, over the Pederson's house, Aydin sees the drone.

"Whoever is flying those things is part of this cluster fuck. How do Robert Walker and Kristy Lewis fit into this trouble? Two more from The Program working for The Service. Drones are not their style. Pops?"

"I have no idea."

"Bryan"

"Not a clue."

Aydin angrily stopped talking and began thinking.

*Just another day in fucking paradise.*

*This is corporate espionage and counterintelligence operations. We got the whole package.*

*Corporate espionage?*

*That's it.*

*The drones are not connected to Walker and Lewis.*

*Miranda.*

*Everything comes back to Miranda.*

*But Bryan had the list?*
*They are both lying.*
*Mother-F-ing-Son-of-a-bitch.*
*They are both lying.*

The hard slap on the back of his hand from Allison pulled Aydin back into the conversation.

"The drones are corporate espionage. Someone is pressing us to open up about our work. I don't know what Walker and Lewis have to do with anything, but it isn't good for us if they are in Colorado. Bryan, when will your taxi arrive?"

"It is scheduled for 07:30."

"Miranda, say your goodbyes inside, do it now. As soon as the taxi arrives, no delays, get in and go. Phil, when Bryan leaves, take Pops to pick up his truck from the repair shop. Pops, head home. I'll have the AI monitor your location."

Allison looked at Miranda but spoke to Aydin.

"What are we going to do?"

"You, Miranda, and I are going to the office to interview receptionist candidates."

"Azima?"

*"Yes, Aydin?"*

"Send a message to KTF: Tow anyone parking in our reserved spots."

*"Message sent."*

"Thank you, Azima."

*"My pleasure."*

# Salt Wounds
## Family Whimsey

*"A sudden bold and unexpected question doth many times surprise a man and lay him open."*

*Francis Bacon*

**Trammel House, 04:20, Clear**

The events of the past six weeks have Aydin lying in bed, unable to sleep or calm his mind.

*Moms is dead.*
*That fuck-wad Arnold is dead.*
*Good riddance.*
*Marina is dead.*
*Who knew she was Mom's and Drakon's handler?*
*Who was Marina's handler?*
*It must be someone in The Service.*
*Fuck, another loose end.*
*The mess never stops.*
*Bryan, the General, is back home in Louisiana.*
*He didn't flinch when he put the bullet in Marina's temple.*
*If Pops is right, Bryan wanted to kill his wife for at least twenty years.*
*She finally gave him a reason.*
*Phil says Miranda's nightmares are terrible, but*

she won't share what they are about or why she has them.

Miranda is lying less and less.

She must have figured out she was in over her head.

She did what she did for Bryan, the only father she has ever known.

The drones are watching.

At least two teams are running the drones.

That must be corporate espionage.

They want us to make a mistake.

We won't make a mistake.

The corporate spies don't understand who they are dealing with nor the immense pain Phil and I can deliver.

They are shit-out-of-luck if they believe they can be successful in getting information.

Phil has never been happier.

Miranda, also being from the deep south, brings out the best in Phil.

He is warming to Miranda now that we recognize who she is and what she is doing in the spy game.

We understand why she was lying all the time.

Inexperience is an m-fer you are in over your head.

Miranda was in way too deep.

Phil can teach her.

Allison can teach her.

We can teach her the spy game.

*Why?*

*Why did Bryan let her take the heat?*

*Pops is Pops and is okay with his life.*

*He and Allison have never been better.*

*Her fucking up the long-con has brought them closer.*

*Being officially retired is his cover.*

*He loves the dual life of being a hitman for a spy.*

*He loves it when I call him.*

*I need to call Pops less.*

Allison's snoring interrupts Aydin's thoughts. He watches his wife for a few minutes until she snorts, then rolls over. His mind is running back to a common theme.

*Allison is trying to get me to open up.*

*She wants more.*

*Twenty years we have known each other, and now we have to talk?*

*She is working hard to make up for the bad deal with the Chinese.*

*She is trying too hard to fix it.*

*We are good.*

*I need to help her appreciate we are okay.*

*She realizes it has always been us.*

*Wait...*

*Ah, fuck snacks.*

*How did I miss it?*

*How did Bryan get the list?*

# Wolves at the Door

### *DTC, Office Parking Lot, 06:32, Cloudy*

Aydin arrives at the Fírinne office in the Denver Technical Center (DTC), followed by Phil. Their parking spaces are open, but the visitor spaces nearest the office are filled. People are waiting for them to arrive.

Two tow trucks are waiting at the edge of the parking lot for anyone to park in a reserved spot.

Stepping out of his car is enough of a signal for the waiting visitors not already out of their vehicles to begin adding to the queue along the sidewalk. Before he reaches the office door, Aydin counts seven deep on the sidewalk.

Pressing his thumb to the pad on the doorframe, Aydin hollers over his shoulder toward the queue.

"Give us five minutes to get settled, and then we can let you in."

Letting the door close behind Phil, Aydin turns the deadbolt.

"Phil, no chairs in the lobby. Close our office doors. We will be polite, but they are to *stand* around and wait."

Phil moves to push the two lobby chairs into his small office. Aydin grabs the receptionist's chair and closes it in his office.

Phil confirms the closet, and the hidden vault,

are closed and locked before he moves to the conference room. Aydin follows, sets down his backpack, and comments before returning to the lobby and the office door.

"Let's see how long they like standing around on the hard Terrazzo."

Opening the office door allows the queue to enter. Aydin counts eleven people. Letting the office door close, he moves to the spot in front of the conference room door and makes a statement.

"There is no IPO. We are not hiring. There is no information. A competitor issued the press release to create precisely what we have here: People looking for a piece of something that does not exist.

"Again, there is no IPO, and we are not hiring.

"We have meetings to attend this morning. If you want to wait around until our meetings conclude, we have time later today to answer your questions."

People began shouting questions that Aydin ignored. He turns his back, enters the conference room, and closes the door.

"Azima?"

*"Yes, Aydin?"*

"Disable the guest Wi-Fi."

*"Guest Wi-Fi has been disabled."*

Phil and Aydin hear the audible groans from the lobby.

"Send a message to KTF: How many cars have been towed?"

*"Message to Kermit sent."*

"Thank you, Azima."

*"My Pleasure."*

Phil pushes Aydin's large black coffee toward his friend. Accepting it with a nod, Aydin opens the sipping tab, sips, then speculates.

"How long before they start leaving?"

Phil points to the window. One of the guests is heading for her car.

*"Aydin?"*

"Yes, Azima?"

*"The message from Kermit says they have towed seven vehicles in the three days since the news report."*

"Thank you, Azima."

*"My pleasure."*

Eyeing the conference room's thermostat, Phil has an idea.

"Azima?"

*"Yes, Phil?"*

"Turn up the heat in the lobby. Make it as hot as possible."

*"Turning up the lobby heat, the maximum temperature is 104 degrees."*

"We'll make hotter'n a blister bug in a pepper patch. Azima, make it 104 in the lobby, and do not turn it down until we tell you."

*"Lobby temperature set to 104 degrees."*

"Thank you, Azima."

*"My Pleasure."*

"Brain?"

"Yes, Pinky?

"When did you install the new entry pad on the office door?"

"Kermit installed it over the weekend."

"Does it do what I assume it does?"

"It does."

## DTC, Conference Room, 09:22, Light Rain

"I emailed you the cell phone number to the business reporter who broke the story of the fake IPO. Miranda sent it to me from work."

Aydin doesn't acknowledge Phil's comment. He uses the conference room phone to call the reporter.

The reporter doesn't say hello. He has correctly guessed from the caller ID who is on the line.

"Mister Trammell, thank you for calling."

"This is not a get-to-know-you call. There is no IPO. You were given false information. Please issue a retraction. Today."

"I have it on good authority that you are very close to a breakthrough in advanced artificial intelligence technology. Would you care to give a statement?"

"I just gave you a statement. There is no IPO. You were given false information. Please issue a retraction. Today!"

"Mister Trammell, I do not believe you. My

viewers have a right to know if the next 'Killer App' is being built right here in Colorado."

"You are misinformed and ignorant. There is no app, and there is no IPO. Issue the retraction."

"Or what?"

Aydin did not take the bait.

"Speak to your colleague, Miranda LaLonde."

Aydin disconnected the phone line and turned to his only true friend.

"Will she do it?"

Turning on the fullness of his and Miranda's southern roots, Phil's response is heavily accented.

"Will she do it? She cain't wait. When I asked her, she was happier than a blue-tick hound chewin' on a big ol' catfish head."

Aydin smiled and looked up to see two more of the guests heading to their vehicles. One is tugging at his shirt, the other wiping her brow.

## DTC, Conference Room, 12:42, Light Rain

Aydin watches Phil waiting for the tow truck to haul away the Prius. The Prius had parked in his space while he was fetching lunch.

The Prius' animated owner is begging and pleading with the tow truck driver not to take her car away.

Phil watches from his Sierra. When the Prius is gone, he pulls in and parks.

Walking through the lobby, Phil counts seven guests. The conference room door is closing as Phil issues a rhetorical statement.

"Only two left from 06:30 this morning."

Putting down Aydin's bag of burritos, Phil points to the Prius driver sitting on the sidewalk. "She offered the tow truck driver a blow job if he let her drive away."

Aydin grunted and pulled the foil from his chicken burrito. Phil continued.

"There is one in the lobby who is not going away. She is sitting on the hard floor in a yoga position, humming. The plain cotton blouse and slacks scream *tree-hugger*. Those dreadlocks look terrible."

"It is the Lotus position in Yoga. She is meditating and waiting."

Smiling around his double beef and guacamole burrito, Phil spoke with his mouth full.

"Lotus, shmotus. How long do we agree to wait?"

Aydin shrugged, bit his spicy chicken delight, and went back to his work.

### DTC, Conference Room, 16:52, Rain

"Aydin, I have an email from Miranda. She is scheduled to be on-air tonight, and she spoke to that business reporter. He will issue the retraction."

"How did she do it?"

"She showed the fuck-nuts pictures of us from the desert and suggested we might not be done blowing shit up."

With one eye closed, the other on Phil, with a

wrinkled brow, Aydin is curious.

"Where did she get pictures of us in the desert."

Phil's response is surly.

"She copied them from my scrapbook."

Both turn and watch Allison pull into her normal parking space.

Entering the conference room, Allison is surprised and confused.

"Have you forgotten, there are four people in the lobby? Damn, it is hot out there."

Neither Aydin nor Phil responds.

"Okay, well then, I've been with Pops all-day. We are good. I feel he and I have never been better. Pops said the end of this drama is close."

Aydin and Phil look up from their PCs with smiles. Allison closes the topic.

"Pops, and I agreed. Moms was always putting tension in our lives. She was not happy, and she made everyone else unhappy. There is sadness but not grief. Everyone is better with her dead. Pops and I are good. I feel good." Aydin's darkness bubbles.

*What is wrong with us?*

*Are we incapable of feeling grief over dead loved ones?*

*Do we love anyone?*

*True love?*

*Is that possible for us?*

*I love Allison.*

*I love Phil.*

*What is wrong with us not being able to grieve?*

Aydin decides it is time to talk to the people in the lobby. He begins packing up, which is the clue for Phil to do the same.

"Azima?"

*"Yes, Aydin?"*

"Return the temperature in the lobby to normal."

*"The lobby temperature is set to 72 degrees."*

"Thank you, Azima."

*"My pleasure."*

Standing in the lobby, with his back to the conference room, Phil on his right, Allison on his left, Aydin is dreading the next few minutes.

"As I said this morning, there is no IPO, we are not hiring, and we are not seeking investors. I may answer your questions, but there is no new information."

He is pointing to the person standing to his left. Aydin indicates the expected order of the questions. His sequence ended with the woman seated in the Lotus position.

Aydin's responses are short, concise, and unwavering.

"No, we are not building a robot.

"No, we are not designing the command and control for the Mars mission."

"No, we do not need investors."

The woman sitting on the floor skipped her turn, allowing the cycle of questions to repeat.

The two men in suits are disappointed with Aydin's answer.

"No, our software is an AI for environmental controls. Not a cybernetic robot."

The guy in dirty jeans, a UFC sweatshirt, and greasy hair doesn't believe the answer he receives.

"No, we have nothing to do with NASA or any of the private space programs."

A man in a grey Armani suit is squinting at the response he receives.

"No, investment funding is a form of hang-cuffs. We do not need investors."

The three people in suits look at each other, shake their heads, then turn to the seated woman.

"I like your new scanner."

Aydin ignores the statement. The woman rocks forward, and without using her hands, she rises to a standing position. The loose cotton blouse falls open enough for those close enough to see she is not wearing a bra. Pressing the wrinkles in her dark maroon slacks, she looks up, steps forward, and extends her hand. Without a word, she shakes hands with Allison, Aydin, and Phil.

Turning to the others waiting, she issues a soft demand.

"I have been waiting all day. Waiting a few more minutes for you to leave is no bother."

The three remaining questioners look to Aydin,

who tilts his head toward the office door. They accept the invitation to leave.

When the office door closes, behind the last of the interlopers, the woman turns to Allison.

"My name is Cathy Lewis. Kristy Lewis is my sister. Aydin, Allison, we met when I was eight at a Fourth of July party in Louisiana."

Allison remains impassive. Aydin's mind is confirming the woman's statement.

*I could be her.*
*Why is she here now?*
*What does she want?*
*Cathy Lewis was too smart for her age.*
*Is this woman Cathy Lewis?*

Phil interrupted the uncomfortable silence.

"Either she's lying, and that dog won't hunt, or she is here to warn us about Kristy."

Cathy smiles and nods affirmation to Phil's statement. Aydin cuts off the discussion.

"I presume you know where we live?"

"Yes."

"Meet us for dinner at 19:00."

Cathy's head bobbed twice, accepting the invitation. Pulling down her sleeve, she covered her hand to pull open the office door.

"Azima?"

*"Yes, Aydin?"*

"Request KTF order dinner for five at the

Trammell house. Make it for 19:00 with two steak and three chicken dishes."

*"Dinner request issued. Is there anything else?"*

"No, thank you, Azima."

*"My pleasure."*


While he is rotating to exit, Phil's question is softly worded.

"Did you teach her to infer context and not confirm common tasks?"

"I added some advanced heuristics to the interpretive sub-processing blocks."

"How does Cathy, if that is her real name, know about the entry pad and its scanning capabilities?"

Allison is through the office door that Aydin is holding open but turns her head to Phil's question and continues to walk, remembering the July 4th party.

"She is Cathy Lewis. It was hard to ignore an eight-year-old who spoke like an adult."

Allison and Phil stop at their cars and look at Aydin. Allison's concern is muted.

"Did you lock the office door?"

"No need, Azima controls access. We can override the lock with your thumbprint or iris scan. We will set you guys up, install your biometrics tomorrow."

Both shrug at Aydin's response and climb into their cars out of the rain.

**SB 125, Aydin's Mercedes, 17:12, Rain and Wind**

*I have seen that car.*

*It is a new BMW 7 Series.*

*It went by the warehouse when we took down the Chinese middleman.*

*It was in the parking lot at Saguaro's when we took down Drakon.*

*It went by on the freeway when the operator recalled the drone to the van.*

*It was driving by when we had the kids on the asphalt in the parking lot.*

*It is following me.*

Reaching over, pressing the correct three icons, Aydin links the communications to Phil and Pops.

*"Aydin?"*

"Phil, stand by for Pops."

*"I'm here, Aydin."*

"I have a tail that has been on me since the warehouse. Mostly, they have been at a distance. This is the closest they have come. I will require some help."

Pops' voice is almost bubbly.

*"Take them down to Wolfensberger Road. Phil, step on it and get behind Aydin. Aydin, make a right on to the first Tessa Drive. We will box them at the top of the second hill, bordered by the trees at the curve's apex.*

"I'll be in the trees on the high ground on the north side."

Aydin merges left, increases his speed,

thinking.

*Pops loves this shit.*

353

# Wolves on Your Heels

***Wolfensberger Road, Aydin's Mercedes, 17:47, Misty***

"*Hey, Aydin?*"

"Yes, Phil?"

"*Does this feel like Chirtok?*"

"No, there are too many trees here. Azima?"

"*Yes, Aydin?*"

"Request KTF and a cleanup crew to our location."

"*Requesting cleanup crew to your location.*"

"Thank you, Azima."

"*My pleasure.*"


Aydin's mind flashes back to the first mission he and Phil were assigned together.

**Bacyak Province 2007, Convoy, 13:17, Hot**

"Aydin, I don't like this."

"Phil, the mission brief was thorough. The road is clear from here to Chirtok."

"I don't like it. I'd feel better if we were on the six and not stuck in the middle of this convoy."

"What difference does it make? On point, on the six, or number four in a line of six. It is random when it pops. This is your first mission, relax."

"It is your second mission, and you get to tell me to relax? Bless your heart. You imagine I don't recognize we are in the shit."

"What are you talking about?"

"What I am talking about is my Spidey Sense is turned up to 11."

"What the fuck does that mean?"

"It means I see things before they happen. I am telling you, we are driving into a shit storm. Hold your horses... What's that?"

"That is the switchback they told us about in the mission brief."

"I can see it is a switchback. They didn't mention it is one-lane with the cliff wall on the right and a drop-off on the left. It is only about 200 meters across that ravine. This is bad. It is so fucking bad."

"RELAX! If you feel it is so bad, slow down. Create space between Martok-3 and us. I'll request opening the spacing."

Keying his mic, Aydin issues the request.

"Martok-6, Martok-4 is requesting additional spacing through the pass."

"Negative, Martok-4, maintain distance. Move through the pass as quickly as possible."

Looking left to his new friend, Aydin reconsidered and realized Phil's sense of imminent danger is accurate. The hair on Aydin's forearms is standing up at the realization of his new friend's ability to know trouble is close.

"Okay, Phil, I feel you."

Aydin reaches across the Humvee and flips the selector to Engine Stop. The Humvee jerked to a halt, narrowly avoiding being rear-ended by Martok-5.

The radio erupted with the Captain screaming.

"Martok-4, what the fuck happened?"

Aydin answers the query.

"Martok-6, the engine died. We are trying to get it re-started. Stand by."

Phil looks right to his new friend with a bent smile.

"Hey Brain, this won't amount to a hill of beans in about five minutes. All you did was piss off the captain."

"Yeah, let him be pissed off. Did you just call me Brain? As in Pinky and the Brain?"

"Yes, and we are fixing to find out if world domination is in our future or an RPG, from across that ravine, ends our global conquest."

Ignoring the captain hollering over the radio, Phil reaches down to flip the selector back to the start position.

Aydin's appreciation for his new partner increased a few notches.

Just as Phil has the Humvee rolling ahead, Martok-3 is rounding the narrow corner. Aydin and Phil watch the APC designated Martok-3, and 13 good men disappear in a cloud of fire, dust, and shrapnel.

Aydin is silent, admiring Phil's cool, calm actions. Before the Humvee has stopped rolling forward, Phil has the reverse engaged. Backing the heavily armored vehicle along the dirt road, Phil's head is swiveling. He is scanning for a space wide enough to spin the vehicle a 180.

Phil does not hear the radio confirmation of Martok-1, 2, and 3 being destroyed.

Finding a spot wide enough, Phil wheels around, putting the Humvee's rear on the right embankment.

Unprepared for the steep action, Aydin is jerked forward when the vehicle's rear wheels rise two feet above the front wheels.

Spinning their Humvee allowed the RPG to whizz by the windscreen. Martok-5 is still backing when the RPG whizzed by the driver's window and flew into the ravine.

The three remaining vehicles were able to turn around and retreat to an area of high ground. The captain called in the airstrike before the three vehicles had turned and fled.

The six remaining Martok mission crewmen watched the SuperCobras scream over the ridge and down into the ravine. Clouds of black smoke rose from the gorge.

The SuperCobras came back over the ridge as the Chinook set down near the Martok mission team.

The Loadmaster jumps out of the Chinook and heads straight to the captain. Hollering, the Loadmaster's tone is commanding over the slow rotor wash.

"We can't get in there, no place to set down. You need to bring them out."

The captain just turns, spins a finger in the air,

and the six remaining Martok mission team members retrieve as many bodies as possible. Each member was thankful for the SuperCobras hovering over the ravine, watching their six.

The bodies retrieved and loaded, the SuperCobras flew over in the missing man formation. The Chinook followed the SuperCobras south. Martok-4 on point for the return to base.

The captain had one thing to say at the close of the debrief. Standing to leave, spinning, and pointing his index finger at Phil, the captain understood what happened.

"It is all in the report. That man saved six lives today."

### *Tessa Drive, Aydin's Mercedes, 18:07, Rain*

"Phil, I hear you. If your Spidey Sense starts acting up, you holler. Pops?"

*"I am in position."*

"Phil?"

*"Five-by-five. Three cars between me and the bogey."*

"Okay, three minutes. Pops, I know where you want me to stop. Give me a 10-meter warning."

*"Roger that, all stop at 10 meters."*

Weaving along Tessa Drive, Aydin's thoughts wander.

*Allison seemed almost happy.*
*She and Pops must have had some quality*

*time.*

*She and I need quality time on a beach.*

*Cathy?*

*How did she know about the sensor on the door control panel?*

*What is her goal?*

*I guess we will find out at dinner.*

*The beach.*

*We need two weeks of sand and adult beverages.*


Pops' voice over the radio yanked Aydin back to the present.

*"Ten meters stop on mark. Three. Two. One. Mark!"*

Aydin spins the heavy Mercedes left, blocking both lanes of the narrow asphalt. The trailing car pulls to a stop in the center of the wet road.

Phil veers left, then pulls right, blocking both lanes with his Sierra.

Aydin is out of his car, half-concealed by the open driver's door. His pistol is drawn. Phil mirrors Aydin from his Sierra.

The black BMW 7 series is new. The dark windows obscure Phil's vision, so he looks to Aydin, who slightly moves his finger twice.

The driver's door and front passenger door open slowly. Two men begin to step out of the vehicle. Aydin and Phil hear Pops through their vehicle's comms connection.

*"I got eyes on. The passenger is holding. If he raises..."*

Pops didn't complete the sentence. The bullet from Pops took out the passenger with a headshot. Brains, skull fragments, and blood spewing across the roof of the German auto.

Using the doorframe to accelerate his egress, the driver attempted to dive and roll away. Phil dropped the driver with a shot to the left thigh. Rushing forward, before the driver could aim, Phil stomped on the driver's hand holding the pistol.

Aydin came around the driver's door and looked down at the man on the ground.

"Hello, Robert."

Phil is noticeably puzzled. Aydin waits for Pops to step out of the tree line and join them. Pops also recognized the man on the ground.

"For fuck sakes, Robert Walker, you were never the sharpest knife in the drawer. Let's make this look like an accident."

Pops begins pulling the dead man to the ditch. Aydin and Phil lift Robert and put him in the cargo bed of the Sierra.

Moving their vehicles to the side of the road, Phil and the BMW moved just as the first car approached, followed by Kermit and his cleanup crew.

The three men return to Robert, who is bleeding onto Phil's new pickup truck. After moving the Mercedes, Pops is waving around the light traffic. Aydin takes up the questions.

"Who is your friend? Sorry, who *was* your friend? Are you crying?"

Robert Walker glares back through tears. Phil pokes the leg wound with a stick he picked up. The pain is intense, his head wrenched back in agony, but Robert speaks.

"Torture? Really?"

Aydin's grin is gnarly.

"Consider it an incentive. Who was your friend?"

"Some guy named Scott, they assigned him to me to help keep an eye on you."

"Why did he come out shooting?"

"This was supposed to be a surveillance-only mission. I did not know he was going to shoot."

"Why are you following me?"

"Because I was told to. Follow you and report everywhere you go and who you talk to."

"Why the drones?"

"What drones?"

Phil, Pops, and Aydin glance at each other, before turning to watch the ambulance pull up. Aydin hollers at the cleanup crew.

"Kermit, is this ambulance one of yours?"

Kermit gives a thumbs up to Aydin's question.

"Robert, these boys will take care of you. No one in the emergency room is going to ask any questions about the GSW. Tomorrow, we'll come to your hospital room and ask a few questions.

"My suggestion to you is for you to have

answers."

Stepping aside, Pops, Phil, and Aydin let the ambulance crew collect Robert. Looking at the blood pooled on his Bedliner, Phil catches Kermit's eye.

Phil pointed to the pickup's bed and received a nod from Kermit, who dispatched one of Sierra's cleanup crew.

Watching the ambulance drive away, Aydin requests Pops join them for dinner.

"Why? I got a porterhouse all marinated and ready for the grill."

Despite his meat-heavy diet and love of a good cigar, Pops is fit, athletic, and just beginning to become grey around the fringes.

"Let it marinate another day. There is someone I want you to meet."

Shaking his head, Pops walks off, grumbling.

"All right, but I will be late. I need to shower first."

Watching Pops walk to his Sierra, which is parked on the side road, Phil chimes.

"He won't be late."

"No, he won't be late."


**Trammell House, Formal Dining Room, 19:27, Rain**

Allison and Miranda have received the delivered food and staged it in the kitchen. Cathy and Pops arrive simultaneously. Pops seems unaware of who the young woman is.

After cleaning up, Phil comes in from the guest

house while Aydin enters from the hallway. No one accepts it is a coincidence Phil and Aydin arrive at the same time from opposite directions.

Pouring the wine, Pops stops and stares at Cathy. She is wearing a lovely blue blouse and coordinated slacks. Her dreads are pulled back into a tight bundle.

"Cathy Lewis?"

"Yes, Pops."

"Last time I saw you, we were at the party."

"I was eight."

"You were never eight."

"No, I don't suppose I was."

Allison interrupts.

"Family style. Take a plate, fill it, and head to the dining room."

The men stand aside, the ladies load up first, then follow with overloaded plates.

## Trammell House, Formal Dining Room, 20:47, Drizzle

"Enough of the chit-chat. Why are you here?"

Allison appears offended by the blunt question from her husband.

"Aydin!"

Cathy defends Aydin.

"Allison, it is a fair question. I am here because I always considered Aydin a friend, and I wanted to warn him."

Allison is focused on Cathy. The others watch

and learn while Cathy and Allison continue.

"Friend?"

"Yes, when I was little, Aydin was the only one who would talk to me. After the party, he and I stayed connected."

"I remember, he liked talking to you. Warn?"

"Yes, warn. Robert and Kristy…"

Sipping her wine, Cathy hesitates, allowing Allison to become impatient.

"What about Robert and Kristy?"

"Robert is five, and Kristy is four years older than you and Aydin. They expected to be the leaders, the A-Team, coming out of The Program. But they knew you and Aydin had taken over the leadership roles."

"Wait, they are two years older than us."

"Not true. Our parents doctored their birth certificates and held them back. Robert and Kristy are not Aydin smart, but they entered school older, with a substantial mental and intellectual advantage. Of course, with the benefit of age, they rose to the top of their class.

"It was not enough. When The Program was dissolved, Robert and Kristy could not stop talking about how you and Aydin backstabbed them and took over."

"But we never took over anything. We went our separate ways."

"Robert and Kristy don't see it that way. They see you two as the enemy."

Allison turns her head on an angle, eyeing her husband. She sees he is somewhere else.

*If Robert is only a tail, where is Kristy?*
*Who was Scott?*
*Who is pointing them at us, and why?*
*How come Cathy knows so much?*

"Aydin!"
"Sorry, Hon, I was thinking."
"Yeah, we get it. Answer the question."
"What question?"
Allison pivots back to Cathy with a look requesting she repeat the question.
"Aydin, at the party in Louisiana, did you tell Kristy that Robert hit on you?"

*Scott was Robert's partner.*
*That explains the tears.*

"Yes, I told her, and he did."
Phil's question is unusually sensitive, coming from him.
"Robert was seventeen, almost eighteen, and hitting on a fifteen-year-old boy?"
Cathy's simple response told everyone the sad truth.
"Robert had and still has many problems. Being gay is not one of them."
Angling back to Allison, Cathy continued.

"That is why she hates you. Robert lies to everyone, and Kristy did not believe he is gay or bisexual. She believed, back then, that he will grow out of the phase. Without Robert being the perfect husband, Kristy's unspoiled life has warts."

The dinner party waits for Aydin to return from his thoughts.

*Aw, fuck snacks.*
*This will not end well.*
*Wait!*
*Kristy!*
*She must be behind the surveillance.*
*That has to be it: Kristy wants a perfect, unspoiled life.*

"Cathy, does Kristy work?"

"Yes, for The Service."

"Beyond that, does she have any other income?"

"I don't think so."

"How does she live? Is it a normal life, or does it feel like she has more than a GS salary can support?"

"I figured she was neck-deep in credit card debt. You don't think?"

"I do. Has Kristy ever mentioned her role at The Service?"

Cathy's long, contemplative thoughts result in a simple sentence.

"She mentioned reporting to Katherine once."

"Moms? She reported to Allison's mother?"

"Maybe."

Instantaneously, Pops, Phil, and Aydin look at each other. They have reached the same conclusion.

"A couple of more questions. You learned Bryan and Marina adopted Miranda. Do you know if Kristy spoke with Marina?"

"I don't know. Kristy went off to college when I was 14."

"One more question. In the past few years, did you see or hear, Moms, Marina, and Kristy talking?"

Leaning her empty wine glass forward, Pops refilled it. Leaning back, holding the wine glass to her lips but not sipping, Cathy is remembering, considering. A long silence ended with one word.

"Yes."

# Kill all the Wolves



"Azima."

*"Yes, Aydin?"*

"Search the list titled Service Directory for anyone with the given name: Scott."

*"I do not understand the request."*

"The given name is another way to refer to a person's first name."

*"Scanning. There are no names on the list with the given name of Scott. There is a Trevor Scott Martin. Designation: Special Operative."*

"Is there a date of birth or age designation for the Trevor Scott Martin entry?"

*"No. There are dates for college graduation and joining the Service."*

"What are those dates?"

*"Trevor Scott Martin graduated from the University of Waxahachie in January. He joined the Service in February."*

"Graduated in what year?"

*"This year."*

"Thank you, Azima."

*"My pleasure."*


Allison is watching the coal train lumbering along, parallel to the highway when she asks a question.

"Even though you explicitly asked for a given name, she knew to ask for clarification and to expand the search. She inferred to look for other dates when she couldn't find a date of birth. You were testing her code?"

"I was not testing, but it was a good result."

"In the wrong hands, she could be dangerous."

Aydin nods in agreement but remains silent. He is focused on the sheets of rain beginning to flow across the highway.

"Will you kill him? Is that why you brought the single-shot .410?"

A long, uncomfortable silence precedes Aydin's gentle response.

"It depends on what he says."

### *Castle Bluff Hospital, Patient Room, 10:01, Clear*

Aydin and Allison are standing next to the hospital bed, on Robert's left, with their backs to the door. Pops is standing on the right of the bed, his back to the window.

Masked as a visit to an injured friend, Aydin opens the interrogation of Robert Walker.

"I am sorry about Trevor."

Tears welling, Robert's response is terse.

"He liked to be called Scott."

"You have always liked them young."

Visibly stealing himself, Robert remains quiet and stares at the ceiling. Aydin's thoughts return to the Fourth of July picnic in Louisiana.

## *BUFF Event Center 2002, Men's Restroom, 11:21, Warm*

"Come on, show me."

"No. Robert, leave me alone."

"Aydin, no one will know."

"I don't care. Now move and let me leave."

"Not until you show me."

Realizing Robert is bigger and stronger, fifteen-year-old Aydin decides to take the initiative. The toe of his right Converse Chuck Taylor All-Star landed squarely on Robert's crotch.

Aydin emotionlessly watches Robert grab his groin, fall onto the concrete, and curl into the fetal position. He continued to hold his groin, moaning. Aydin stepped around and exited the restroom with a warning.

"If you ever try to hurt me again, I will kill you."

## *Castle Bluff Hospital, Patient Room, 10:11, Clear*

"Robert, I am giving you one chance. You have been following us. That means you recognize I am not making an empty threat.

"Do you remember that day, in the bathroom in Louisiana? The promise I made."

Robert refuses to answer.

"Of course, you remember. That kick in the nuts was painful. You are about to learn a new level of pain."

Pausing, Aydin notices Robert is staring at the

ceiling, attempting to remain composed.

"I am sorry about Trevor. You should not have let someone so young jump out, ready to shoot. Gun battles never end well. I will give you one chance to help me. Who assigned you to follow us, and what were your orders?"

With a scowl and glaring from Allison to Pops, ending on Aydin, Robert sealed his fate.

"Fuck you. They will kill you and her before they take the code. You think you are so smart. I was number one in the Program. Me! You took it from me. I will drink a toast when they kill you. If they don't kill you, I will."

Allison moved to stand in the open doorway with her back to the room.

Robert's face wrinkled, sterner, and colder at Allison standing in the doorway.

"You won't get away with it."

Aydin's response is soft and pointed.

"Kristy is your handler. You would do anything for her to make up for breaking her heart."

The tiny twitch in Robert's neck told Aydin he poked the soft, painful truth. Looking over her shoulder from the doorway, Allison waited for Aydin to look at her. When he looked, she checked both ways along the corridor, turned back, and nodded positively.

Pops did not need the signal. He inserted the syringe into the IV port. Robert's eyes flickering, his body convulsing, was the signal for Allison to dash into the hallway and begin screaming.

"NURSE!"

### *DTC, Conference Room, 14:11, Rain and Sleet*

Phil and Cathy are in the conference room when Aydin and Allison arrive. Two people are standing in the lobby, waiting.

A bag of cold burritos is on the table at Aydin's spot. A grilled-chicken salad at Allison's place. Iced teas with no ice remaining are growing warm. Unwrapping the cold burrito, waiting for his PC to boot, Aydin asks Phil about the guests.

"How long have they been waiting?"

"They were here when I arrived at 09:00."

"What do they want?"

"I have no idea."

After entering his password, opening the email app, burrito in hand, Aydin leaves his PC for the lobby.

"There is no IPO. We are not hiring. There is no information. A competitor issued the press release to create precisely what we have here: People looking for a piece of something that does not exist."

The two men appeared to be mid-twenties, rail-thin, unkept college students. When the one on the left looked to the other, Aydin realized they were together. The taller, skinnier guest on the right spoke for the duo.

"We are not here to ask for anything. We are here to offer something."

The statement from the guest causes Phil and

Allison to rise and join Aydin in the lobby. Phil, picking up and handing Aydin his second burrito. Cathy remained seated in the conference room, listening.

Peeling the foil from half of the tasty delight, not looking up, Aydin issues the request.

"I'm listening."

"We did our homework. You are working on an advanced AI. We have been working on a similar tool and might have something that can help you. I am Teo Timmons, but people call me T-Square. That is Amp Willcox. I don't know why he is called Amp. We are graduate students at CDU."

Interrupting with a mouthful of spicy chicken, Aydin is impatient.

"Get to the point."

"Have you heard of Game Theory? Of course, you have heard of Game Theory. Anyway, Amp and me built an algorithm that functions non-linearly."

Ignoring Teo's point about non-linear computational functionality, Phil interjects.

"Amp and *I* built an algorithm."

Teo looked at Phil, skewed his head in annoyance before looking back to Aydin, and continuing.

"We call the algorithm, FourSight, F-O-U-R-S-I-G-H-T."

Crushing the paper napkin into the foil wrapper, Aydin tossed it to the trash can next to the reception desk. He stood tall and dismissed the pair.

"Let me guess, *four* because that is the limit of

variant outputs to your algorithm. You applied the limitation because you had two problems. First, your code is shitty and consumed all of the processing power on the supercomputer. You pissed off a lot of scientists when their processes ran out of memory and crashed.

"Second, your code does not have the distinguishing capability to stop looking for new variant outputs. You can create an infinite number of outcomes but cannot select one outcome over the other. All results are equal. Therefore, all results are invalid.

"Finally, you believe our AI can control your FourSight and heuristically select worthwhile outcomes."

Stunned, Amp speaks for the first time.

"How did you know about the processes crashing?"

Grinning widely, Aydin ignored the question before eyeing Teo, expecting a response.

"Mister Trammel, you have that all correct. Obviously, you have access to the supercomputer. You are one of the classified remote users. But that doesn't mean we can't help you. We can help you with the AI and non-linear analysis. You can help us by removing the limitations.

"Together, it is a win-win."

Disgusted and rolling his eyes, Aydin closes the discussion.

"I was listening until you decided to quote

stupid business journal jargon. Fuck you and your *win-win*. Get out."

"Mister Trammel, please, we need your help, and we can help you."

"Teo, what makes you imagine I need your help?"

"Because we have code that produces non-linear results."

"Teo, Amp, about five months ago, you made a mistake."

Amp is fidgeting, looking at his friend for answers.

"Mistake? What mistake?"

"You posted a snippet of your core on the *AI Is The Future* forum, in the subforum, *Break This Code*."

Teo's eyes narrowed. Aydin continued.

"You should have read the fine print of the forum. Everything posted is public domain."

Aydin stopped, waiting. Amp filled the silence.

"He has our code."

Responding to Amp but looking at Teo, Aydin's tone is academic.

"No, we built *our* code using the seed in the crap you posted. I understood and refined your base. Our code works. Your code sucks."

Teo is indignant.

"We are going to sue you. Copyright infringement. Theft of intellectual property. Corporate espionage. Anything we can think of, we are going to sue you into the dark ages."

Almost laughing at the outburst, Aydin moots the tension.

"One, you have no money for the number of lawyers it would take to sue us. Two, you are not a corporation. Three, I'll pay Amp to side with us and shut you down before you start. Four, you are free to leave now. With a promise..."

Amp lights up.

"How much?"

Over Phil's chuckling, Aydin continued.

"Teo, you have learned a life lesson. Take it and run, with a promise. If our code becomes commercially viable, I guarantee you and Amp will receive something. You promise to leave now and never come back. If I hear or see you again, my offer is off the table."

Amp remains intrigued.

"How much?"

Simultaneously, Teo and Aydin respond.

"Amp, shut up."

Agreeing, Teo grabs Amp's upper arm and turns him toward the office door.

"Deal."

Before the door closes, the trio hears Teo's response to Amp's question.

"Millions Amp. Millions. Now shut up and drive."

Phil snickered and chimed while he followed Allison, who trailed Aydin, back into the conference room.

"That Teo, he might be college smart, but he

don't know shit from Shinola. Amp could throw himself on the ground and miss."

Sitting, Aydin looked to Cathy.

"I could look it up, but I am sure you have a direct line to Kristy.

"I have her private cell phone number if that is what you are asking."

# Jigsaw Puzzles

*DTC, Conference Room, 15:21, Lessening Rain*

The conference room phone rang, startling everyone except Aydin. Allison, Phil, and Cathy watch Aydin press the green button, answering the call.

"Fírinne, how may I help you?"

"Hello, Aydin."

"Hello, Kristy. Thank you for returning my call. I am sorry about Robert."

"No, you are not sorry, but I don't care. I am past that. What do you want?"

"I want to meet. Anywhere you like, I'm buying."

"With the money you stole from the Chinese, you damned well better be buying."

"How about Saguaro at 19:00?"

"Why, so you can blow my head off like Drakon? How about The Gray Dog café at 19:00?"


*Bold.*
*Kirsty is making a power statement.*
*She wants me to believe she has the high ground with information and power.*


Phil lit up at the name of one of his favorite diners. Alison and Cathy are both shaking their heads in the negative when Aydin responds.

"The Gray Dog café, 19:00. You are closer. Get

a table in the back, away from the windows."

"Are you afraid something bad might happen to the wonder boy Aydin Matthew Trammell?"

"Not afraid but not stupid either, 19:00."

"You and Allison, no one else."

"Allison and me, 19:00."

Aydin disconnected the call.

Allison and Phil remain quiet, letting the anticipated conversation between Cathy and Aydin unfold. Cathy does not wait.

"She is setting you up."

"I am aware."

"Then why are you meeting her on her terms?"

Aydin continues to focus on Cathy.

"Azima?"

*"Yes, Aydin?"*

"Initiate comms protocol Alpha-Three."

*"Initiating comms protocol Alpha-Three."*

"Thank you, Azima."

*"My pleasure."*

"Why am I meeting her on her terms? Because I am going to shift the paradigm and take control of the meeting."

Her right eyebrow arched high, Cathy is intrigued.

"Oh?"

Looking down, Aydin reads the pop-up from Azima on his PC.

*"Protocol Alpha-Three confirmed."*

Lifting his head to Phil, Aydin receives a nod of confirmation.

"Phil, the single-shot .410 is in my car. Try not to hurt the drone's internals. Let's take a look at that drone."

Cathy's and Allison's heads spin toward the window and stop, focusing on the drone hovering above the trees. The drone's camera pointed at the Fírinne office windows. Phil stands to complete Aydin's request.

Steely-eyed, Aydin summarizes the situation for Cathy.

"I always play by my rules because my rules keep us alive. No exceptions. Our AI code, coupled with the automated targeting code, is one of our two big problems."

Phil stopped, smirked, commented, then exited the conference room.

"Only two?"

Aydin continued.

"When the AI is ready, we will sell it to the highest bidder and give it to DARPA. Hell, they probably already have it and are waiting for us to refine it."

The muted sound of the small shotgun turned Cathy and Allison again. The three watched Phil run over and grabbed the downed drone.

"DARPA?"

Mildly surprised, DARPA is a new term to Cathy. Aydin chalks it up to naïve Millennials.

*The American education system creates automatons.*

*No one thinks deeply anymore.*

*No one reads the news.*

*Real news.*

*Not Twitter and Facebook.*

*Real fucking, unbiased news like it used to be every day at six o'clock.*

*Fucking TikTok and Instagram and reality TV dumbing down America.*

*We need more real news with facts and impartial reporting.*

*Everyone should understand, the American government provides almost unlimited funds to secret projects.*

*How can an adult not know that?*

*Fuck it.*

"DARPA: Defense Advanced Research Projects Agency. Black funding for defense and military research. They will get the targeting code also. We are not selling the targeting code.

"As soon as we sell the AI code, the corporate espionage games will stop."

Allison disagreed.

"Why will they stop?"

"Okay, they won't stop, but they will stop trying to intimidate or kill us to get the AI code."

Aydin stops and points toward the parking lot.

The women turn around for the third time. The trio sees Phil stop on the asphalt, just short of the sidewalk. He holds the drone in one hand and the small shotgun in the other. The drone's camera is pivoting up toward Phil's face.

Phill tosses the drone onto the sidewalk, upside down, the camera begins to swing left and right. The trio in the conference room see Phil talking to the drone but does not hear the words.

Phil uses the butt of the .410 to smash the camera lens and plastic actuator housing.

Bending to lift the drone, beaming a Cheshire Cat grin at the windows, Phil returns to the conference room.

Placing the drone and the 4-10 on the conference table, Phil takes his seat.

Aydin resumes his summary while beginning to dismantle the drone.

"We sell a version of the AI code. Take a month off to go and play in the sand. Selling the AI code and giving the full version with targeting to DARPA will solve problem one."

Stopping to pull the SD-Card from the drone, Aydin turns back to his PC. After several keystrokes, he slides the SD-Card into his PC.

"I was saying, problem one solved, and we get some beach time."

Phil does not look up with his comment.

"Assuming Kristy does not do something stupid."

Aydin continues without a retort to Phil's dark comment.

"Kirsty is now the source of problems two and three. Problem two is the hole we put in the heroin cartel's supply chain by taking out Drakon and Arnold, and Moms."

Phil continues to focus on his PC but comments.

"Technically, we took out Drakon. Someone else took out Arnold and Moms."

"True, and it looks like it was Kristy. She probably had Robert and Trevor-Scott do it, which brings us to problem number three and Kristy. The Program."

Aydin stops talking, looking at his PC. Cathy and Phil suppose he is studying the SD-Card. Allison understands. Aydin is somewhere else.

## Flat River Woods 2005, Secluded Alcove, 14:31, Warm

"Kristy, why did you bring me here?"

"I wanted to be alone and talk to you. Aydin, do you ever think about us?"

"Us?"

"Yes, us. You and me."

"No. I never see you. We only see each other at these picnics. What are you talking about?"

"Our parents have this all planned. I am supposed to marry Robert. Chrissy Nelson will marry Matt Thomas. You and Allison. They have a plan. But, Aydin, what about you and me?"

Kristy has moved to stand over Aydin, who is reclining on his elbows. She is rubbing her hands along the inside of her thighs. The older girl is applying a full-court press to get Aydin's agreement.

"We could get together, have some fun, and do some real work."

"Work? What are you talking about?"

"The Program. You and me. We could lead the Program."

*Lie. Lie. Lie.*
*Dad said someone might try to recruit me.*
*Keep her talking.*
*Learn what she wants.*

"What Program?"

"You don't know about The Program? Your father runs The Program. We are all part of it. Everyone at the picnic is part of the Program. I don't believe you didn't know."

*I am not telling her I know about anything.*
*How does she know?*
*Get information.*
*Dad will want the information.*

"What are you talking about?"

"Our parents have this all planned. We are supposed to grow up, become important scientists, and take over The Program. That's it, simple."

*She knows about Robert.*
*She is looking for a new plan.*
*She is afraid.*


"You know about Robert?"

"What about Robert?"

"He is gay."

Kristy throws herself on the ground, next to Aydin. She is crying before her butt hits the ground, speaking through the sobs.

"How?"

"He hit on me a couple of hours ago."

"Is that why he had to go to the hotel?"

"Yes, and put ice on his nuts. He would not take no for an answer."

"Robert has problems. Real problems. You don't want to know what he does to me. Aydin, what am I going to do?"

"What do you mean? You will graduate in the spring. Then college. You will meet someone and live a good life."

"No. I mean, what am I going to do without The Program?"

"I don't understand. Why do you need The Program?"

"Because without The Program, we lose everything?"

"Everything? I don't understand. Kristy, you are not helping. What are you talking about?"

"I heard my parents talking a few months ago. I told them I wanted to go to college without Robert. They freaked out. I heard them talking. They agreed, if Robert and I didn't stay together, The Program would cut us loose, and our parents would lose their funding."

*Aw, fuck snacks.*
*I can't let her leave thinking like this.*
*I have to tell her.*

"Kristy, The Program is ending. The funding has been cut-off, which is why my dad arranged this picnic. He wanted to tell everyone in person. They are discussing it right now."

"You *do* know about the Program!"

"Yes."

"What will happen?"

"I don't know, but we will be okay. My dad has a plan, I think."

"But, without Robert..."

"Here's what you will do. You tell Robert to keep his secret. Also, no more of anything with you. Tell him you and I will keep his secret, but he has to do whatever you say. My guess is: He knows he hurt you and will follow the plan.

"If he comes out, his dad will disown him, and he will lose everything. His dad will take away college, no support, nothing.

"You keep moving forward. My dad will keep

The Program running for as long as possible. Do whatever your parents tell you to do.

"If you need anything, call me."

"Aydin? The Program is about more than creating super-smart people."

"Let's head back. Do whatever your parents tell you. Promise me. You will talk to Robert."

"I will talk to Robert. But you have to help me."

"Kristy, I will help you."

### DTC, Conference Room, 15:21, Lessening Rain

The group hears a car door close over the speakerphone, followed by the office door chime buzzing, surprising everyone in the conference room. Aydin stepped out of the conference room to open the office door. The others hear him greet the woman they see standing on the sidewalk.

"Hello, Kristy."

# Start With The Edges

**DTC, Conference Room, 17:21, Clearing**

"This conversation is a dead end. Kristy, unless you open up and tell us what you want, I suggest we head out and get something to eat."

"Aydin, what I want is to talk to you alone."

Allison sees her husband go somewhere mentally.

*Kristy is afraid.*
*She wants something.*
*What does she want?*
*She wants me!*
*Aw, fuck snacks.*
*She is jealous of Allison.*
*She never liked Allison.*
*How did she get hooked up with the Service?*
*Didn't she get a degree in English Lit, or Art Appreciation, or something?*
*What am I missing?*
*Revenge!*
*I knew it!*
*I thought the revenge was for breaking the drug cartel's supply chain.*
*It was always Kristy hating Allison.*

"You guys go-ahead to the house. I will meet you there later. Kristy and I are heading to The Gray

Dog Café."

Allison and Phil start to object, but Aydin held up a palm. He spoke with unblinking eyes directed to Kristy.

"It is okay. We wouldn't want to disappoint Kristy's handler. Would we?"

Not waiting for a response, Aydin closes his PC, packs up, and begins to exit.

"Phil, take Allison home. Cathy, do whatever you want. Kristy, we will take my car, I'll drop you back here, or you can Uber back for your car after dinner."

## NB 125, Aydin's Mercedes, 17:51, Colder, Misty

"Aydin, we will be too early."

"Are you worried? Will we be too early for your friend?"

"No, I suppose not."

She is sitting upright in the front passenger seat, her head turned left, and Kristy's tone is businesslike.

"You abandoned me."

*Oh fuck, here it comes.*
*Let her vent.*

"What are you talking about?"

"That day in the woods. You promised to help me. You never helped me. For fifteen years, I have been alone. That fucking Robert was no help. He used

389

me to hide. Good riddance.

"Aydin, The Program is still running. Do you know that? Do you know who runs The Program?"

*What the fuck?*
*Oh shit.*
*I missed something.*
*Something big.*

"I didn't realize The Program was on-going, but I am not surprised. Do you understand the true goal of The Program?"

"I have an idea."

*She doesn't know.*

"Tell me about your idea."

"They designed The Program with two goals. One, to create super-smart people by immersing the subjects in an enhanced environment. Nurture intellect starting in the womb, continuing through adolescence. Two, direct the product, the super-smart people, into the spy game. Create and train domestic and international espionage and counter-espionage agents."

*She doesn't know the whole story.*

"There is more."

"More?"

Aydin's tone is flat and even.

"Some of us, a select few, were trained in the art of assassination."

Kristy turned her head forward, staring and the lines on the highway, considering the facts.

*She is figuring it out.*

Kristy states her conclusion.

"They knew about Robert."

"Of course, they knew. They monitored everything about us all the time."

Learning, she continues softly.

"They used the cartel's drug money to fund The Program?"

"They did."

"How did they do it?"

"We are about to find out. Do you know who your handler is? Will your handler meet us?"

"I do not. Everything is done through an online portal. Aydin?"

*Oh no.*

Aydin turns his head to find Kristy looking at him with tears running down her cheeks. She speaks delicately.

"I realize why you never helped me."

"Why?"

"Because you spent all your time trying to keep

it all together. Everyone in The Program was, is, trying to keep it together. Every day is a struggle. That is why they all killed themselves. I understand why you stayed away.

"You love Allison. You two kept each other balanced. All these years, like you helping Allison, Robert helped me. When I told him about you and me talking, he agreed to help me. He wanted to kill you."

"I am aware."

"Why did you put him on us?"

"I didn't."

*Not Kristy!*

*Fuck. Fuck. Fuck.*

*I have spent weeks tracking the wrong paths.*

*I am missing something.*

*Who?*

*Who the fuck is playing me like an overstretched snare drum?*

"We are here. Kristy, do whatever I tell you. This is a setup, and we are in trouble. Your handler has been manipulating us from the get-go. If you want to stay alive, do whatever I tell you.

"We are a little more than one block from the diner. Stay as close to the building as possible. I will be on your left shoulder. Don't stop walking. Get inside as quickly as possible."

Kristy rocked an agreement to Aydin's instructions and opened the passenger door.

The block and a half walk was tense, even using a quick step.

Standing inside the second door, they see one person is waiting on a wooden chair.

### The Gray Dog Cafe, Rear Booth, 18:41, Clearing

"Hello, Miranda."

"Aydin? What are you doing here?"

"I could ask you the same."

"I received a message. Dinner here at 19:00. Who is this?"

"You don't recognize her?"

"No."

"This is Kristy Lewis."

"The Kristy Lewis?"

"Yes. This is a setup. Kristy, why did you pick this place?"

"I was told, in an email, this is your favorite place."

"That is wrong. Someone has crossed their facts. Phil loves this place. The question is, do we eat and wait for the attempt, or do we run?"

Miranda's voice cracks.

"Attempt?"

"Yes, someone got us together to take us all out. We run. Miranda, where is your car?"

"At the station, I Uber'd over here."

"Okay, my car is on the next block. Stay next to the building, in a single line. The high ground is that building to the right. The car is on our left. Miranda,

393

you go first."

The trio breaks into a run when they hear the gunshot. They practically dive into the car. Aydin has the engine running and pulling a 180 before the automatic door locks engage.

### *SB Broadway, Aydin's Mercedes, Clear*

Miranda, in the right rear seat, responding to a phone text.

**Phil**: Cover Kristy when exiting the car. Confirm.

**Me**: Confirmed. Danger?

**Phil**: Worse than a hair baked in a biscuit.

**Me**: Understood.

### *Trammel House, 19:41, Clear*

Pulling into the garage, Miranda is out of the car before it stops. Her pistol is out of her purse, pointed at the front passenger door. Phil opens the door leading from the house to the garage. He is pointing his pistol at the windshield and Kristy.

Aydin calmly exits the car and steps to the front, waving for Kristy to step out of the vehicle.

Slowly opening the door, she steps out and puts her hands on the roof. Phil steps around the open car door, creating a direct line to the target.

Miranda does not take her eyes from Kristy but asked Phil a question.

"How did you know I was in the car?"

Phil ignores the question, and Aydin hollers.

"Allison?"

Allison opens the door and stands on the first step, allowing the entry door to close behind her. Reaching over, she flips on the lights and pushes the glowing button, closing the overhead door.

Aydin begins an interrogation.

"Kristy, you are the only person I have seen today, a cold, windy, rainy day, wearing a skirt. Do not move."

Allison catches Miranda's eye. Leaning and tilting her head toward Kristy, Allison is silently requesting Miranda frisk Kristy. Miranda responds with a negative head shake.

Allison steps down, walks around, and begins frisking Kristy. Pulling up the shorter woman's skirt with her left hand, Allison reaches around with her right hand. She finds the pistol on Kristy's inner left thigh. Strapped much too high to be comfortable, Allison's hand has to become intimate with pantie-less Kristy to remove the weapon from its holster.

Kristy's snide comment goes unanswered.

"Oooh, we should do this more often."

Allison steps back before moving to the front of the vehicle. Aydin continues his interrogation.

"You had me fooled for a moment. I believed you when you said you did not order Robert to follow us.

"You put him on us because you knew he would not control himself. He'd either kill me, or I would kill him. You hated him for what he did to you when you were teenagers. Either way, you win.

"Kristy, you may have missed something important. But we will get back to that later. Why were you going to kill Miranda?"

"Isn't it obvious?"

"Indulge me."

"How long before Pops arrives?"

*Fuck!*
*She has a lot of information about us.*
*What the fuck is happening?*

"In a few minutes. Answer the question."

"I'll wait for Pops."

"Miranda, get some wire-ties."

### Trammel House, 20:01, Clear

Kristy is wire-tied at the wrists and ankles. Sitting on the leather sofa, she seems unconcerned.

Pops enters from the garage. Looking around, Phil is pointing a pistol at him. Aydin grasps command.

"Sit down."

Pops responds to the gun pointed at him as he has every time someone points a gun in his direction: He ignores the threat, sits in the chair to Kristy's left, and begins speaking. Internally, Aydin admires the old warrior.

*He is so fucking cool.*
*Pops loves this shit.*

"I was worried she'd point you at me. This bitch has been a fucking pain since she was five. Do you know what she did when she was young? I will tell you. She broke Albert's foot with an iron. Everyone said it was an accident, but Albert and I knew better."

"Is that why my father has a slight limp?"

"Yes, Aydin, she crushed the bones on the left side of his left foot. Didn't you, bitch?"

Kristy remains unphased and unresponsive.

Pops looks up to Aydin.

"She said she wanted you here before she answered any questions. Why was she waiting for you?"

"Because I have the truth of who she is and why she is here."

Aydin and Allison look at each other, then turn to Miranda, who shrugs. Aydin looks down at the woman he judges is the missing piece.

*It must be her.*

*Who else could it be?*
*Pops is not the missing link.*
*It must be her.*

Phil catches Aydin, gently tapping his finger on his jeans. Phil moves closer to Pops.

"Kristy, indulge me. Why were you going to kill Miranda?"

Kristy answers, with a face that is happy to tell a story,

"Because I can. Fuck her."

Looking up and over to Allison, Kristy continues.

"Fuck you, too. All of you bitches. I was first, and I will be first. No red-haired step-child or bimbo orphan will take what is mine."

Phil interrupts.

"You're so fulla shit your eyes are brown. Bitch, you better start telling us something we can believe, or it will get ugly like ten miles of bad road."

Kirsty's snarky comment is intended to antagonize Phil.

"What did the idiot say?"

Aydin held up a hand, keeping Phil from moving at the insult.

"He said he doesn't believe you, and if you don't start telling the truth, it will become painful for you."

"Pops, you can stop acting. This is a show for me."

Pops leaps up and, in one motion, backhands

Kristy across the face. Phil Grabs Pops and pulls him away.

Sitting straight up, blood trickling from a busted lip, Kristy's tone is jovial.

"Is that all you got, old man? Robert hit harder than that when he was 14."

Pops holds up both hands, surrendering before he speaks.

"Aydin, Allison, Miranda, what you are unfamiliar with is what happened to Robert and Kristy. They failed the psych and intelligence exams. Over and over. Their parents kept at it. They refused to believe both Robert and Kristy failed the Program for the same reason: The psych exams."

Pops stopped speaking, took a deep breath, looked to the slider, and waves in the man no one noticed was standing on the patio.

# Fill In The Image

"Dad?"

Hugging Allison, shaking hands, Albert Clark Trammell acted like no big deal that he appeared at his son's house. Greeting each person, he called out their name, confirming an unspoken bond.

"Hi, son. Allison. Phil. Brandon. Miranda, Kristy."

"Azima?"

*"Yes, Aydin?"*

"Why was I not alerted there was an intruder?"

*"Pops asked me to keep it quiet. He wanted to surprise you."*

"Thank you, Azima."

*"My pleasure."*

Phil's tone is harsh.

"Fucking-A, we will fix *that* little flaw. That artificial bitch better not keep secrets from us."

Aydin's response seemed offhanded but was on-point as he looked from Allison to Pops.

"Now you appreciate why the AI code is so dangerous. Back to the topic. Dad, why are you here? What do you have to do with Kristy?"

"Did you scan her DNA?"

*Fuck!*

*He knows about the entry pad on the office door. What else does he know?*

*Everything.*
*Dad always knows everything.*

"How do you know about that?"

"I am familiar with a lot of your work. Who do you think Kermit works for?"

*Holy mother-fucking, fuck snacks.*
*This has all been an effort to source information for the Program.*
*What information?*
*What is Dad looking to find?*
*No wonder I was lost.*
*I never looked in the right direction.*

Kristy interrupted the father and son.
"DNA?"
Albert smiled at the bound woman.
"When you rang the buzzer and the Fírinne office, it collected a sample of your DNA. Azima..."
*"Yes, Albert?*
"Nothing, Azima. Thank you."
*"My pleasure."*

With a crooked smile, Albert chastised his son.

"You have got to fix that. As I was saying, the buzzer panel collected a DNA sample that the AI sent off for analysis. But we will get back to that in a few minutes.

"Brandon was telling you about the troubles we

had with Robert, Kristy, and their parents.

"At first, Robert failed the intelligence exams. But they worked hard at tutoring him. Eventually, he met the minimum scores. The psych exams uncovered Robert's sexuality when he was about 11 or 12. Despite what you would think, his sexuality was a plus to the Program. Unfortunately, Robert was heavily influenced by Kristy. He lost his way and, eventually, stopped the tutors. When he failed the annual intelligence assessment, he and his parents were dropped from the Program. It was no matter. Robert failed the year the Program's funding was cut. He was already off-the-rails when we all met in Louisiana that summer."

Pausing, Albert waved to the chairs, allowing everyone who desired to take a seat. Everyone remained standing. Aydin, Phil, and Pops, silently and strategically covering everyone in the room from the triangle they formed. Aydin's father waved a dismissive gesture, sat in the overstuffed leather chair to Kristy's left, and continued.

"Kristy passed the intelligence assessments easily, but she failed the psych exams. Her psych profile reflected a high-intellect with a strong bias toward violence and a narcissistic need for control. She broke my foot when I went to warn her parents. Just before her tenth birthday, Kristy was supposed to be in her room studying. She had snuck down and was hiding in the pantry while her father, mother, and I chatted in the kitchen."

Snapping his fingers, Aydin barked.

"Hold up. Azima?"

*"Yes, Aydin?"*

"Terminate comms protocol Alpha-Three."

*"Comms protocol Alpha-Three terminated."*

"Thank you, Azima."

*"My pleasure."*

Silent until this moment, Miranda asked meekly.

"Comms protocol Alpha-Three?"

Phil answered his lover.

"Comms protocol Alpha-Three connects Aydin, Pops, and Me on all of our devices. That is how Pops knew to cover you at the Gray Dog Café and I knew you were in Aydin's car."

Pops bent over, face to face with Kristy.

"She's dead."

Kristy turned away from the cigar breath inches from her face. Allison queried.

"Dad, who is dead?"

"Her lover, the patrol woman. Juanita Menéndez. But don't' worry, Kristy, the Denver police found the track marks on Juanita's feet and the empty Dime Bags. They figure she shot herself over the loss of her lover. She is just another lousy cop with an addiction, a broken heart, and a drug deal gone wrong. They will search her apartment, and guess what they will find? Never mind, I will tell you. They will discover Katherine had been living there, on-and-off, for a couple of years.

"Katherine thought I was too stupid or no longer cared. Both are wrong. I knew what she was doing and with whom. Katherine liked sharing Juanita with you. She figured Juanita's relationship with you would eventually pay off with information."

Pops stopped when Albert stood, stretched, and stepped closer to his decades-old friend. Pops gently put his hand on the shoulder of his friend of forty years. Pops moved away from Kristy while Albert returned to the overstuffed chair.

"Back to my story. Kristy was a young girl, but she understood the implications when I told her parents that she would need intense counseling. She would not be permitted to see Robert.

"She lost it and came running from the pantry, holding up the iron. She'd have hit me in the head if her father had not tripped her. She toppled over, and the iron crushed my foot."

Kristy added some color commentary.

"I remember that day. Good times."

Ignoring the comment, Albert continued.

"Azi… The AI has checked Kristy's DNA. But we already knew the results: Kristy is a half-sister to Allison and Miranda. Now that we have the DNA, we confirmed the father: Timothy Michael Arnold."

Allison is incredulous.

"What? Kristy was not yet ten years old when Arnold met Moms."

Pop's held up an 'I got this' hand to his friend

Albert.

"Arnold was the lifeguard at the pool. Remember when you were little, 5 or 6, one summer, your mother went every day to the pool?"

"Yes."

"Did she ever swim?"

"I don't remember."

"She didn't swim, but she took a shower every time. Kristy is not the oldest daughter. Allison is older by four years. Miranda is four years younger than Kristy. The Program manipulated the subject's ages as part of the experiment to achieve academic and athletic success. Allison and Aydin don't know it, but Allison was almost two when Aydin was born."

Allison, Miranda, and Kristy are each looking at each other. The three half-sisters realize they are all pawns in their mother's long-game.

Albert accepted the chin point from Pops to complete his story.

"Kristy learned to control the psych tests. She became a model student and stopped being cruel to Robert. She didn't realize, and what we didn't tell her parents is, we knew she was faking. We let her and her parents continue to hide her problems to keep the peace.

"The final piece is the most important. Either Kristy is, or she has the name of who is pulling all the strings. Whoever she reports to in the Service is the person out to get Aydin.

"So, Kristy, there are no more secrets. Tell us,

to whom do you report?"

"You have the list. You know who I work for."

"The list is bogus. There is no organizational chart or reference in the list."

The slider explodes, sending shards of double-paned glass spewing into the room. Everyone dives to the floor and the cover of the reinforced furniture.

"Aydin?"

"Yes, Dad?"

"I thought you had a plan to do something about that sniper perch?"

"Yeah, well, Pops was supposed to take care of it. I have been a little busy, staying alive."

Aydin recognizes Phil's mission tone.

"We need a target, someone closer to the slider, hold up a pillow."

"Why, Phil?"

"Because the sniper's mission is over."

"Why is that?"

"Because I have Kristy's brains on my face."

Miranda puked.

Pops held a throw pillow over his head. Nothing happened.

Aydin resumed command.

"Azima?"

*"Yes, Aydin,"*

"Get KTF here *right the fuck now*. Code Alpha-Alpha-One."

*"Requesting Code Alpha-Alpha-One."*

"I suggest we crawl into the kitchen and wait."

No one needs encouragement. They all crawled over the shattered glass to the tiled kitchen floor. Picking glass out of her palms and knees, Allison is curious.

"I thought your codes with Azi... your codes with the AI need confirmation. I thought the specialized orders require two-factor approval?

Aydin's response is flat.

"I added a protocol to avoid the two-factor authentication. If you, or Phil, or I say, 'right the fuck now,' as a precursor to the command, she will execute the order immediately."

*"KTF reports an ETA of 22 minutes."*

"Thank you, Azima."

*"My pleasure."*


"Dad?"

"Yes, Aydin?"

"Who is killing everyone in our bubble of friends and family?"

Reaching up, pulling down a dish towel, Phil is wiping his face and talking through the towel.

"Yeah, Dad. Who wants your boy D-E-A-D, dead?"

"I have an idea, but I am not able to confirm my theory."

# The Reality of Family

*Trammel House, 23:49, Clear*

Everyone is cleaned up, sitting at the formal dining table. Working around Kermit's clean-up team, Phil and Allison make sure everyone eats and is comfortable.

Aydin cedes the head of the table to his father, Albert. Pops is seated on Albert's left, between Albert and Allison. Aydin is to Albert's right, Miranda next to him. Phil is one open seat to Miranda's right.

Kermit appears, catches Aydin's attention, gives a thumbs up before leaving without a word.

Allison's attention is on her husband. She knows his mind is racing from the expression and thousand-mile stare. Expecting something profound to emerge, she remains quiet.

Before the conversation begins, Miranda moves over one seat, next to Phil, and puts her hand on his knee. Everyone waits in silence, watching Aydin's slow breathing. They are waiting for him to return from his zone.

*That has to be right.*
*What else could it be?*
*But if I am wrong, there is no coming back.*
*They will never get over the accusation if I am wrong.*
*If I am wrong, it will destroy everything.*

*If I am not wrong, all the threats will stop.*
*Maybe, the threats will stop.*
*What if the threats don't stop?*
*They will stop and stop now.*
*Fuck.*
*We need a beach.*
*We need lots of sand and too many drinks.*
*Fuck it, here it goes.*

"Dad, how long have you been running The Service?"

Albert does not flinch.

"I don't run The Service. I am what the corporate world calls a COO. I am the Chief Operations Officer. Your next question will be about The Program.

"I accepted the role with The Service because it gave me the ability to continue The Program."

Pops fidgets but remains quiet. Aydin catches Pop's fidget.

*Pops kept Dad working for The Service from me.*

*He must have a good reason.*

Albert continues.

"Aydin, Allison, The Program has always been the priority of our families. From the beginning, we wanted to achieve the goal of improved intelligence through selective nurturing. The Program came apart.

409

It came apart, not because of funding. It came apart because we did not keep up with the changes in society.

"The psychologists failed to help the others in The Program. The high suicide rate within the group scared everyone. The rash of suicides was the tipping point that triggered the funding to be cut off.

"We were devastated at our inability to understand why The Program failed so many. Aydin, you, and Allison are the apex, the pinnacle of the Program's success.

"For the others…"

Albert paused, thinking. Everyone remained still. Bobbing his head in agreement to an internal decision, Albert continued.

"For the others, we missed the value of the technological changes unfolding in society. Technology begets technology. The requirement to be highly educated has become a commodity. The value in nurture, the core value contribution in raising intelligent adults, is in teaching them the ability to find information.

"Aydin, your mother and I, along with Pops, decided to stop pressuring you and Allison about your academics. We began narrowly focusing The Program for you two. It was a focus on your broad knowledge. We didn't teach you to remember reams of data. We instructed in a way that resulted in your ability to think critically.

"You two did the rest."

Stopping, sipping his Jameson, Albert waited. It was Miranda who spoke softly.

"What about me?"

Setting his tumbler down, Albert answered.

"Bryan and Marina refused to accept The Program would not continue and that you were not going to receive the training. Marina was livid. She threatened us if we didn't let you in The Program.

"Bryan stepped in and began your training. Brandon and I gave Bryan the outline of what was required at each stage of the guidance.

"But something went sideways with Bryan. I think Marina became impatient and pressured him to alter The Program outline we provided.

"When he flipped and accepted Marina's pressure, is when he changed your name. He pulled a lot of strings to get you into the training at Quantico. He did a good job. We have followed you closely. What you did in Washington State with the depleted uranium deal was brilliant."

Aydin softly interrupts his father.

"This is a nice history lesson but does not answer the question of who is coming after us nor why they are killing everyone around us."

Sipping the last of his Jameson, Pops refills Albert's tumbler when he set it back down.

Shifting from winking a thank you to his long-time friend, Albert focuses on his son.

"Aydin, I know you think I ordered the hits. I did not. That is why I came here. Brandon and I think we know who is behind the attacks, but we need to prove it."

Hearing Albert's response, Miranda squeezed Phil's thigh, digging in her bright red fingernails.

"Hey!"

Miranda apologizes to her new love before rotating her bowed head back to Albert.

"Sorry."

Albert's tone is parental.

"Brandon, she knows."

"I think she does. The question is: Will she admit it? Despite her training and the mission in Washington State, she is too inexperienced for this level. I don't think he knew the depth of her inexperience. Maybe he didn't care. She was not ready."

Allison and Aydin are staring at each other, listening, and beginning to comprehend.

Albert continued.

"Miranda, call Bryan, put him on the speaker."

"Albert, it is 2 am in Louisiana. You want me to wake my father?"

"Your father is not in Louisiana. He has not been home for several weeks. Bryan goes home every few weeks but never stays in Louisiana. He followed you to LSU, to Virginia, to Washington State, now Colorado."

Reeling, Miranda is buoyed by Phil squeezing her hand.

"You have been following my father?"

"Yes. We found that Marina forced him to initiate your training. He learned to like the mission and being part of Marina and Katherine's plan. Marina and Katherine were creating an empire. They were grooming you and Allison to join their cadre and eventually take over. They considered Kristy also. We think Marina vetoed recruiting Kristy. Behind Marina's back, Katherine kept after Kristy through Juanita."

Allison requested clarification.

"Empire?"

Albert smiled behind his tumbler before answering.

"Marina and Katherine, with Mikhail's help, took over the opium distribution. Mikhail accepted his new role: Number 3 in their syndicate. Marina controlled her brother Mikhail. They had a special relationship in which Katherine fit easily. However, a tertiary opium syndicate on the world market was not enough. Marina and Katherine wanted more. They turned to espionage and assassinations."

Aydin stands, grabs three tumblers from the sidebar, puts round ice balls in each tumbler, unlocks, and reaches in the cabinet before returning to the table. Setting down the tumblers, Aydin lifts the bottom of the bottle he is holding, indicating his father and Pops to finish their Jameson.

He begins pouring Dewar's 32, sliding the first to Allison, the second to Phil, the third for himself. His father and Pops are beaming at Aydin's choice.

Aydin's tone is even and controlled when

speaking and finishing the pour.

"Miranda, I know you don't prefer Scotch. If my hunch is correct, this conversation is about to become intense. What would you like?"

"If my hunch is the same as your hunch, I want one of those."

Aydin retrieves a tumbler, ice and pours the small woman a short drink with a dry smile. Sitting, he holds up his glass for a toast.

"Here's to seeing the sunset on a beach."

Everyone sipped. Miranda coughed at the burn in her throat but smiled. Setting her phone on the table, she unlocks it and dials her father.

"Hello, honey. It is late. Is everything okay?"

"Hi, dad. Everything is okay. I have you on the speaker."

"Oh? Is Phil with you?"

"Yes, and Aydin, Allison, Pops, and Albert."

Miranda's response is met with silence. Albert takes up the conversation.

"Bryan, why don't you come by the office tomorrow morning, about 08:30?"

"Albert, that would be hard to do from Lafourche Parish."

"Don't play games. We know you are in Colorado."

"Why should I come to the office? We can talk now."

"Because, Bryan, I have an offer from The Service for you. We can discuss the proposal at the office. Don't be a jerk. Accept the peace offering and say yes. We will see you at 08:30."

"Miranda?"

"Yes, dad?"

"Are you okay?"

"Yes, I am fine."

"Good. You come to the office also. With you there, I will know Albert is acting in good faith. Do not trust him. Do not trust any of them. Do you understand?"

Hesitating, not sure, afraid, Miranda plays along with her father's request.

"I understand."

The line goes silent. Miranda confirms the connection closed before slipping her phone back into her pocket.

Everyone is quiet, sipping. Miranda's drink goes untouched. Pops drains his glass and silently toasts Aydin. Albert does the same before joining Pops in leaving the Trammel house.

Phil stands, grabs Miranda's tumbler, her hand, and they depart for the guest house.

Aydin is swirling the ice in the remnants of his drink, looking at his wife.

*Why do I feel nothing?*
*What is wrong with us?*
*All the suicides?*
*How did Allison and I escape?*
*Miranda needs help.*

*Phil will help her.*
*Why am I sweating?*
*I am sweating because it must be true.*
*I can never tell anyone.*
*Not Allison.*
*Not Phil.*
*No one will ever know.*

Breaking her husband from his funk, Allison finishes the last of her drink before she sums up the evening.

"Did you send the request?"

"I did."

"Did you get a response?"

"No, but I offered to pay."

"How much?"

"A grand. In cash."

"That will do it."

"Yes."

"Aydin, the only people I trust are you, Phil, and me."

## DTC, Conference Room, 08:15, Clear and Bright

Aydin and Allison are settling into their seats in the conference room when Phil and Miranda arrive in his Sierra.

Setting down the cardboard coffee holder before Phil can unload his PC, Pops, and Albert arrive in Pops' Sierra. Allison retrieves the coffees with hers and Aydin's names written on the side.

Aydin points Pops and Albert to chairs opposite the door. When Bryan arrives, he will sit with his back to the door.

Pops and Albert retrieve their coffees.

Phil breaks the tension.

"Good thing Miranda knows how Allison prefers her coffee ruined. I'd never have remembered Café Latte Mocha Frap No Whip All In No Room."

Allison and Miranda roll their eyes at Phil's tortured attempt to remember Allison's coffee order. The men hold up their sleeved paper cups full of dark, black, hot coffee.

"Azima?"

*"Yes, Aydin?*

"Stop all surveillance in and outside the office. Immediately."

*"Stopping all surveillance requires authentication."*

"Azima, *right fucking now*, stop all surveillance in and outside the office.

*"All office surveillance has been discontinued."*

"Thank you, Azima."

*"My pleasure."*


The group remains quiet, waiting.


**DTC, *Conference Room, 08:30, Clear and Bright***

Precisely on-time, General Bryan Michael Cole, USAF Retired, walks into the Fírinne conference room and sits in the designated seat. Without saying hello

417

or greeting the daughter he raised, Bryan jumps right into the discussion.

"Albert, I have a plane to catch. Make your offer."

Pops gently slides his hand from under the table and points his Colt 1911 at Bryan. Albert responds.

"Bryan, there is no offer. We want to know what you planned to do when Aydin and Allison were out of the way. Is it your plan for Miranda to step in and assume the leadership of the team? You must know, The Service would never consider giving Miranda the missions they would assign to Aydin and Allison."

Bryan does not hear the woman come into the office. In the window reflection, he sees someone standing behind him in the conference room doorway. Seeing the others looking over his head, Bryan turns and sees a heavyset brunette standing.

"What is she doing here?"

Aydin responds to the question Bryan directed at Albert.

"I asked Kimber here to clear up a few details. Bryan, I could not get it out of my head that Moms hired Kimber to follow Miranda. It occurred to me, following Miranda is not Moms' style and not necessary. I did a little digging and found Madame Kimber's web page. It is a lovely page, but that is not the point.

"The point is, I realized, Moms was the middleman between Kimber and someone else. That someone is you, Bryan.

"Taking the logic forward, I realized how you know Kimber. Sorry, Madame Kimber. You are a customer.

"Kimber, is the guy?"

Kimber does not move. Her hands are shaking slightly, but her face is stone. She is suspicious of being too close to the seated Bryan.

"Oh yeah, that's the fucker."

"Are you sure?"

"I am sure. It took Deanna and Bobby a week to recover from what he did to them."

Bryan's face is impassive while he looks through the windows. He is following the birds and ignoring the conversation.

Albert shuffles in his chair, getting ready to speak, but Aydin holds up a hand, indicating his father should remain quiet. Pulling an envelope from his backpack, he holds it up for Kimber.

Shaking her head negative, looking at the back of Bryan's head, Kimber refuses to get closer to Bryan.

Aydin hands the envelope to Phil, who walks around the room and gives it to Kimber with a message.

"Kimber?"

"Yes?"

"I know you know how to keep a secret. If anyone asks, you accepted our apologies for stepping on your hand."

"Why would anyone ask?"

Phil pointed to the windows. The drone is

hovering above the trees on the other side of the parking lot.

Kimber's question is a request.

"We will never see him again?"

"You will never see him again."

Kimber nodded to Phil, then to Aydin, before she left as quickly as possible without breaking into a sprint.

Phil's sitting was Bryan's clue to begin speaking.

"So fucking what. I beat up a couple of whores. What do you mean there is no offer?"

Albert turned to Aydin, giving over control.

"Bryan, there is no offer. The team will be here soon to arrest you. If you give me the storage drive in your pocket, I will make sure it is destroyed and not used at your trial."

Bryan smiles at Miranda but makes the mistake of patting his front pocket, confirming the storage device is safe.

Pops saw the hand movement and raised his pistol with an order.

"Hand over the flash drive."

"And what if I don't?"

Aydin's tone is flat.

"I will kill you and take it."

"Boy, fuck you. You were always too big for your britches."

Miranda finally spoke.

"Dad? What are they talking about?"

"Nothing, Honey. They are trying to intimidate me."

"Dad?"

Aydin does not let Bryan respond.

"You give me the device, and I give you my word. It will be destroyed. No one will ever know."

"Not a chance."

Everyone except Pops and Phil turns their head to the two white vans and the black sedan pulling into the parking lot and stopping in front of the office. Aydin tries again.

"If they find it on you, you will never see daylight again."

The side door to the first van is open, three men in tactical gear are piling out. Seeing the two men in black suits from the black sedan walking toward the office, Bryan slides the flash drive to Aydin.

The conference room feels thick and tense for the few seconds it takes for the agents to enter. Standing on either side of the retired General, the taller agent begins speaking.

"General Cole, I am Agent Cooper, and he is Agent Durant. We are here to arrest you. Colonel Trammel, Colonel Kearney, it is good to see you both again."

Albert and Pops silently accept the Agent's greeting. Agent Cooper continues after Pops puts down his pistol.

"General, we are going to take you with us. Please come quietly."

Bryan is staring at Miranda but stands and puts his hands behind his back for the cuffs. Agent Durant is cuffing Bryan when Agent Cooper makes a request.

"Miss LaLonde, a word, please?"

Miranda is nervous and looks to Phil, who nods encouragement.

Miranda stands. As she is moving to follow the agents and her adoptive father, Pops hands her his pistol. The four exit the conference room and the office.

The group remaining in the conference room watch as Bryan is wire-tied to the wall of the van. Miranda is talking with Agent Cooper and is joined by Agent Durant. Looking from one to the other, both agents are faintly exhibiting positive affirmation.

Miranda looks to the window before walking to the open van door.

"Why?"

"Honey, I never touched you. It was Marina who hurt you. I protected you. I made sure you got into LSU and the training. I was there for you."

"Protected me? Not well enough. Why did you let her?"

"I don't know. When I get out of this, we will start over. Me and you. Like it was before."

"No. It will never be like it was before. Just tell me why."

After a too-long pause, Miranda's adoptive father's response is too soft for the agents and tactical officers to hear.

The agents, and tactical commandos, turn their backs to Miranda and the retired General.

Through the tears, Miranda puts a bullet in her adoptive father's forehead.

Phil meets Miranda at the office door, takes the pistol, and hugs her tightly. Standing in the lobby, holding the gun out, Pops jumps up and takes it. Allison has Phil's PC loaded in his backpack and hands it to him.

Phil waits for the black sedan and the vans to leave before he half-carries Miranda to his pickup.

### DTC, Conference Room, 15:00, Clearing

"Azima?"

*"Yes, Aydin?"*

"Connect me to Phil."

*"Stand by."*

"Hello Aydin, I suppose you want an update?"

"How is Miranda?"

"She is sleeping. I now understand some of the nightmares she has and why she has trouble sleeping. This is the first time she has slept and has not struggled to stay asleep. No, I don't know what her father said, and I didn't ask."

"That's okay. I know what Bryan said. We will be home at about 18:00. Pops is taking Dad to his hotel to check out, then to the airport. It'll be us four for dinner if Miranda feels up to it. We'll bring home dinner."

"Sounds good. Aydin?"

"Yes, Phil?"
After a long gap, Phil closed the conversation.
"Never mind, we can talk about it later."
"Azima, close the connection."
*"Connection closed."*
"Thank you, Azima."
*"My pleasure."*

# Good Riddance



## BREAKING NEWS

IN TODAY'S BUSINESS NEWS, A LOCAL COMPANY HAS CONFIRMED IT PROVIDED THE TECHNOLOGY FOR THE PENTAGON'S RESEARCH PROGRAM LOOKING INTO REPLACING HUMAN HACKERS WITH ARTIFICIAL INTELLIGENCE, ALSO KNOWN AS AI.

DARPA, THE EXTREMELY SECRETIVE DEFENSE ADVANCED RESEARCH PROJECTS AGENCY, ISSUED A PRESS RELEASE IN A HIGHLY UNUSUAL ANNOUNCEMENT.

IN THE PRESS RELEASE, DARPA THANKED THE LOCAL COLORADO COMPANY: FÍRINNE, FOR DONATING THE ADVANCED SOFTWARE REQUIRED TO CONTINUE THEIR RESEARCH.

ADDITIONALLY, FÍRINNE AND COMMSECARC, THE GLOBAL SECURITY GIANT, AND DARPA ANNOUNCED A TRILATERAL AGREEMENT FOR COMMSECARC TO ACQUIRE FÍRINNE'S ADVANCED TECHNOLOGIES.

WE'LL STAY ON THIS COLORADO FIRST

STORY.

Now, the weather with Stormy.

Phil, Miranda, Allison, and Aydin are watching the news from the breakfast bar. Phil is picking up the used breakfast dishes.

For her breakfast, Miranda insisted on eating the baked Halibut Aydin brought home for dinner. She had slept through dinner into the morning, then went for a run with Phil.

Aydin reaches over and presses the power button on the television remote.

"Azima?"

*"Yes, Aydin?"*

"Change the standard response message. Inform any callers and replies to external email messages with: The Fírinne Offices are presently closed. A reopening date has not been determined. All inquiries will be addressed when the office reopens."

*"Standard response message updated."*

"Thank you, Azima."

*"My pleasure."*

Allison is beaming, and Phil is almost bouncy. Miranda is cautious and looks to Phil, who looks to Aydin before commenting.

"This time of the year, it'll be hotter than a hooker's doorknob on payday."

"Yeah, but what do you care? Miranda loves the

swamp heat, and didn't you grow up in the south? What's a little summer sun? The only one here who should be worried is our Ginger."

Allison does not back down.

"I have 100 SPF."

Miranda finally understands and turns to Aydin.

"We are we going to? What about the house in Louisiana? Don't I need to go close it down?"

"Don't worry about the house. Kermit's team will take care of it. You can decide what you want to do on the beach. I booked us at Bucuti & Tara Beach Resort in Aruba. No kids allowed, plenty of adult beverages, a lot of sand, and warm Caribbean water. We will stay as long as you like."

"I don't know what to say..."

Allison stands and takes over the conversation.

"You can start by calling me 'Sis.' I'd like that if you are okay with it. Then we are going to Park Meadows and buying a shitload of beachwear and some of the smallest bikinis these boys have ever seen. Then we are going to get waxed and painted."

Grabbing Miranda by the forearm, Allison tugs her toward the garage and her Rover.

"Hold up, let me run and get my purse."

Miranda dashes out toward the guest house.

Phil hugs Allison.

"Thank you. She needs a friend."

"Phil, she has us, and by the way she looks at you, she may never leave."

Miranda darts back into the house with her

purse and a smile.

Allison kisses Aydin and notices his face. Walking toward the garage door and her Rover, she hollers.

"Phil, find out what Aydin is up to now."

When the garage door closes behind the women, Phil complies.

"Brain?"

"Yeah, Pinky?"

"This world domination thing, it's not over, is it?"

"No, Pinky, it is not over."

Aydin points to the slider and the distant small hillside. Kermit's team is putting up a side fence, planting some flowers, and installing hidden surveillance.

Phil's response is deadpan.

"At least we will know when they show up to shoot at us."

Aydin's response is expressionless.

"Pinky, those are not just birdhouses. They are putting on those poles."

"Not birdhouses, Brain?"

"Azima?"

"*Yes, Aydin?*"

"Let me know when the target parameters are installed and tested for Bird-1, Bird-2, and Bird-3."

"*Kermit anticipated your request. The ETA to complete the ranging and targeting of Bird-1, Bird-2, and Bird-3 is one hour.*"

"Thank you, Azima."

*"My Pleasure."*

"The drones are gone. At least, they are not here now. The miniguns in the birdhouses will help us with anyone else who thinks they want a dead Aydin.

"Agents Cooper and Durant got what they needed from the Drones. They wanted Bryan."

"Brain, you don't think they will stop coming, do you?"

"No, Pinky, I do not."

# Thank you!

*"Anyone who says they have only one life to live must not know how to read a book."*
*Anonymous*

Dear reader, please accept my sincere gratitude for spending your precious time reading the words I was able to patch together. The story of Aydin Trammell continues with Volume Two, The Kintsugi Protocol.

I am often reminded of how lucky I am to write and do more than I ever imagined.

*"O Lord that lends me life,*

*lend me a heart replete with thankfulness."*
*William Shakespeare*

I have my health, a loving family, a wonderful wife, and an overwhelming yearning to keep them all.

R. C.

# About R. C.

Fortunately, in secondary school, my interest in reading was sparked. A close friend and an instructor who took an interest in a boy he later called 'The rebel without a clue.' were instrumental in learning the value of a good book. Both piqued my interest in reading.

My lifelong friend inspired me to read J.R.R. Tolkien, and I became addicted to the fantasy genre. The instructor required me to read exciting historical novels for academic credit. Frank Norris, Leon Uris, and Ken Follett are inspirations and fuel my love of history.

Born to a military family, it was logical that I follow the military tradition. However, after four years of "yes sirs" and scraping the wax off floors, I decided there must be more fun in a corporate career.

After thirty-plus years of work experience across the globe, the corporate career landed me in Colorado.

# Contact R. C.

Website
www.rcducantlin.com

Facebook
www.facebook.com/rcducantlin

Twitter
twitter.com/rcducantlin

LinkedIn
www.linkedin.com/in/rcducantlin

# Books by R. C.
## Novels

Summitate Series
Biomass
Dominion
Connections

*The Plan: Create A Pandemic. Use A Designer Drug To Cure The Flu And Kill Six Billion People. Hope For Humankind Fell On Me To Control The New Humans.*

The Carina Series
Time is an Illusion
A Calm Mind
Our Place
BairnGefa
Ho' Ma' Utz

*The Blessing Of Interstellar Travel Has Become A Curse. With The Powers He Received from the Designer Drug, Corb Has One Chance To Save Earth, But It Has Become Impossible To Tell Friend From Foe.*

Aalborinn
The Reluctant First
The Girl of Light
Ka'i: The Second First

*To Become A Plentari Warrior: Survive The Brutal Training. Can Corb's Daughter, A Human Girl, Become A Plentari Warrior? How Many Will She Slay To Survive? Is She The First?*

# Short Stories

## MAX AND THE DREAM TIME
### THE FIND
### THE EVERWHEN
### THE TONTINE
### THE LOST YEARS
### THE PRICE OF LOVE

*Jamie's future will break Max's heart. Understanding the Orb becomes Max's obsession. With the Orb, he can make sure the future he sees never happen. Can His Friends Save Him From the Pain? Will Their Plan Work? Is The Pain Too Great To Endure?*

## MIRANDA EVERLASTING
### GRIS-GRIS
### FÒ MIRANDA
### ENVIE

*Young Miranda is going to be famous. She is going to be in the movies and fly aeroplanes. The dreams of children destroyed, Albee helps Miranda become famous.*

*Not all voodoo is bad voodoo.*

*Some voodoo is for the dead.*
*Some Voodoo Is For The Living.*
*Voodoo Is Eternal.*

## THE AYDIN TRAMMELL CHRONICLES
## VOLUME ONE
### SHINY LIES

*A former Special Ops Commando thought covert missions in the desert were rough. Then he married a spy who wants him dead.*

*When Aydin Trammel becomes an international intelligence operative, he quickly learns his new career is considerably more complicated than when he was a special ops soldier. Back then, problems were solved more straightforwardly: Hike in, blow something up, hike out. He was good at that.*

## VOLUME TWO
### THE KINTSUGI PROTOCOL

*How do you fix that which can never be the same?*